TIC

'Sorry, AJ,' I said meekly. 'I will try to be obedient, but please don't tickle me again, please?'

'Why not?'

'I hate it!'

'Tough. I still owe you one.'

'No! You just did me!'

'No. I said I was going to do you in the street, and I'm going to. This isn't a street, Dumplings, in case you hadn't noticed.'

Why not visit Penny's website at
www.pennybirch.com

By the same author:

THE INDIGNITIES OF ISABELLE
THE INDISCRETIONS OF ISABELLE
(writing as Cruella)

PENNY IN HARNESS
A TASTE OF AMBER
BAD PENNY
BRAT
IN FOR A PENNY
PLAYTHING
TIGHT WHITE COTTON
TIE AND TEASE
PENNY PIECES
TEMPER TANTRUMS
REGIME
DIRTY LAUNDRY
UNIFORM DOLL
NURSE'S ORDERS
JODHPURS AND JEANS
PEACH
FIT TO BE TIED
WHEN SHE WAS BAD
KNICKERS AND BOOTS

TICKLE TORTURE

Penny Birch

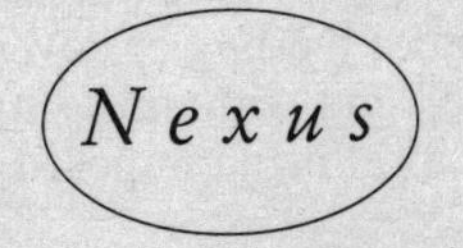

This book is a work of fiction.
In real life, make sure you practise safe, sane and consensual sex.

First published in 2004 by
Nexus
Thames Wharf Studios
Rainville Road
London W6 9HA

www.nexus-books.co.uk

Typeset by TW Typesetting, Plymouth, Devon

Printed and bound by
Clays Ltd, St Ives PLC

ISBN 0 352 33904 7

You'll notice that we have introduced a set of symbols onto our book jackets, so that you can tell at a glance what fetishes each of our brand new novels contains. Here's the key – enjoy!

Author's Note

Tickle Torture is fiction, but the cabaret featured at the beginning is based on a real event, held at a club which had better remain nameless. Ryman's reaction in refusing to believe that a woman would have put together such a perverse event is also drawn from fact. The main difference is that we got away with it, leaving the club while the angry bouncers searched for the non-existent male organiser, some of us still in our wet panties.

One

Penny sighed as she realised she was finally going to get it. She'd been so lucky, avoiding a slippering and six of the cane, while she hadn't even been made to remove any clothes. Not me. I'd had to take my jeans and panties down immediately and sit like that, bare behind on the floor. Next I'd been spanked, kneeling with my bum stuck up for fifty firm swats that left me warm and fidgety. As if that wasn't enough, I'd been forced to take a plum in my pussy. Penny had watched me insert the fruit, grinning, and promptly climbed a ladder to escape having to strip, so even if she did get a whacking she would be able to take it on the seat of her jeans – probably.

Only it hadn't worked that way. I'd landed on a blank. She'd hit the very next snake and gone all the way back to the bottom. I'd got a little ladder, going up one level. She'd hit the nastiest square on the lower part of the board, twenty smacks of the hairbrush on the bare and left with the handle up the bum. It was my turn to grin.

She was looking seriously sorry for herself as she kneeled up and put her hands to the button of her jeans. I just watched as she pushed them down, panties and all, over her sweet little bottom and her pussy at the front, baring herself with that lovely shyness she never loses, however often she does it. A year and a half we'd been together, and it still set my pulse racing to watch her, and faster still as she went down on all fours, her bum lifted, her pretty face set in rueful consternation as she looked back at me.

'You chose it,' I reminded her as I picked up the hairbrush.

Her response was a weak nod, and to close her eyes. It was typical. However much she loves rude, painful sex, she can never quite come to terms with it. She must have had her panties taken down for spanking a thousand times, and peed in them a hundred. She's licked other girls' bottoms, and let men up her own. She's even been done up as a pig, nude in a mud wallow, with a snout and tail. She still finds it all utterly humiliating. If she didn't, she wouldn't do it. Dirty bitch.

'Count them,' I ordered.

Again she nodded, and I began to spank her, applying the hard wooden hairbrush to her lovely round cheeks to make them bounce and wobble, showing off her pinkish-brown bumhole in its nest of hair. Her pussy showed too, furry little sex lips pouting out behind with the centre pink and creamy. When it came to sticking the hairbrush handle up her bum, she wasn't going to need any lube but her own.

She had started to count, choking out the numbers in between little gasps and sobs as I spanked merrily away, one cheek at a time as they turned gradually pink. I didn't bother to hold back my laughter at the way she looked, because I knew my amusement would just humiliate her all the more, and make the spanking that much better. By ten she was beginning to shake, and to snivel. By fifteen she had begun to stick her bottom up for more. As I gave her the twentieth her hand went back to her pussy. I slapped it.

'Oh no you don't, slut,' I told her. 'Not yet. Now pull your cheeks open for me.'

I turned the hairbrush in my hand as she obeyed, leaving her pussy to reach back and spread her bottom. Her hole was open, the mouth stretched wide, with a trickle of juice running down between her lips. I slid the hairbrush handle in, drawing a long sigh of pleasure from her, then setting her gasping as I began to fuck her with it. In no time she was clutching at her smacked bottom, but I waited until she tried to sneak a finger to the little pink hole in the middle before I stopped.

'Uh, uh,' I chided, 'that's for the hairbrush handle, not your finger.'

It didn't stop her, the top joint of one finger disappearing into the tight ring of her anus. I pulled the handle out, white and slimy with her juice, and slapped her hand.

'Behave, slut.'

Her finger came out and once more she stretched her cheeks wide, her bumhole now a moist pink cavity. I put the hairbrush handle to it and pushed, watching her flesh go in, then spread around the shaft as she took it. She groaned and began to squeeze her cheeks, kneading her reddened flesh as I entered her. I eased the handle as deep as it would go and left it, the business end of the brush sticking up obscenely from her buggered anus.

'Bring me off, please, Jade,' she begged, 'like this.'

I slapped her on the back of her thigh.

'Wait for it, you dirty bitch. We've only just started.'

'Yes, but just making the game up turned me on.'

'Me too, but we're going to finish before we come, aren't we?'

She nodded and let go of her bottom cheeks, allowing them to close around the brush. I sat back, and so did she, very gingerly, so that she was squatting on her heels with the brush between her feet. I was ready too, and very conscious of my own spanked cheeks and the plum in my pussy. We exchanged looks, both thinking the same thing, but I resisted and took up the dice.

I threw. Five. It put me on the base of the longest ladder on the board, leaving me just one level below the finish and the possibility of having Penny as my pet for the rest of the evening. Even as I considered the delicious possibilities of what I could do with her there was a touch of disappointment. I do love her, and there's a lot to be said for going out with a fellow submissive, but with the snakes and ladders game it had always been inevitable that we'd both want to lose.

She was bright eyed and smiling as she took the dice up again. It came down on one, moving her onto a blank. Before I could throw again the doorbell went, but I was in no mood for company and ignored it. I got a six, landing me on one of the last punishment squares, twelve strokes of the cane. My tummy tightened. She was going to hurt me, if only to make sure she really suffered once I'd won, which now looked inevitable. The doorbell went again, a single long ring.

'Aren't you going to see who it is?' Penny asked.

'No,' I told her. 'Don't you want to cane me?'

'Yes, but it might be important. At least check who it is, or they'll just keep ringing.'

She was right. I stood, quickly pulling up my panties and jeans, and went to the window. It was dark outside, windy and wet, with raindrops glittering orange as they passed through the glare of the streetlights, making me glad of the warmth and comfort of my flat and my girlfriend. As I lifted the window my feeling of contentment vanished abruptly. There was a fuck-off big motorbike parked right outside, tight between two cars, and the rider was the person ringing my bell. Tall, slim in black leathers, her helmet tucked under one arm, her shaved head glistening in the wet, she looked every inch the sadistic diesel dyke she was, AJ, aka Alice Jemima Croft, but never to her face. She'd heard the window, and she looked up.

'Open the fucking door, Dumplings!'

'Who is it?' Penny asked from behind me.

'AJ,' I answered, then called down, 'Hang on, I'll throw you the keys.'

AJ gave me a dirty look, and as I ducked back into the room I found Penny hastily rearranging herself, her panties held up in one hand even as she extracted the hairbrush from her bumhole. It was the sensible thing to do. If we kept playing, things were likely to get heavy, and AJ had a nasty reputation for not respecting submissive girls' limits.

By the time I'd got the keys from the bedroom Penny was decent and had begun to tidy up, shovelling the pile of implements and sex toys we'd laid out into a draw. I threw the keys down. AJ caught them one handed and quickly let herself up, so that Penny had to push the snakes and ladders board under a chair to hide it. The room still smelled of sex, but at least it wasn't obvious we'd been kinky with each other. I still had the plum in me too. Penny went to make coffee.

'It's pissing down out there,' AJ said as she let herself in. 'Get us a towel.'

I hurried to fetch one, and by the time I came back she'd taken off her jacket and sat down. All she had on underneath was a tatty black T-shirt, which left her arms bare, the long, smooth muscles showing under her skin, and her tats. She had a new one, stark black and white like the others, a female symbol shaped from twists of barbed wire. With her head shaved she looked harder than ever and, if it was scary, it still made me want to get down at her feet and lick her boots. She took the towel and rubbed the rainwater from her face, speaking as she threw it back to me.

'I swear your tits get bigger every time I see you. Get them out.'

'AJ!'

'Do it.'

I made a face, but I did as I was told, hauling up my top and bra to flop my boobs out for her. They are big, but they felt huge as I stood there showing them off for her amusement. She took her time, her mouth curled into what looked more like a sneer of contempt than a smile of admiration as she inspected me. At last she looked away, and I hastily covered myself up.

'Who's in the kitchen?' she demanded.

'Penny,' I told her.

She laughed and turned around in her chair, calling out. 'Grown your hair back yet, Muffet?'

'Yes, thank you,' Penny answered, sounding as sulky as ever when the subject of her forced depilation was brought up.

AJ laughed and put her feet up on the table we'd been playing our game on. She stretched, emphasising the muscles in her arms and also the shape of her breasts, bare beneath her T-shirt, the outline of nipples and the rings in them quite plain. I've met bigger girls, a few stronger girls, but nobody quite so blatantly, viciously butch. It made me want to melt, and rather than sit in a chair I curled myself up on the floor, feeling it was right. She took no notice, and stayed silent until Penny had put a mug of coffee in her hands.

'Cheers, Muffet.'

Penny didn't look too happy as she went to sit down, but she said nothing. For all her experience, she's never really accepted that sometimes you just have to give in and take what's coming to you. Not that it stops her getting it, but she likes to retain ultimate control, something AJ delights in taking away.

I took my own coffee, not really sure what to say, half hoping that AJ wouldn't realise what we'd been up to, half that she would. She took her time, blowing at her coffee and sipping it before she spoke.

'I want you two sluts to do a cabaret for me.'

My stomach tightened. I could imagine exactly the sort of thing it would be, doing filthy, humiliating things to each other on her orders until she was horny enough. Then maybe she would piss on us as we wriggled together on the floor, or tie us head to tail and give us enemas, or have us fight to see who got the privilege of licking her pussy and make the loser clean her bumhole, even make Penny tickle me . . .

'Do . . . do you mind?' I asked Penny. 'We could be pigs if you like, or . . .'

Penny gave me a dirty look, but AJ cut in before she could answer.

'No, too weird. You have to be schoolgirls . . .'

'I don't have a uniform with me,' Penny pointed out.

'Not now, you tart,' AJ answered her. 'At a club.'

'Which club?' I answered doubtfully, although I knew full well I'd end up doing as I was told even if Penny didn't.

'A new one,' AJ told us. 'Bolero's, it's called.'

'What, up at the Palace?' I asked. 'It's straight, isn't it?'

'Yeah, it's straight, but Bob Ryman, that's the bloke who's running it, reckons he can cash in with a bit of lessie chic, and you know how the little shits love to watch.'

'How do you fit in?' Penny asked her.

'He runs the courier firm I've been working for as well as the club,' AJ answered. 'Wanted me to do it, he did. As if!'

'How can you ask us to do it then?' Penny answered her.

I winced, wondering if AJ would hit her. She didn't, but there was a hard edge to her voice as she answered.

'I'm not asking you. I'm telling you. You're bi anyway, so what do you fucking care?'

'What does he want us to do, AJ?' I intervened hastily.

'That's down to you,' she answered, 'but he says to make it hardcore, the harder the better. He claims he's unshockable, but nothing too weird, just nice and sleazy, that's what he said, and you've got to be in school uniform. That's the theme for the club. There's two hundred in it for you.'

'And how much are you getting?' Penny asked.

'You're going to get a smack in a minute, Miss Muffet,' AJ answered. 'I get fifty on top, OK? You can ask the fucker if you don't believe me.'

Penny shrugged. I knew she wanted to do it, underneath. If it hadn't been AJ asking, and if the audience had been a bit more select, she would have gone for it. As for me, the thought of performing in front of straights, and men at that, was making me feel sick. It didn't matter how I felt. I knew I'd be doing it because I couldn't refuse AJ, and the two hundred pounds was tempting.

The thing was, she wanted me as her lifestyle submissive, which spoke right to my deepest fantasies of being under another woman's absolute control. She hadn't said anything, but she'd been hitting on me more and more often, and testing me. That meant doing what I was told, when I was told, and, if that meant having sex in front of straight men, then that was what I had to do. Not that I'd have had the guts to refuse anyway, but that didn't stop me trying to wriggle out of it.

'Of course I'll do it,' I answered AJ, 'but what about the venue owners?'

'The venue owners!' She laughed. 'The Palace is leased to Ronnie Miles!'

'Never heard of him.'

'Ronnie Miles used to own *Piccadilly* magazine. He was in porn when you were in nappies!

'That would be last weekend, then,' Penny remarked dryly. 'Jade, I really don't think this is a good idea. You've met Morris Rathwell, AJ, why don't you ask him? Melody will get a team together for you, not for two hundred pounds maybe, but . . .'

'Bob's not going any higher,' AJ answered her, 'and he's my boss. I need this, and you're going to fucking do it, that or find somebody else. Naomi's up for it, and I reckon we need five.'

'So forty pounds each?' I asked, my vision of two hundred pounds for an evening of humiliation fading. I knew Penny wouldn't accept any, even if she did do it.

'Yeah,' AJ answered, 'and you get your drinks free. Get little Zoe if you can, she won't speak to me, fucking baby dykes, and that cute blonde slut, Sophie.'

'They might be up for it,' I answered. 'Come on, Penny, for me?'

'It's a mainstream club, Jade,' she objected. 'What if one of my students is there?'

'What's the chance of that?' AJ answered her.

'Quite high,' she responded. 'There are over thirteen thousand students at the university, a lot of whom know me by sight and a lot of whom go clubbing in London. I'm a senior lecturer for goodness sake, I can't be seen in a lesbian sex show at some rundown club! You do it, Jade, but I can't.'

'Who else then?'

'I don't know. Perhaps we could ask Poppy?'

'Who's Poppy?' AJ demanded.

'She used to go out with Anna Vale,' Penny answered. 'You must have heard of Anna?'

'What, the mad bitch who thinks she's living in the twenties?'

'Poppy's dead cute,' I put in, 'and very dirty. Anna used to keep her on a short leash, so now she's up for just about anything. Don't be hard on Penny, AJ, please?'

'OK,' AJ answered, and for all her toughness I could sense her relief as she sat back in the chair.

As she drained the rest of her coffee I was wondering if there wasn't more to it than she was letting on. Normally she'd have told any man to piss off, even if he was her boss, but on the other hand I knew she'd done her time stripping in bars, so she wasn't as prissy about men seeing her naked as she claimed to be. I was, especially in front of the sort of straight laddish types who would be at the club, and I knew it would take a lot of the free drink before I could do it. Not having Penny to play with, or at least to support me, would make it worse.

That was another problem. AJ didn't approve of Penny, for being bisexual, for not buying into the lifestyle, but above all for wanting submissive sex without absolute submission. Penny was as bad. She thought of AJ not as the experienced lesbian dominant she was, but simply as a bully. That didn't stop them fancying each other, because Penny adores just the sort of extreme humiliation AJ loves to dish out. I knew that to be AJ's bottom would mean surrendering Penny, or at least my right to play with her when I wanted, and I was not prepared to do that. Then there was Sophie, and Zoe, and other girls I liked to play with, or top me, like Melody Rathwell. I need my playmates.

I was definitely going to need them for the cabaret, especially Penny.

'You'll come anyway, yeah?' I asked her, sure what the answer would be. She was not going to spend a night alone in her flat while I was out with Sophie, never mind Zoe and Poppy.

'Of course,' she answered, 'just not on stage.'

AJ leaned to the side to put her empty coffee mug down, and I realised too late that the corner of the snakes and ladders board was sticking out. She'd seen it too, and was looking puzzled, then amused as she drew it out.

'What's this?' she asked. 'Been playing games?'

'Rude board games, our own type of snakes and ladders,' I admitted, feeling a little embarrassed and a little scared too.

AJ began to examine the board.

'You get these punishments then?' she commented after a while. 'Pretty tame, "Go Bare", "Go OTK", "Twenty with a slipper"?'

'They get harder as you go along,' I explained.

'It can take for ever to reach the end,' Penny pointed out.

'And you dish it out to each other?' AJ asked, her voice full of disdain.

'Penny spanks hard!' I protested.

'Besides,' Penny went on, 'the woman who lives below has been complaining about the screams.'

'So? Stick your panties in your mouths.'

'It still gets noisy. She's even threatened to report us to the noise-abatement people.'

AJ gave a snort of pure contempt. She was still looking at the board, and I was wondering if she was going to make us play, with her dishing out the punishments, a terrifying yet thrilling prospect. She would be a lot harder, merciless, and it wouldn't matter who won either, because both of us would end up getting what we needed. I glanced at Penny, hoping she was thinking the same thing, to find her looking nervous and more than a little stubborn. AJ threw down the board.

'Crap,' she announced. 'If you want to do it, why don't you just do it?'

'Playing the game builds up the tension,' Penny answered.

'It's fun,' I added, trying not to sound too apologetic, 'that way you don't know what's going to happen, what you're going to get. It makes it unexpected.'

AJ made a face, then stood up, her hands going straight to the button of her leather jeans. She stepped towards me, and my tummy tightened into a hard knot at the prospect of being made to lick her, then and there, with my girlfriend watching. My mouth had already come open, my body responding to her dominance by sheer instinct. I leaned forwards, my knees wide as she came between them, her trousers open at the front to show a leather thong pulled tight over her pussy. The smell of leather caught my nose, and of her, making me keener still to lick, and to submit to her utterly.

Her thumbs found the waistband and down came her jeans, taking the thong with them. She was shaved, and she'd had her pussy mound tattooed, replacing her bush with a tangle of barbed wire, stark black on her pale flesh. As she pushed her belly out into my face her pussy spread, showing the pink centre and the twin silver rings in her lips. I poked my tongue out, awaiting her order as the muscles in her belly tightened.

'How's this for unexpected?' she said, and just let go her bladder, sending a stream of hot piss right into my open mouth, then exploding into my face as I stupidly closed up on her.

I should have tried to drink it, but it was such a shock, and I was choking immediately, blinded too, with piss up my nose and in my eyes. She just laughed at me, pushed me back in the chair and cocked one leg up, aiming her stream onto my tummy as I fought for breath, completely unable to help myself as she casually urinated all over me. I heard Penny's yell of protest, but that didn't stop AJ, and I could only bat my hands pathetically at the stream of piss, spattering it over my face and legs as well as my middle. AJ was still laughing, and began to do it over my boobs as I finally managed to get my breath back, and between them, filling my cleavage and plastering my top to my skin, hot and wet and sticky. I didn't even fight, but just let her do it, my eyes still closed, pee dripping from my fringe and out of my nose.

She finished off over my belly and the mound of my pussy, leaving me sodden and sitting in a pool of it. Not that it was over. I felt her climb onto the chair, a hand twisted into my hair and my head was pulled forwards, against her pussy. My eyes were stinging horribly; my mouth was full of the taste of her piss and I felt I was going to be sick, but she didn't care, rubbing herself in my face as I struggled to stop myself from doing it.

'Lick it, bitch,' she drawled, and I did, my tongue in the salty folds of her sex, lapping up her pee and her juice.

I could feel her rings against my tongue, and the little hard bud of her clit. Her spare hand came down to grab one of my boobs, groping me and squeezing piddle from my sodden top. The pool in my cleavage broke, running warm pee down my belly and over my pussy, onto the ruined chair beneath me. Still I licked, broken to her will with the scents of piss and leather and girl strong in my head, my nipples hard, my pussy aching and stretched on the plum I'd put in myself.

AJ came, full in my face, her pussy tightening against my mouth, her grip painfully tight in my hair, her nails digging into the flesh of my boob. I didn't even try to fight it, now wanting the pain, and the humiliation, of being pissed on, of being made to lick her, of being hurt and degraded in front of my girlfriend . . .

I was going to masturbate the instant she'd finished, in front of them both, with my hands down my soaking panties and my boobs pulled out. As she climbed off, my hands went straight to my jeans, popping the button. AJ laughed as my fingers pushed down my panty crotch to find my pussy, wet with her pee, my hole agape around the plum.

'That's right, frig off, you little slut!' She chuckled. 'No, get your face in there, Muffet, you're not getting away with it.'

Penny didn't answer, and I paused to pull my tits out, hauling my soggy top and my ruined bra high to spill them onto my chest, naked and wet with piss, my nipples straining up. I wanted to play with them while Penny licked me, and AJ laughed at us, maybe beat Penny to encourage her, maybe made her piss to add to the mess . . .

'Please, Penny, darling, do it,' I begged. 'Lick me . . . please . . .'

Again she didn't answer, but I had to come, one way or the other. I lifted my bum, to push down my jeans and my panties too. My thighs came wide as my bare bottom settled onto the pee-soaked cushion beneath me and I was spread, open for them both, the plum showing in my hole.

'Why have you got a plum in your cunt?' AJ demanded, more derisive than ever.

'It was part of the game,' Penny answered defensively.

'A right pair of little tarts, aren't you?' AJ answered her. 'Go on, Muffet, eat it out of her, now, or do I have to drag you over and stick your face where it belongs?'

'There's no need to be like that,' Penny answered, but she had stood up, her voice coming from a different place.

I spread my thighs wider, encouraging her, letting my wet panties and jeans down to my ankles. AJ gave a sour laugh. I had to see, and to open my eyes before my lids got stuck down, so I forced myself, revealing the room in a pissy haze, AJ a dark blur, standing over me, Penny kneeling between my legs. My body was steaming gently.

Penny went down, lapping hesitantly at my pussy as I once more took my boobs in hand, feeling my now sticky skin and my taut, sensitive nipples. I spread my legs as far as they would go, offering myself to her, determined to get her over her reluctance. Her licking immediately became firmer, right on my clitty and my mouth came open in pleasure.

Above me, AJ had folded her arms over her chest and was watching us with amusement, cool and poised as I prepared to come off in a pool of her urine. I was wishing she had more, lots more, enough to fill my mouth and soil my hair, to leave Penny a sodden, dripping mess the way I was, to fill my belly until I was sick, to engulf us in a torrent of lovely hot piss . . .

I would have come, but Penny stopped, leaving me right on the brink. Her lips found the plum, sucking on it, and I felt the cool juice spurt over my pussy as the skin burst, and trickle down onto my bumhole. For one brief instant she hesitated, and then she was licking between my cheeks, slurping up plum juice from my crease and lapping it out of my hole. I knew then she'd given in, her dirty instincts getting the better of her. She loves to lick my bottom.

She took hold of me, her arms around my thighs, pulling herself in as she lapped up the mixture of juice and piddle from my bumhole. AJ could see, and Penny didn't resist when her top was pulled up, or as her jeans were undone and pushed down off her bum. Her panties followed, and AJ began to spank her, just as I'd hoped, encouraging her to lick as her bottom danced and jiggled to the slaps.

Not that she needed much encouragement. Her tongue was deep up my bottom and her nose was rubbing on my clit, bringing me back up to the edge. My hands tightened on my boobs as I felt my pussy contract. The plum squeezed free, plopping into Penny's mouth. I was there and she was pushing cool, mushy plum flesh into my pulsing bumhole as I came in her face, screaming in ecstasy, my hands locked on my sticky, pissed-on boobs, her nose wiggling on my clitty, her tongue so deep I felt my ring close on it.

I'd started to squirt, as I always do, fluid erupting from my pee hole into Penny's face, but still she licked my anus and still she rubbed my clit, and all of it was to the sound of slaps as the woman who had urinated over me spanked her. It was so good, so dirty, pissed on and licked to ecstasy, my clothes ruined, my chair ruined, my body taken right out of my control . . .

My orgasm broke to the realisation that AJ really had made a serious mess. Not that it stopped Penny, who was playing with her breasts as she licked, and I had to take her by the hair and pull her off when my pussy had become too sensitive to be touched. AJ didn't care, grabbing her by the collar and heaving her bodily onto me to carry on the spanking. Penny was already masturbating, her hand down between her legs as she was punished, and I took hold of her, cuddling her close. Her body was jerking to the smacks, and as she took a nipple in her mouth to suckle me I knew she was nearly there, only for AJ to stop abruptly. Penny's mouth came off my nipple and she was begging the next instant.

'Don't stop! Finish me off, AJ!'

'Shut it,' AJ answered. 'Here, look at this, looks like I've spoiled your silly game.'

She bent down, and came up with the snakes and ladders board. It had been under the edge of my chair, and it was soaked with pee. We'd drawn it on a piece cut out of a box, and the cardboard was so wet it had already started to come apart, but I couldn't see what was so funny that it was making AJ grin like a wolf. Then I found out.

'Open wide, Muffet,' she ordered. 'Keep a good hold on her, Dumplings, I'm going to make her eat this stupid thing.'

I'd have let go if Penny had tried to fight, but she was too far gone. All she managed was a miserable sob and her mouth had come open, looking back towards AJ, with her fingers still moving on her pussy and her spanked bottom pushed up. AJ's grin grew broader still as she tore off a chunk from the ruined game. I held on, not to restrain her, but to comfort her as she was forced to degrade herself, because I knew that, for all that she would do it, her mind would be burning with humiliation.

AJ pushed the piece of piss-soaked mush into Penny's mouth and she was doing it, holding it in her mouth as she masturbated, yellow trickles already running down her chin, and pale ones from her eyes where she had started to cry. She was still rubbing though, her muscles starting to twitch against me and her bottom moving up and down. It was going to make her come, in tears of humiliation, spanked and made to hold the soggy remains of our game in her mouth, but that wasn't enough for AJ.

'When I say eat it, I mean eat it!' she snarled, and pushed the cardboard hard into Penny's mouth.

Her eyes popped as it was jammed into her throat, and a froth of yellowish bubbles sprouted from her nose. For a moment she was resisting, wriggling in my arms and trying to cough the pulp in her mouth back up even as AJ pushed it deeper. Then she'd given in completely, chewing, starting to masturbate again, and swallowing, her eyes popping again as she took her mouthful down. AJ laughed and tore off more, forcing it into Penny's gaping mouth, and once more starting to spank her. Penny just stuck her bottom up, chewing on the cardboard with piss streaming down her chin and over my boobs. The tears were running freely from her eyes, and when she swallowed her filthy mouthful she retched, but she held it down, and the next instant she was coming.

Penny went wild as AJ stuffed the rest of the ruined game in, a great ball of piss-soaked pulp that left her cheeks bulging. She started to writhe on my lap, squirming and bucking to the spanks, wriggling her bottom with her legs cocked wide and her fingers working hard in the wet folds of her sex. I held on, cuddling her as she shook in her miserable ecstasy, to the tune of AJ's laughter and the slaps on her punished bottom, coming over and over as she chewed on her disgusting mouthful.

It took her for ever, and AJ didn't stop, Penny's orgasm riding on the spanking to peak after peak of ecstasy. Only when she tried to swallow the cardboard in her mouth did it break, the ball simply too big to take down. She began to choke. AJ stopped, slapped her on the back, and Penny was coughing up the whole filthy mess, all over my boobs.

I squeaked in alarm, sure she was going to be sick all over me, but I held on, torn between the urge to comfort her and my horror at what I was sure was about to happen to me. She didn't, coughing and retching until both my boobs were covered in bits of mushy cardboard, but at least holding her dinner down. AJ went on slapping, until in the end Penny had got her windpipe clear and found her voice.

'Sorry,' she gasped, and spat the last of the pulp out into my cleavage.

The moment AJ saw that Penny was OK she was laughing again, loud and high, her cool dominance starting to crack over the ludicrous sight we made. Penny slumped down on top of me, her breath coming out in a long, satisfied sigh, indifferent to her face being right in the mess or the state of her top. My flesh was beginning to get seriously sticky, and I was less than comfortable, but I wanted to hold Penny until she'd come down properly, and stayed cuddled onto her. AJ leaned down, bracing herself on the arms of the chair to keep herself well clear of the mess, and kissed me.

It was so sweet, and exactly right after the way she'd treated us, and I opened my mouth under hers and reached up to hug her. Instantly her hands went up under my armpits, tickling me. I screamed in shock, managed one desperate plea for her to get off as our mouths came apart, and then it was too late. Her weight was on Penny, pushing us into the chair, and I couldn't get up. I couldn't control myself anyway, giggling stupidly with my muscles already jerking in helpless reaction.

Penny knows, and she tried to squirm away, down between AJ's body and mine. Only we'd stuck together, her tits firmly glued to my tummy as AJ's pee dried. I heard her squeak in pain and she began trying desperately to ease our flesh apart as I jerked and kicked beneath her, with AJ's fingers pushed deep up under my arms and tickling hard. I couldn't stop myself. I couldn't do anything but giggle and squirm and kick my legs and thump ineffectually on AJ's back. Even my desperate pleas for her to stop only came out as a ridiculous bubbling noise, and I knew I couldn't hold . . .

It happened. My bladder burst, all over Penny's tummy, down her legs and onto her pussy, into her lowered jeans and panties, and my own, on the floor. AJ heard the hiss of pee and Penny's shriek of shock and disgust, and was laughing wildly as she went right on tickling me. Penny broke free with a gasp of pain as our skin separated, only to catch my stream full in her face and over her head as she squeezed out from underneath AJ, who moved quickly aside. My legs were wide, kicked up in helpless agony at the tickling, and with Penny gone my stream squirted high, all over the living-room floor.

AJ stopped, but it was far too late. I felt too weak to move anyway, and just let it all come out, spraying over the floor, then into the chair beneath me as it died to a trickle. She was still laughing, and she knew full well that I can't take being tickled and, if there's anything at all in my bladder when I am, it comes right out. There had been plenty, and now it was all over me, and Penny, and the room.

'You . . . you . . .' I managed, still unable to get the words I wanted to say out of my mouth.

She slapped my face and thrust her finger up in front of my eyes.

'You fuck up the cabaret, Dumplings, and you get that again, not in private, not in a bar, but in the street.'

Two

We had eight days to get the cabaret ready for the following Saturday night, which was not a lot. It was also left to me, with Penny not fully involved and AJ's only contribution her threat of what she'd do to me if I failed. She wasn't joking either. I knew she'd do it and, after all, there's no law against tickling your friends in the street. There's no law against wetting yourself in the street either, but that didn't make the prospect of being made to do it any better for me.

Penny did at least help on the Saturday, coming with me to the flat in Victoria where Poppy lived with her girlfriend, Gabrielle. I'd met them, but only briefly, and was worried that Gabrielle would object. She didn't, and Poppy was full of enthusiasm, even offering to run up some matching school skirts so that we could all be in the same uniform. We left after agreeing to meet up on the Saturday afternoon to decide the details. I was in a great mood as we travelled back on the Piccadilly. She was no more keen on men or straights than I was, but the idea of stripping and playing in front of them didn't seem to bother her at all, and that made it a lot easier.

Poppy was fun and, if we hadn't got down to anything, it was plain from her manner, and

Gabrielle's, that it was possible. She had also recommended a friend as another member of the team, a bi-girl called June, who sounded just right. June lived out in Beaconsfield, but Poppy had called and the invitation had been accepted like a shot. That made three of us, and we could be sure of Naomi if she'd already promised AJ, so we could afford either Zoe or Sophie to turn us down.

Sophie had taken a job working for Morris Rathwell's property concern, but she wasn't at home, or answering her mobile. Zoe was easy, because she was at college and still living with her parents, but bringing in some extra cash by stripping at Sugar Babe's. Her parents had no idea what she got up to, and she kept her gear with me. She was coming over that evening.

We went into town with her, discussing the cabaret on the tube. She wanted to join in, but it meant missing a night at Sugar Babe's, which generally brought her in a lot more than the miserable amount Bob Ryman was offering. We were on late though, and in the end she agreed to come up if she could. That made four definite and one probable.

Sugar Babe's had changed since I'd first been there, from a hangout for strippers and peep-show girls to a slick and expensive night-spot packed with wannabe celebs, minor-league footballers and so on, all keen to bask in the bad reputation it no longer really had. Zoe's strip was great, with her peeling down from a Japanese sailor-girl costume to just her tiny white panties, which was as far as she was allowed to go. She was on later too, but by then Penny and I had been hit on by so many men we decided not to wait, but moved on, intending to go to Whispers. I was horny enough to be thinking about putting on a show for the girls in the back room, and half-hoping AJ and her friends would be there.

We never got there. As we turned into Old Compton Street, an enormous man emerged from a pasta restaurant, nearly knocking into us. I turned to tell him to watch where he was going and realised I knew him, 'Fat Jeff' Bellbird, a dirty bugger if ever there was one, and with him was a petite girl with shoulder-length blonde hair – Sophie Cherwell. We didn't really need her, and I wasn't at all sure about letting Fat Jeff know what was going on, but Penny spoke before I could do anything about it.

'Hello, Sophie, just the girl we've been looking for.'

'What's up?' Sophie answered, and kissed her, then me as Penny went on.

'We're doing a cabaret next week . . . well, Jade is. Would you like to be in it?'

'Yeah . . . probably. What are you up to?'

'It's for a new club, at the Palace in Muswell Hill,' I explained. 'They want us to do some lesbian schoolgirl stuff.'

'What, flashing my bum and tits for hundreds of horny clubbers? Yeah, I'm up for it!'

'Schoolgirl stuff? Nice!' Jeff put in. 'When is this?'

'Saturday night,' I told him, knowing it was pointless to lie. 'We're meeting at my flat on Saturday afternoon to go through it, Sophie. No men allowed, I'm afraid, Jeff.'

Sophie went on as the beaming expression on Jeff's huge, bearded face changed to a sulky frown. 'I'm free. Who else is in?'

'Zoe, who you met at Morris's. Naomi, who was there too, punky-looking girl. Poppy, and a friend of hers I haven't met, June.'

'June, as in Boots June?' Jeff asked.

'I . . . I'm not sure. She's half-Indian apparently . . .'

'Yeah, that's her, fat tits, big round arse . . . not as

meaty as you maybe, but pretty close. She'll be good, filthy little mare, she is.'

I opened my mouth to protest at the way he was talking about me, but shut it. It was pointless, as much use as resenting the wind for blowing my skirt up. Penny knew, and quickly tried to change the subject, speaking to Sophie.

'We were going to Whispers.'

'Lezzer bar, ain't it?' Jeff broke in. 'They're not going to let me in, are they?'

'Well, no,' she answered. 'I didn't mean to imply . . .'

'We're going dogging,' he carried on, oblivious, 'up your way as it goes. Want to come?'

'Dogging?' Penny queried.

'Yeah, you know,' he went on, 'sex in cars so voyeur types can watch. We were out with Monty last night, at this great place some of the boys from his company go to. You should've fucking seen it! Six blokes, I swear, all tossing off like they're demented or something while Soph gives 'em a bum and tit show.'

Sophie made a wry face, obviously embarrassed by the admission of what she'd been up to with him. I could understand it though. Exhibitionism was her thing and all the better outdoors, but she knew better than to take risks. With Jeff there were no risks, his bearlike bulk enough to give anyone second thoughts about trying to push their luck. He wasn't the type to start getting possessive over her either, so all in all he was the ideal companion for her dirty games, despite being a sort of human butter mountain.

Flaunting herself so that some dirty old men could get off might have turned her on, but it was not really my thing, even if they were kinky. Getting put on the cross in the back room at Whispers by the butch girls was far more appealing. Still, Penny was a bit bruised from the spanking AJ had given her, and she'd done it before even if she wasn't up on the current term. We didn't have to join in anyway, and watching Sophie get rude did appeal, a lot. The offer also meant a lift home. I threw Penny a glance. She shrugged.

'OK, let's go,' I said to Jeff, 'but I'm not up for anything, just watching.'

'Whatever,' he answered, and went on as we turned north into Dean Street, 'a lot of the sites are listed on the web now, so you get loads of blokes, but you get police too. That's what's good about Monty's place, strictly local. So's the one we're going to. We got talking to one of the blokes who jerked off over Soph afterwards, and he recommended it. Says he might even be there. Hey, am I going to be the man or fucking what, with three chicks!'

Sophie threw me an arch look, and I stuck my tongue out at her. Penny says I get her into trouble, but it works two ways, especially with her taste for humiliation. Sophie was no better, maybe worse. Still, all I had to do was be cool and enjoy the view, then I could get my own fun back at the flat with Penny, maybe Sophie too, and, well, if Jeff wanted to watch I could be sure AJ wouldn't find out.

His car was parked well north of Oxford Street, where they'd left it before going to the restaurant. The three of us got in the back, leaving Jeff to drive, and were soon cuddled up together as we made our way north through the traffic. Jeff stopped in Kentish Town to buy beers, and I thought he was going to take us onto the Heath, but he turned east, finally parking near the bottom of Muswell Hill, no more than a mile from my flat.

It was very quiet, a big empty car park with a wooded slope on one side and open space leading down to a railway on the other. He'd locked the doors, but I still felt nervous, and was scanning the bushes for movement as the engine died and the lights faded. For a moment I could see very little, but there were lights, dull orange, and brighter ones in the distance on the railway, casting coloured shadows and making patches of absolute black. It was easy to imagine the men there, watching us expectantly, their big, ugly cocks already out of their trousers, thinking how much they'd like just to take us out and fuck us . . .

I'm no virgin, having had my fair share of boyfriends before I started to come to terms with my sexuality, but I can never really get into the idea of sex with men. They're so ugly, and their cocks are just grotesque, however good one feels inside. Just thinking of what they would want to do to me had me scared, and I was very glad we had the doors locked and Jeff with us, who could at least be trusted not to force me.

Jeff turned the interior light on, meaning we couldn't see a thing, but we could be seen. I scrambled quickly into the front seat beside Jeff, wanting to make it very plain that I was not part of the show. Penny looked doubtful, scanning the now dark bushes with one finger in her mouth and her hand on her tummy. Not Sophie: her eyes were glittering and full of mischief as she kneeled up on the seat and shrugged her fleece off.

'Penny?' she asked and took her tits in her hands, offering them.

Penny gave a nervous nod and grabbed hold, feeling the outline of Sophie's breasts under her top. Sophie had a hold-up bra, and she's not small, making them really stand out, with her nipples poking up through the material as they came hard under Penny's thumbs. Sophie giggled, her eyes flicking between Penny's caressing hands and the window, for all that we couldn't see a thing.

Jeff had half turned in his seat, watching them as I was, and squeezing his crotch. I moved a little away, but there was a lump in my throat and my pussy felt ticklish, just from the tension of what we were doing and the way Penny was exploring Sophie's breasts. We'd played together, many times, but this was different, less intimate maybe, but somehow dirtier, because they were doing it for men.

'Take them out, Soph,' Jeff grunted.

Sophie responded with an odd little noise, half sigh, half whimper, but immediately pulled her top up, to show off a pale pink bra with her boobs held in by rounded, lacy cups. Her nipples stood out as little bumps in the cotton, and it was just a little small for her, making her flesh bulge over at the tops. She took hold underneath to flip it up and free her boobs into Penny's hands, each the size of a big orange, and as round as they get. Penny hesitated only an instant, and then she'd taken one nipple into her mouth and she was sucking, with Sophie holding her breast up and deliberately turned to one side so that anyone outside could see.

I was enthralled, just watching Penny suckle, and knowing how humiliating she would find the idea of doing it for unknown male watchers. She'd put a hand between her thighs, caressing herself gently through her jeans, and my own pussy wanted attention, but I could only think of the unseen eyes watching us. I took a moment to peer out of the window, my hands cupped around my eyes, and found myself staring full into the wrinkled face of an old man, balding, his skin red and sweaty with excitement, his eyes bulging. I very nearly screamed, and my hand went to my heart as I jerked back, to find my pulse racing.

'There's someone out there!' I managed. 'An old man . . . just a few feet away!'

Sophie's reaction was to giggle and turn her body so that her back was to the seat, giving anyone looking in from my side a better view. Penny had to move, and I could see that she was shaking as she laid herself into Sophie's lap and once more began to suckle. There was a huge lump in my throat, which I struggled to swallow, thinking of the raw, desperate lust I'd seen in the man's eyes. He'd vanished from sight, but I knew he would still be there, in the bushes, probably with his dirty, ugly cock in his hand, wanking.

'Give him a bit more then,' Jeff urged, glancing down to Sophie's waist.

Sophie nodded, and her hands went to her jeans. Her mouth was a little open, her neck flushed, and her fingers were trembling as she popped open her button and drew down her zip. She kneeled up, pushing her bottom out to the window and peering back over her shoulder. Her low-rise jeans barely covered the top of her crease as it was, and her bum made a full rounded ball under the black denim.

'Nice and slow,' Jeff advised. 'The dirty old sod'll love that.'

The 'dirty old sod' wasn't the only one who was going to enjoy it. Jeff had his hand on his cock, which made a big, rigid bar in his trousers. He looked huge, and I was sure he was going to try and make me take him in my hand, even my mouth. I swallowed again, shaking at the thought and at the horrible compunction actually to do it. Telling myself that if I did it would be just to make sure he didn't fuck me, I turned back to Sophie. Her thumbs were in her waistband, and I could see the top of her panties – bright red ones.

'Ready?' she asked. 'Is he watching?'

Jeff grunted, and quickly reached up to turn the light off. It took an instant for my eyes to adjust, then I could see. The bushes were as before, shapes of shadow and dim light, only in different patterns, and in a moment I had begun to make out the men, standing motionless, their faces pale ovals, their eyes glued to the car.

'Five of the fuckers,' Jeff said with satisfaction. 'Go on, Soph, give 'em what they want.'

He flicked the light back on. Sophie was biting her lip as she began to push her jeans down, taking her panties with them, eased slowly off her bum to reveal her rounded cheeks and the deep cleft between, inch by inch. Soon her whole gorgeous peach was on show, but she didn't stop, pushing it all the way down to her knees so that her pussy would be on view from behind. I could smell her, and I badly wanted to touch myself, but held back, determined not to give in.

Sophie was bare from her neck to her knees, and she held her pose, half turned to let them admire her tits. I was sure they'd be tossing their dirty cocks, determined to come while she was in such a rude position, maybe already with their filthy spunk running down their hands. The thought sent a shiver right through me, and again I had to resist the urge to put my hand between my legs, although I didn't know if it was more for protection or the need to touch myself.

'Go on, Pen,' Jeff urged, 'touch Soph up. They love a bit of lessie action.'

Penny made a wry face, but took Sophie gently by the shoulders, to turn her over the back seat, bum up. Sophie's cheeks came open, showing off her sweet little pussy, with her lips shaved and just a little puff of golden blonde hair left on her mound, her bumhole too, pink and glistening where her juice had run down. Penny began to spank. Jeff gave a grunt of appreciation. I heard the rasp of his zip being pulled down, and caught the smell of his cock.

I had to look: it was more than I could do to stop myself. It was right out, his scrotum too, a column of thick meat over a big, hairy, wrinkled bag with his balls moving about inside, at once utterly disgusting and utterly compelling. He began to wank and I turned back to watching Sophie get her spanking, her cheeks already flushed pink, her tight little bumhole winking, her pussy running juice in her excitement. I could hold back no more, I just had to touch myself, and my hand went down between my legs to feel the swell of my pussy lips through my jeans.

The denim was pulled well up into the groove of my pussy, and I knew I could come, just as I was, rubbing myself through them without having to go bare for the men. I began to do it, and I saw that Penny was at it too, surreptitiously masturbating even as she spanked Sophie's quivering bottom. We exchanged a smile, both knowing what the other was thinking.

Sophie was getting hot, her cheeks glowing pink, and her pussy absolutely sopping. I wanted to spank her too, and to kiss her cheeks when she was done, to soothe her after her punishment. I wanted to lick her, to swallow down her juice and make her come under my tongue. I wanted the same treatment myself, bent over with my bottom bare for spanking in the dim light of the car . . .

So did Penny. She abruptly stopped spanking and stuck her face in between Sophie's cheeks, buried deep. I could see her tongue was up Sophie's bottom hole, licking wantonly at the tight pink ring the way she loves to, but she kept her tongue in for just a moment before she had moved again, over the seat, side by side with Sophie. She wriggled herself quickly out of her jeans and panties, exposing her bum, and looked back hopefully.

Jeff didn't need any further encouragement. He swivelled round, still tugging at his cock, left-handed, as he began to spank them both, clumsily, but hard, one after the other, his fat red hand slapping down on their cheeks. I wanted to join them, and if it had been a girl doing the spanking I would have done, dirty old men or no dirty old men. It was the thought of exposing myself to Jeff's great ugly cock that stopped me. If I went over, and when I'd got hot, there would be nothing to stop him mounting up on my back. I'd be helpless under his weight, and he'd fuck me, ramming himself home up my ready pussy. He might even bugger me, forcing my poor little bumhole despite my pain and my protests, to spunk deep in my gut, and I wouldn't even put up a fight . . .

I grabbed his cock, jerking hard at him even as my skin crawled to the sensation of touching a man's penis. He responded with a pleased grunt and turned his full attention to the girls' bums, leaning over the back of the seat with a hand to each. Penny was getting pink, and making a lot more fuss about it than Sophie, but both of them had put their hands back, rubbing their pussies in wanton ecstasy. I heard a grunt, right outside their window, and the next instant it was splashed with spunk, even as Jeff came in my hand, hot spunk dribbling down my fingers as I finished him off with a series of hard tugs.

He was done, which made me safe. I wiped my hand on his leg and began to scramble into the back, eager for my share. I was so turned on, but I still felt I was betraying myself, and AJ, as I pushed down my jeans and squeezed in between the girls, lifting my bottom for Jeff's attention, but I had at least kept my panties up. Penny kissed me and I responded, our mouths opening together as I got comfortable, ready to rub off through my panty crotch as I was warmed behind. Jeff's hand found my bottom, his fingers sticky with spunk, and a fresh shiver of disgust ran through me.

It did feel awful. There were men watching me, a man about to spank me, and I was going to rub off for them. No, I was going to rub off for me, and with Sophie and Penny to either side of me, their soft, sweet flesh pressed to mine, teasing the men, giving only what we wanted to, and I did still have my panties up. They weren't very big and most of my bum cheeks were sticking out at the sides, but the top showed even with my jeans up, on purpose. My pussy was covered, and that was what mattered . . .

. . . until Jeff jerked them roughly down, exposing me completely, my bare pussy and my bumhole too, nude for all to see with my fingers tangled in my dropped panties. Penny was holding me, our mouths together, and for a moment there was nothing I could do but kick out behind, an utterly futile gesture. As we broke apart I cried out in protest, just as he started to spank me, landing a slap across my bum so hard it knocked the breath from my body.

'Sorry, love,' he said, as I heard the smack of his palm on one of the others' targets. 'I'd heard you liked it hard.'

'No . . . not that . . . it's not that . . .' I managed, breaking to a squeak as my turn came again. 'My . . . my pussy's showing . . . I . . .'

'Yeah, cute,' he drawled, and stuck one fat finger right up my hole.

I screamed, but he began to finger me, and he was still spanking us, the slaps and Penny's cries echoing out around the car. Sophie had begun to squeal; I knew she was coming, and as she grabbed my head and forced her mouth to mine my protests were abruptly cut off, with Fat Jeff's finger still working in my hole. My control had been taken away from me, and I gave in, with a last stab of bitter resentment as I began to frig, masturbating myself through my panty crotch in front of the watchers, not just with my bum bare, but with my pussy hole penetrated.

They were there too, watching, and wanking. I saw a fat dun-brown cock pressed to the glass, the man with his balls in his hand and a pair of grubby dun-coloured trousers open at the crotch, as if he was trying to get as close as possible to Sophie's body. He'd have heard the shrill squeals she'd made as she started to come, and she'd have been willing, if not for the window, and so would I, the final strand of my resistance snapping as I imagined what could happen as my own orgasm hit me.

Our door would come open. We would be dragged out, thrown down in the mud, stripped nude, Jeff just laughing at us as our jeans and tops, our panties and bras were torn off. They'd fuck us, all five of them, in our pussies, in our mouths, up our bums, using us until every one of them had come. We'd be left there, on the dirty ground, soiled and filthy, spunk in our mouths and over our faces, in our hair and on our tits, up our pussies and up our bottom holes . . .

I broke from Sophie and screamed as the hideous prospect of one of the men outside spunking up my bottom hit me. There is simply nothing dirtier, nothing ruder, than to let a man put his erection up your bottom and spunk in your rectum, except maybe to make you suck his cock clean afterwards, and that was the awful, filthy thought I was holding in my head as I rubbed myself up towards orgasm.

Sophie was still there, and Penny too, their piping squeals and wanton cries joining my screams and the sound of our spanking as the three of us came together. I was so, so high, my brain fizzing with the thought of all the awful things that could be done to me, and all the while with Jeff spanking my bare bottom and working his finger in and out of my sopping pussy as fluid squirted over and over from my pee hole.

He'd put a second finger in just as I started to come down, and a third, then a good half of his fat fist, stretching me to bursting point. I cried out in shame and pain too, and he pulled back, to leave my pussy gaping behind and me sobbing over the thick, paint-smeared blanket in the back of his car. I really thought it was over but, as I began to get up, one last obscene detail was added to my experience.

The man at the window had pushed closer still, jamming himself up against it so that his cock and balls were squashed out on the glass, also his dirty trousers and an expanse of hairy, lard-coloured belly. He'd come, and the crevices in his flesh and the folds of his trousers were filled with sticky, white spunk.

Three

My Sunday was spent in bed with Penny, just cuddling and drinking coffee until late in the afternoon. She had to prepare a lecture for first thing on the Monday morning, so she left as darkness started to fall and I got an early night in an attempt to catch up on my sleep. It was just as well, because the agency phoned at half-eight with a booking in the Farringdon Road. It was for the full five days, and from nine to six, which more or less swallowed my week at a gulp.

I didn't even have much time to think, because the work was in a mailroom with a dozen other temps all packing Christmas decorations for a rush order from one of the supermarkets. It was simple enough, tedious really, but what with talking to my work mates and avoiding the lecherous attentions of the overseer, who was obsessed with my boobs, I barely had a chance to work out the cabaret.

We were on for half an hour, which is a long time to keep an audience amused, even with a sex show. It can't be too slow, or they start to lose interest, and it can't be too fast or you run out of things to do. I don't really have much experience with stage shows either, and the only solution I could think of was to bring the focus onto each of us in turn, so that there would always be some new flesh to show. It seemed to make sense, because if there's one thing I've noticed about men it's that they love the idea of seeing a girl used up, in the sense that once she's performed a particular act she is somehow spoiled. After all, that's what the whole virginity thing is about.

The other thing I could be sure of was that Naomi would expect to top us. That was OK, and I could easily cast her in the role of prefect or, better still, school bully, which went with her punky look, currently spiked green hair in a Mohican. If she dealt with us one by one, with a slightly different and slightly harder punishment or humiliation each time, it would certainly take up half an hour, with just six minutes each.

That was as far as I'd got by Saturday morning, and I was so knackered after my week's work that I lay in until lunchtime, and was still wandering around in my robe and a pair of fluffy slippers when the doorbell rang. It was Poppy and Gabrielle, both holding large bags, and a third girl, who from her coffee-cream skin colour and dark chocolate hair had to be June. I threw the keys down and went to put the kettle on as they came up.

June was every bit as cute as Jeff had made out, and as much fun. She was a little taller than me, and very nearly as curvaceous, with big boobs over a tiny waist, full hips and a lovely fat bottom, with her jeans worn so low the top of her crease showed. So did the top of her bright green thong, and her crop top left her little round tummy bare and the maple leaf tattoo in the small of her back showing. She was giggling over what we were going to do from the moment she came in, full of enthusiasm and determined to make a night of it.

By the time we'd finished our first coffee she and I were swapping stories about the outrageous behaviour of Fat Jeff, who had managed to seriously freak her out despite her being on the straight side of bi. Poppy and Gabrielle knew him too, and we spent a happy half hour which must have made his ears burn white-hot, discussing him and his equally gross friend Monty. There was irony in it though, because, one way or another, they'd had all four of us.

We were still talking about them when Penny turned up, and it was only then that Poppy began to unpack her bags. The skirts were lovely, pleated bright red tartan and short enough to get any real schoolgirl sent home on the spot. She hadn't stopped at skirts either, but had bought dark green ties with embroidered crests and, as a final cute touch, little Tam O'Shanters to match our skirts. Along with the white blouses, white knee socks and little black shoes we were to supply ourselves, we were going to drive the men mad, perhaps some of the girls too, with any luck.

Penny was delighted with the outfits, and obviously wanted to join in, immediately trying on a Tam O'Shanter and giving Poppy a friendly swat on the bottom for making the skirts so short. Poppy had made her a uniform too, completely ignoring her request, but after a moment of hesitation she declined, promising to look after our gear during the cabaret but nothing more.

I went to put the hot water on, and glanced out of the window as I came back, to find Naomi's old blue BMW reversing into a parking space a little way down the road. She can be a vicious bitch, if nothing like as bad as AJ, and I felt my stomach tighten as she climbed out, as tough as ever in her leathers, but fortunately on her own. With AJ around my ability to do anything but grovel crumbles pretty fast, and I needed to stay in control, at least until the cabaret was over.

She was going to need my keys, and I opened the window, but she didn't come over, going into one of the stores across the road instead and emerging a minute later with a pack of beers in each hand. I could see Sophie too, further down the street towards the tube station, and I waved. Both girls saw me at once, Sophie waving and Naomi responding with a smug grin. I let them up and returned to the others, who now had the uniforms spread out over the floor.

I only had one comfy chair; AJ had completely wrecked the other one as there is simply no way to get pee out of cushion stuffing. So we were sat in a ring on the floor, Gabrielle the only one in a chair until Naomi brought one out from the kitchen in what I was sure was a conscious effort to exert her dominance. Only Penny and Sophie knew her, and that strictly from clubs, but they all knew her reputation, which brought about an instant change in the atmosphere. Not that it was a bad thing, as such, but she had brought in that nervousness which is inevitable when you know somebody is likely to be applying their hand or a cane to your bare bottom before the evening is out.

We still had no idea what we were doing, so I took advantage of the lull in the conversation caused by Naomi's entrance to get down to working it out. The beers she'd bought had come straight out of the fridge, so I fetched an opener as she dished them out, trying to get my thoughts together as I took my first swallow. June got in first.

'So what are we doing? A schoolgirl strip or something?'

'It's got to be hardcore, hasn't it? You said, Jade?' Poppy asked.

'In a straight club?' Sophie queried. 'No way.'

'That's what the bloke who's running it said,' I confirmed.

'Yeah, as hard as we can go,' Naomi answered, 'that's what AJ's boss said.'

'Yes,' Penny put in, 'but does he realise what hardcore means to us? Is he straight, Naomi?'

Naomi just shrugged.

'He will want what is popularly perceived by men as lesbian sex,' Gabrielle stated, 'situations that pose your body for their voyeuristic pleasure first and foremost.'

'She's right,' I cut in, 'and it is a show, after all. It's half an hour long too, so this is what we do, OK? There are bound to be chairs, so we set up the stage as if we're in a classroom, maybe waiting for the teacher, who doesn't come . . .'

'How're we going to get that across?' June asked. 'This Bolero place doesn't sound like the sort of club where you can exactly hear each other speak.'

I'd been making it up off the top of my head, and she was right. The audience wouldn't be able to hear a thing.

'We'll keep it visual,' I went on, 'and they're not going to care why there are six schoolgirls sitting around on chairs, only that it gets dirty.'

'It's a school theme anyway, isn't it?' June went on.

'Yes,' I told her, 'so it's no good just posing around, when all the other girls are dressed the same.'

'We need to shock them,' Sophie put in. 'I want to piss my panties.'

June burst into giggles and suddenly they were all talking at once, each stating what she'd like to do or thought we ought to do. I put my hands up, desperately trying to get them to pay attention, and shouted over the noise.

'Hang on! Look, we each get to do our own thing, but one at a time. Shut up, will you!?'

They went quiet and I carried on quickly.

'Naomi's the school bully, right? She's picking on us one by one, pretending she's the teacher and punishing us. We haven't got the guts to fight back, and we just let her do it. So we need five different punishments, getting stronger as we go along. Any ideas?'

'We'd better let Zoe go first,' Penny put in, 'just for a plain spanking. She can't really take much.'

'OK, that's one,' I answered. 'Assuming she comes.'

'You have to be tickled, you do,' Naomi suggested.

'No, that's not fair,' I answered quickly. 'I hate it, I really do. I'm bound to wet myself if we've been drinking, and I think watersports is going a bit far for this Bob bloke.'

'Bollocks,' Sophie answered me. 'There'll be beer all over the floor, so a bit of piss won't make any difference. Naomi can cane me and I'll go in my panties as if it's an accident. Have you ever had a girl wet herself while she's caned, Naomi?'

I was going to try and dissuade her, but the doorbell went. Hoping it would be Zoe, I went to let her in, leaving Sophie to explain how the cane strokes needed to be even and not too hard so that she could concentrate on her bladder control. It was Zoe, and I threw down the keys.

'. . . you don't let go because of the pain, you clam up,' Sophie was saying as I sat down again, 'at least, I do.'

'I really don't think –' I began, but Naomi raised a hand to shut me up.

'It's good,' she said. 'AJ said hard, so we give them hard. There's going to be sex in the loos and shit anyway, and I think there's a striptease too, so we have to go further than they think we will.'

'You can make me lick you, Naomi,' Poppy volunteered, 'and I can take it hard.'

'I can't,' Zoe said from the door as she let herself in. 'What's happening?'

I began to explain, again, and slowly it started to come together. It made sense to shock, and we certainly had to go further than anything which was likely to be going on offstage, so that meant everything showing, and the kinkier the better. As there were going to be straight girls and men there, I put myself second, after Zoe had taken a spanking across Naomi's knee, to have my panties pulled up tight between my cheeks for a dose of the hairbrush. It would let me keep my pussy hidden, but it was going to hurt, and the prospect had my stomach fluttering the moment I'd consented to it.

By then June and Poppy were arguing over who could take the most, both of them sure that once drunk and horny they could handle anything Naomi could dish out. Poppy backed down suddenly at Gabby's suggestion that she ought to be put in a nappy instead for the sake of variety, and that was that. It was a fine piece of humiliation, and even surprised Naomi, so we agreed that June should be thrashed, Poppy given six hard ones and put in her nappy, and Sophie done last, wetting herself as she was caned. Naomi would then line all five of us up with our smacked bottoms to the audience and give us six each as a finale.

It had to be good enough, for Bob Ryman, for the audience and, most importantly, for Alice Jemima Croft. Not that there was any guarantee that she wouldn't subject me to public tickle torture anyway. I knew her well enough to be sure that once she'd got the idea of doing it into her head it was likely to happen regardless, but at least it wouldn't be in the street.

With the routine worked out we began to get ready, taking turns in the shower and changing into our uniforms. With the seven of us running around the flat naked or near naked and the prospect of showing off and getting punished, it was inevitable that we got horny. I also got nervous, thinking of the people who'd be watching, and I could tell Poppy felt the same for all her bravado. Zoe was scared, not of the men but because she was going to be caned at the end, but she likes to dish it out herself and was determined to learn to accept it. Sophie and June didn't seem to care.

It was dark by the time we were dressed and made up, and my pussy was damp and my stomach tying itself in knots. I felt deliciously rude in my uniform, but seriously vulnerable as well. I'd picked up a six pack of plain white school panties at lunchtime on the Friday, just to be sure we matched in every detail, but they were too tight for me, leaving my cheeks bulging out at the sides. They showed at the back too, a slice of white panty material visible below the red tartan, because Poppy had cut the skirts to just cover her own bottom, and mine was simply too big. If I bent over, anyone behind me got a real eyeful.

June looked just as rude, which was some consolation and, like me, her boobs were threatening to burst out of her blouse. It was good not to be the only busty girl, but I still had a few inches on her, and I was pretty sure Naomi wouldn't let me keep them covered even though she'd agreed not to show off my pussy.

Zoe was no younger than June, but she had a lot less on top, and bottom. She also had an innocence about her, and of all of us she was the only one who might have been let through the doors of a school. Her skirt covered her bum, just, and the same panties that were cutting into my flesh were a little baggy on her. She'd done her blouse right up and put her tie on properly as well.

Sophie hadn't, and for all her pretty blonde hair and sweet face she looked the dirty little slut she is, with her blouse knotted above her bare tummy and generous slices of her boobs showing between. Poppy went for the same style as Sophie, but she was too sweet to look anything more than wayward, with her curly black hair and her little snub nose. Anyway, next to Naomi she looked positively wet.

For one thing Naomi had three inches on any of us except Gabrielle, who wasn't dressed up. Her hair, her tats, her piercings, all combined to make her look the sort of girl who generates enquiries about delinquency in the education system. It was very easy indeed to imagine her as a school bully, especially as I knew full well that, if it had been a few years since she was at school, there was no doubt whatever about her sadistic leanings.

We ordered pizza to get something inside us, and I couldn't resist telling the delivery boy to bring it up. He was one of the regulars, a pasty-faced fat boy with greasy hair who went around with an expression of perpetual astonishment on his face. When he saw us the expression cranked up a good few gears, and with June bending at the mirror to touch up her eye-shadow it was hardly surprising. Her panty seat and plenty of plump, coffee-coloured bottom was sticking out under the hem of her skirt, enough to make the coolest stare, never mind Dough Boy.

The club was open from eight, but there didn't seem a lot of point in getting there early, so we ate our pizza and drank beer until we felt good and ready. Penny and Naomi both had their cars, but neither wanted to be used as a taxi service, so we ordered two cabs. The local company was practically next door, so most of the drivers know me, including the one we got, an enormously fat Greek guy – Lardo, as we called him – who forever had his eyes on my boobs. With me, Penny and Sophie in the back and Naomi beside him, his eyes were absolutely popping, and I was seriously worried he was going to crash on the short drive up to the Palace.

He didn't, and the effect we'd had on just two men was getting to all of us, myself included. I have got better about men ogling me. At least, I'd prefer to be stared at by a dirty man thinking what he'd like to do to me than by a straight girl thinking what a pervert I am. I'd had plenty to drink too, and with the seven of us together I felt OK, and we were going to be on stage. My stomach was still tying itself in knots as we entered the club by the back door. The bouncer there was a huge black man, maybe a head taller than Fat Jeff and just about as big around, only with a lot more muscle. He drew an appreciative glance from June as he gave us our passes, and she stayed back for a little before catching us up inside.

The club was much as I had expected, the huge hall lit with coloured lights that moved over a great throng of young men and women, just about all of them dressed in school uniform. Some of the girls were as cheeky as us, and there was plenty of panty on show. We didn't even stand out, especially as red tartan seemed to be the in-thing for skirts. Sophie had been right. There was a long bar to one side, and the music was so loud we had to shout to order our drinks. Bob Ryman proved as good as his word, the barman taking a quick glance at our passes and serving us for free.

Ryman himself turned up as we were getting the drinks, a slim, hard-faced man in a sharp suit and shades. There was another man with him, older, and much sleazier, with dyed black hair combed back around a balding crown, deep wrinkles in his artificially tanned face, and shades. I'd guessed he would be Ronnie Miles even before Bob Ryman had shouted it into my ear, and as he ran his eye over our figures it was less with lust than cool appraisal, as if weighing up our value for one of his dirty magazines.

We held a brief, shouted conversation, both of them urging us to be good and dirty. I promised we'd do our best, but their attitude left me unsure if we'd got it quite right. I went to Poppy and Naomi to make sure there was some pussy licking at the end, and suggested the others get a bit ruder if they felt up to it. It was as much as I felt I could do. Ryman gave us our money too, peeling ten-pound notes from a roll in his pocket, and I quickly distributed them.

The place we were performing in was an upstairs room, really a huge balcony overlooking the main hall. The floor was perforated steel, and the whole thing appeared to be suspended from the original iron roof girders, which was a bit unnerving. Beneath us was the 'VIP lounge', with assorted minor celebs and their cronies hanging around looking smug. They had the only chairs or tables in the place too, and it took all our powers of persuasion to get the bouncers to bring some up.

The stage was a platform of the same steel, raised a couple of feet. There was no backstage, as such, so Penny and Gabrielle made a pile of our coats and bags and tried to look inconspicuous in the corner. We still had over an hour, but I was getting seriously nervous, and took every advantage of the free drinks, knocking back beers and breezers as fast as they came. Sophie was on pints of cider, and her belly was soon bulging with it, so that by the time we were due on she'd had to lie down to ease the pain in her bladder.

By then I was drunk enough to be ready to take what was coming to me. We'd set out our 'classroom': six chairs set in two widely spaced rows in front of a single table, so that the audience would have a good view of each girl as we were punished. I took my seat right at the back, by force of habit, with June in front of me. She leaned back as the others took their seats, signalling to me. I leaned forwards, knowing full well the position left the seat of my overtight panties on plain view but too drunk to care any more.

'We're going to get Naomi at the end,' she whispered. 'Yeah?'

'Get Naomi!?' I gasped. 'What, spank her? June, she'll kill us!'

'Not all five of us she won't. Come on, we need you!'

'Yes, but –'

'Come on, Jade! We've got to do it, and it's only fair, after she's done all of us. Sophie's in already.'

'Well . . .'

I broke off as Bob Ryman's amplified voice boomed out over the PA, announcing 'lezzer action on the balcony space'. Dealing with Naomi did appeal, a lot, and, yes, we could do it easily enough. The trouble was she was not going to forget it in a hurry and at some point she would catch up with me when I didn't have any friends to help. Yet I wanted to do it, and if it was going to happen anyway . . .

'. . . it's gonna be hard, so get up there and feast your eyes!' Ryman ended, and I realised we were on.

There were already a lot of people watching us, and more were coming up the stairs, packing onto the balcony space. My stomach was still churning, and I was telling myself to remember Zoe's advice when stripping – to blank the audience from your mind. It was not easy, and I could hardly imagine it was easy for her, considering Naomi was about to spank her bare bottom in front of several hundred laughing, drunken clubbers.

They thought it was hilarious, jeering and catcalling from the moment they realised we were going to get kinky. I could hear the contempt in their voices too, disgust even, as Naomi hauled Zoe down over her lap and put her in a leg lock. We'd got it wrong, completely, but it was too late to back out, and I didn't want to either. It's about time straights learnt to accept kinky sex.

Not that I could expect them to understand, not the way Zoe reacts to a spanking. She was fighting like a she-cat from the moment Naomi took hold of her, and scratching and kicking out as she was forced into spanking position with one arm twisted tight into the small of her back. She quietened down a bit when her leg had been locked off, but the other one was still kicking as her skirt was hauled high to show off her panties. They came down; her little pink bottom was put on show, and the crowd went crazy.

She did look ridiculous, with her panties at half-mast and one leg pumping frantically up and down in the air as Naomi began to spank. Most of the audience just thought it was funny, and, if there were calls of appreciation, there were hoots of derision too, even demands for it to stop. Naomi didn't seem to care, slapping away at Zoe's bouncing bum cheeks with all her force, so hard she was making them part to give us all flashes of pert pussy lips and wrinkly pink bumhole.

Inevitably Zoe burst into tears, as she always does. It was obvious too, because she was howling like mad with her face screwed up in pain and misery and the droplets glittered in the light as they ran down her face. Immediately the crowd's attitude changed, with voices yelling for Naomi to stop, even threatening to give her a dose of her own medicine.

Naomi stopped and let go of Zoe, who tumbled over to sit down hard on her smacked bottom. She had tears streaming down her face, and for one awful moment I really thought the crowd were going to rush the stage, but she picked herself up and came forwards, smiling, to give them the sweetest little curtsey. Her panties were still around her thighs, and it showed her pussy off, her lips pink and bare in the bright spotlights they'd turned on the stage. Her face was a mess, her bottom red and blotchy, but there was no mistaking her pleasure. The crowd's aggression died abruptly, to my relief, but it was short lived. Naomi was coming towards me.

Immediately I felt I was going to be sick. It was worse than being done in front of the dirty old men, who had at least appreciated me. Most of the audience were laughing as Naomi hauled me to my feet by one ear, and I squeaked in pain as she abruptly spun me around and stuck a knee into the small of my back. It wasn't agreed, and it took me an instant to realise what she was doing, an instant too long, as her fingers caught in the front of my blouse and ripped it wide, buttons flying out into the audience.

I screamed in protest, but she just tightened her grip on my ear, really hurting, took a firm hold under my bra and jerked it high, flopping my boobs out for all to see. A great storm of catcalls, rude suggestions and insulting remarks rose up from the audience, men and women both, calling me 'melons' and 'udders' and asking how many they'd get to the pound. I was held, my chest thrust out, my boobs stark naked and shaking as I began to go into uncontrollable sobs.

They thought it was fake, but it wasn't, and the tears were starting in my eyes as Naomi twisted my ear, forcing me down and around as she started back to the front. I could do nothing, only hobble along behind her, bent double, my boobs swinging bare under my chest, my panties on show behind where my skirt had come up. She got to the table and threw me over, so hard I was left panting, then gasping in pain and shock as she grabbed the waistband of my panties and hauled them up, right up.

My feet left the ground, my whole lower body suspended from my panties, the material pulled up between my pussy lips agonisingly tight. I was squealing in pain, and kicking frantically, with the tears rolling down my cheeks. They all just laughed at me, now sure it was just part of the act, but my pain was real, and my humiliation, with my boobs squashed out naked on the table top and the full globe of my bottom naked behind. Worse, my panties were so tight up between my pussy lips, not even that was covered.

She just laid in, applying the hairbrush hard to my bare flesh as I writhed and squirmed in her grip. It hurt like anything, because I just wasn't ready for punishment, and in seconds I was gritting my teeth and hammering my fists on the table top. Slap after slap hit me, each one sending a shockwave right through my body. She'd taken my control away from me, but the raucous laughter and crude yells of the audience were too much. I was being called a tart, and a tramp, and a pig, all the things that get to me most . . .

. . . and I'd broken, blubbering pathetically in Naomi's grip as she thrashed me, my head tossing, my boobs slipping in my own tears and spit, stripped and spanked for the gloating attention of hundreds of callous bastards, and in unbearable ecstasy. My orgasm had hit me from nowhere, with the panty material jerking in my crotch and the hairbrush slamming over and over into my bottom. I was screaming as it tore through me, with my legs kicking out backwards, together and in time to the spanking, and as my ecstasy rose to a peak someone called out that I looked like an electrocuted frog.

The insult brought a sharp hit of humiliation, taking me to what I thought was the peak, that it could get no worse, and no better. It wasn't, and it did. The cheap panties I'd bought in Chapel Market finally parted under the strain, dumping me on the table, rear-end up, the whole fat moon of my bum flaunted to the lot of them, my pussy and anus pink and rude between, still twitching in orgasm. A grunt of shock and horror escaped my mouth, and a full-throated scream as Naomi brought the hairbrush down between my legs, right on my pussy, and again.

I was still coming, with my pussy spanked in front of all of them, and the pain and the exposure and the terrible humiliation all came together in a final, blinding peak as fluid squirted from my pee hole, adding one last, awful touch. My ears were singing; my vision had gone, and when Naomi at last let go of the tattered remnants of my panties I just collapsed on the floor, in a sweaty, broken, tear-stained heap, heedless of my exposed body and even my pain.

Some were clapping as I crawled away, others jeering. I managed a weak smile as I hauled myself up into my chair, but that was all. June was on, and already standing, pretending to face Naomi down as agreed, but I wasn't really paying attention. My bottom stung furiously, and I just had to rub, regardless of what I was showing off behind. I couldn't cover myself anyway, and it hurt to sit, so I stayed lifted, knowing my rosy cheeks were naked to the audience but too far gone to care.

She'd spanked me really hard, and, if my bad reaction to the audience wasn't her fault, she had hardly helped. It was impossible not to feel resentful, and I could see why the others wanted to make her take her turn afterwards. June didn't seem to want to wait, putting up a serious fight as Naomi struggled to get her down over the table. The audience were loving it, chanting 'Bitch Fight! Bitch Fight!', and it certainly looked real. Even when Naomi had finally put June in an arm lock and forced her face down over the table, she was still fighting.

Like me she'd had her blouse torn open, and like me her big tits were squashed out on the table, only still in their bra. But not for long. Naomi hauled the blouse back to trap June's arms, snipping her bra catch and wrenching it off, all the while with June swearing furiously and calling her every name in the book. Her bra went into the audience, her skirt was lifted and her panties came down, baring her bottom, with the full, coffee-cream cheeks open to show off every rude detail between.

It did look good, enough to take my interest off my own smacked behind. Her legs were kicking, and they began to kick faster as Naomi reached down to draw the cane from beneath the table, and faster still as the first stroke lashed down on her unprotected flesh. Her swearing got worse as she was thrashed, and her legs pumped ever faster, but she wouldn't break, still struggling in Naomi's grip. It only made things worse, the cane strokes catching her thighs and wrapping around her hips because she wouldn't keep still enough to present a decent target, but it just made her angrier, calling Naomi a bitch and a whore and worse.

She was yelling for it to be done harder too, challenging Naomi to do her worst, despite her whole bottom already being a mass of angry red and purple welts. Naomi laid in, her face red with effort and anger too, but it did no good, June screaming at her to beat harder, to really hurt her. The cane was a blur, slashing up and down on June's blazing cheeks, and every cut leaving a fresh welt, and June still screaming for more. I saw her hand come back, and she was frigging, with her pussy lips deliberately spread to show herself off and one finger on her clit. I could never, ever have kept so cool while I was being thrashed so hard, and as she went into a bubbling, writhing orgasm I was staring in amazement. So were the audience, a few of the crudest still chanting, but most of them in awe. I caught astonished comments from among the nearest, and doubts as to June's sanity.

Naomi realised June was coming, and stopped when it was over, to stand back, panting slightly, with her hands shaking from the effort of dishing out the beating. June stayed down for a moment, her fingers still rubbing in the wet folds of her sex, then stood and turned, a little unsteady on her feet but no more as she curtsied to the crowd. Her panties had fallen right down around her calves, and she slightly spoiled the effect by tripping over them as she went back to her seat, but the audience were clapping.

For all her bravado I noticed that she kept her caned bottom off the seat to spare her bruises, leaving it showing under the hem of her skirt as she hadn't bothered to pull her panties up. Poppy was already standing, and looking very meek with her head hung and her hands folded in front of her. Naomi looked knackered, but managed a derisive laugh and beckoned her up. Gabrielle tossed out the piece of towelling that was to be used for the nappy as Poppy came forwards.

Poppy was the opposite of June, completely meek. She was ordered to bend over and she did, to lift her skirt at the back and she did, to take down her panties and she did. Her legs came apart without her having to be told, showing off the puff of black fur between her legs, and the soft pink dimple of her bumhole. Naomi tapped the cane across her cheeks, lifted it and brought it down hard, but Poppy barely flinched, one thigh muscle twitching slightly, nothing more.

She took the second in the same stoic silence, and the third, each long red welt laid neatly across her chubby little peach. The fourth caught her low and finally brought a sob to her lips, the fifth lower still, under the tuck of her bum to make her squeak and jump on her toes. Naomi responded with a wicked grin and laid the sixth full across the meat of Poppy's thighs, which finally got to her, sending her jumping up and down on her toes with her hands clutched to her well-marked bottom.

The audience clapped her, and I was wishing I'd been as brave, which I normally am, only the situation had broken me. There was an abrupt change in attitude when they realised what the towelling square was for though, with laughter and calls of disgust as it was pinned up around her hips to make a nappy. Naomi added a final touch of humiliation by pulling the panties back up to leave them bulging under Poppy's skirt as it fell into place, and it was Sophie's turn.

I'd thought she would fight, like June, but she didn't and I could see the strain on her face as she stood up. Naomi beckoned her and she hobbled into position, one hand pressed briefly to her straining belly as she readied herself. She was told to get bare, and she lifted her skirt as she bent herself over the table, tucking it up into her waistband. Her thumbs went into the top of her panties and down they came, low enough to get her bum ready for caning, but not all the way. As she bent a little more her anus came on view, but her pussy stayed hidden among the folds of white cotton where her panties got in the way.

Naomi stood a little back, took careful aim and brought the cane down firmly across Sophie's bottom. Sophie jerked as it hit, one leg kicking up, and gave a squeal, but she was back in position as the second stroke fell, and held herself as Naomi set up a rhythm. I realised I was biting my lip as I watched. Sophie's bottom cheeks started to tighten in time to the cane smacks, then suddenly went loose. She gasped. I saw a little yellow trickle running from her panty crotch, and suddenly a great fountain of pee had erupted backwards into her panties, soaking them in an instant and spraying over the floor as the cane thwacked into her flesh one more time.

Gasps of shock and disgust went up from the audience as Sophie wet herself, pee running from her now sagging panty crotch and down the insides of her thighs, into her shoes and onto the floor. Naomi paused, just long enough to twitch the panties down another inch and give us a better view, of the pee bubbling out from Sophie's open pussy. Again the caning started, harder, with Naomi calling Sophie a filthy slut and telling her she should be the one in nappies.

Sophie just let it all come out, with her head hung and her breathing deep and even, her bottom pushed up to meet the cane, until the strokes grew too hard for her. The pee was still coming, and began to spray out behind her as she started to kick and writhe. Naomi pushed down on Sophie's back, forcing her face onto the table and her bottom up, to leave the pee squirting out in an arch over the stage, which was how she held her until it was all done, still whipping the cane in over and over.

The audience had quite obviously never seen a girl wet herself before, and they were stunned. They had expected boobs and bums, girls kissing, maybe sucking each others' tits or even licking pussy, but nothing like what they had got. As I turned, I found that the balcony was packed, every one of them staring, some fascinated, some disgusted, some shocked. We'd taken the rowdiness clean out of them, and it wasn't over.

Sophie stayed put, pee still dripping from her panties, and Naomi beckoned to the rest of us and flourished the cane. I held back, not wanting to be seen as one of the ringleaders, letting June and Poppy reach the table before I stood fully. I saw Sophie nod, and June grabbed Naomi around the waist, hurling herself sideways at the same time. Naomi went down, taken completely by surprise, and in the next instant she had all but disappeared, just her legs sticking out from beneath a pile of girls.

She was kicking like anything, and I could see right up her skirt, as could the audience. I had to do it. Darting quickly in and avoiding her furious kicks, I snatched up under her skirt, caught her waistband in both hands and hauled. She gave a scream of rage as she realised her panties were coming down, but down they came, and off. I tossed them quickly into the audience and grabbed her legs, throwing my whole weight onto them to roll her up, leaving her bottom spread to the room and her pussy lips sticking out rudely between her thighs.

The sheer fury of her response as she realised how much she was showing nearly made me let go, but it was abruptly muffled as Poppy sat her nappy-clad bottom down, full in Naomi's face. Even that didn't stop her fighting, but we had her pinned, June and Zoe clinging on to her arms, Poppy and Sophie mounted on her, and me clinging in desperation to her legs.

'Spank her, Jade!' Sophie yelled, pushing the hairbrush at me.

'I can't!' I protested, but Sophie had already grappled onto Naomi's legs, and I knew I could.

It had to be done. I owed it to her, not just for the earlier spanking, but for a long string of beatings and humiliations, ruined clothes, the embarrassment and discomfort of going about with bruises, and more. OK, she'd made me come many, many times, but that wasn't the point. I laid in, laughing as I spanked her, smacking the brush down on her upturned cheeks as her body jerked in her furious but utterly useless attempts to break free. We had her, good and proper, and we were going to spank her, and make her come in front of everybody . . .

'. . . and piss on her!' June laughed, and I realised I'd been thinking aloud.

It was good, ideal in fact, just the sort of mean thing she liked to do to girls herself: spank them, frig them off, then piss all over them. She'd done it to me, and to Zoe. Now it was her turn. I forced a hand round her tummy and between her legs, onto her pussy, to spread her lips, still spanking. She was wet, her clitty swollen, and I started to rub.

Her struggles grew stronger still as she realised what we were going to do to her, and that she couldn't stop it from happening, her pussy and bumhole already tightening rhythmically as I frigged her. I was laughing, and spanking as hard as I could, completely carried away. Poppy had pulled her nappy aside, smothering Naomi's face in bare bottom, anus to mouth by the look of it, and she gave a sudden crow of triumph.

'She's licking me, the little slut, up my bum!'

She was too, her tongue pushed well in up Poppy's bottom hole, and she was coming too, her own anus and her pussy pulsing, the muscles of her thighs and bottom locked tight in ecstasy. I gave her a final salvo of hard spanking, twisted the brush in my hand and stuck it up her, deep into her sopping hole while she was still coming. She'd stopped fighting, but I knew she'd start again in a few seconds, and wasted no time, fucking her briefly, pulling the brush free and jamming it just as deep up her juice-slimed bumhole.

That got her kicking, but we had her, my legs already spread over hers, pussy to pussy. A second of concentration and I let go, full on her sex, my pee gushing out between her lips and into her open hole. She gave one furious jerk as she felt herself fill with pee, throwing me back, and I sprawled on the floor, still pissing, all over her. It hit Sophie too, right in the face.

She squealed and let go, losing her grip, but it did Naomi no good – June and Zoe still had her arms, and Poppy was squatting over her face, ready to do it, the nappy pulled aside, pussy poised, bumhole pouting. It came out, Naomi thrashing her whole lower body and tossing her head frantically from side to side, but she still caught it full in her face, in her mouth, in her eyes, up her nose and in her hair.

Poppy was laughing as she soiled Naomi's head, and so was I, so hard I couldn't even think about trying to hold my own pee back. I wanted to do what was left over Naomi, but I couldn't even move, and it all came out onto the floor beneath me, and through it.

I'd realised people were shouting, but I'd thought it was just our stupid audience, and didn't expect anything better from a bunch of straights. It wasn't. They were still gaping in horror at what we were doing to Naomi. The shouting was coming from below, and it was only then I realised what was going on underneath us. I'd completely forgotten about the VIP lounge, and Sophie, Poppy and I had just emptied the full contents of our bladders onto their heads.

Four

Our exit from Bolero's was far from dignified, but fast. Gabrielle and Penny had realised what was going on and had been frantically collecting up our things even as we took our revenge on Naomi. Around the time that what had happened was sinking in for me, they had been forcing open a blocked fire door at the rear of the balcony, and were frantically beckoning us to follow. I saw, and I didn't need any encouragement to join them. Nor did the others, all six of us tumbling pell-mell through the door and down the iron fire escape outside. Opening the door had set an alarm off, a din audible even over the music, and the sprinkler system had started too, adding a deluge of water to our own efforts just as we left.

We didn't even see Bob Ryman, Ronnie Miles or any of the bouncers, not until we were halfway down the park and turned back to see a cluster of men standing at the door from which we'd made our escape. I was still laughing, and couldn't stop giggling all the way back to my flat, and even Naomi thought it was hilarious, smiling and chuckling in between bouts of threatening to do horrible things to us.

It did not seem so funny in the morning. My head hurt, my bottom hurt and my body was stiff from sleeping in between Penny and Sophie, but those were the least of my problems. Sophie was already awake, lying on her back and staring at the ceiling. She put my thoughts into words.

'AJ's going to kill us.'

'No she's not,' I answered her. 'She's going to catch me in the street and tickle me until I pee myself. Actually no, that's what she'd have done if we'd just fucked up a bit. You're probably right.'

'Just tell her to go away,' Penny suggested sleepily as she tumbled herself out of bed.

'She won't,' I answered. 'You know what she's like.'

Penny didn't answer, but made for the bathroom, her arms hugged around her middle against the cold. Her bottom was pristine, pink and smooth, very unlike mine, but my bruises were nothing compared with what I was likely to get when AJ caught up with me. Bob Ryman was going to be furious. Maybe he'd even sack her.

The others had left, and Naomi was sure to tell AJ what had happened in order to push the blame away from herself, that or Ryman would ring her. It was gone ten, so possibly he already had. If I stuck around I was going to catch the full force of AJ's anger, but every day I could delay it would make it a little less bad.

'Can I come back with you, Penny?' I called out.

'Of course,' she answered, her voice muffled through the hiss of the shower.

I got out of bed, willing myself to hurry but not really up to it. An inspection of my bottom in the mirror showed just how sorry a state I was in. Naomi is strong, and she'd laid the hairbrush in with a will. Both my cheeks were suffused with bruising, a mess of reds and purples and dull blacks. It would be a week before I could even go OTK, but that was not going to stop AJ. She was more likely to make a point of beating me on my bruises.

A whole range of excuses were running through my mind as I joined Penny in the shower, but they were all useless. It had been my responsibility, and shifting the blame onto Sophie for starting the pissing games or Penny and Gabrielle for opening the fire door was just going to get them in trouble as well. Not that I'd have done it anyway, but it was impossible not to think about it. Besides, all three of them had the guts to face AJ down, or at least try. I didn't. They like submissive sex, but I'm submissive.

I'm also a working girl, and, while I could commute from Penny's, it was going to be expensive. It still had to be done. A week, and then I would come back and take my medicine, because short of leaving the country I was going to get it sooner or later. The best I could do was ensure I got it in a situation that was ultimately pleasurable, for all the undoubted pain. That did not mean being made to pee myself in the street.

The plan made sense, and it evolved in my mind over the morning. Sophie left us to walk to the tube, and Penny and I drove west. As we waited at the lights to join the North Circular, an all-too-familiar black motorbike passed us going the other way, at speed – AJ. My heart went straight into mouth, but fortunately she didn't recognise Penny's car. We'd got out with maybe ten minutes to spare.

My pulse was racing and my tummy felt weak as we drove on. Penny was trying to be helpful, pointing out that AJ had no right whatever to do anything to me, but she was wrong. To be considered as a genuine bottom in my set a girl had to accept her position to the established dominants, and that meant AJ. It was bad enough with them knowing that I'd occasionally given in to men, although in fact they didn't know the half of it. To refuse to take what would be seen as a just punishment would get me ostracised, and that didn't bear thinking about. Not that it mattered what I thought. AJ also had her position to think about, and if she didn't deal with me she was going to lose a lot of respect. It was going to happen, no question at all.

Not in the street. If AJ caught up with me at a club, she would be obliged to do me then and there, and the more of her fellow diesel dykes were there the more that would be true. I had to pick my moment, just as soon as my bottom was better, and there was an obvious choice. Most Sundays AJ went off to meet other girl bikers somewhere north of London. I'd never been, but I did know it was strictly girls only, no exceptions.

It was a scary thought, but a turn-on too, just the sort of thing I like to fantasise about, when I have no control whatsoever over what happens to me. Now it was for real, and all the way to Penny's I was thinking of the horrid things AJ might do to me. A whipping would be the least of it. I'd certainly be stripped and humiliated in a variety of ways, maybe made to lick out every girl there, used as a grease rag for the day . . .

By the time we reached Penny's I was sick with fear, but desperately wanted to frig off. She was a bit surprised when I asked for a lick as soon as we were through the door, but obliged, going down between my thighs as I sat on her bed with my boobs out and my eyes closed. As her tongue began to flick over my pussy lips I thought of how it would be, my clothes ripped off, my body naked in front of ten or twenty diesel dykes. AJ would use chains, heavy-duty chains, thick with grease, to bind my wrists and string me up from a beam, dangling helpless and in pain, my toes just touching the ground.

No, she'd stand me on an oil can, so if I kicked it would fall over and I'd be hanging free. She'd lay in, with a leather belt, cracking it down across my poor bare flesh, and not just my bum, but also my thighs, front and back, my belly, my boobs, all the while with her friends watching in approval. I'd lose my balance, the can would go and I'd be swinging from my wrists, in agony as I was lashed harder and harder, into a kicking, thrashing frenzy of pain, torn and bleeding . . .

I came, right in Penny's face, screaming aloud and clutching at my boobs so hard my nails went in, leaving two bloody crescents on my flesh. It had got to her, and the moment I'd come down I rolled my legs up to let her lick my bumhole out as she brought herself to a much more discreet climax. I lay back, enjoying the feeling of her tongue up my bottom and wondering if I would be made to do the same for AJ. It was quite likely, if only as a mild prelude to my real punishment.

Telling Penny was out of the question, as I knew she wouldn't approve. Her idea of consent and mine differ. To her, it has to be asked for and given in each instance, at least if anything extreme is going to happen. For me, to have taken my place as a dyke bottom meant giving blanket consent to a partner to treat me as she saw fit, but, as Penny was my girlfriend and she wasn't one of us, that meant to whoever claimed me as hers, and that was AJ.

Penny was due for Sunday lunch at her mother's, and after a slightly awkward phone call managed to get me invited. It was a strange experience, the three of us eating together in the quiet old house with

Penny's mum, Geraldine, explaining to me how best to store apples for the winter when a few hours before her daughter had been tonguing my bottom hole. She had to have realised that Penny and I were lovers, after over a year, but nothing was said. To her, as Penny had explained, lesbian affairs might happen, but were never, ever mentioned, an attitude a world away from what I was used to.

Odder still was that I could quite easily imagine Geraldine taking Penny, or me, or AJ for that matter, across her knee for a damn good spanking. There was something uncompromisingly strict about her, and the way she spoke to Penny suggested not so much a proud mother on equal terms with her successful academic daughter, but patient exasperation with a wayward twelve year old. Admitting that I was a temp was deeply embarrassing and, despite the fact that she was as polite and friendly as she could possibly have been, I left feeling very small indeed.

It left Penny in an odd mood too, and we didn't even have sex that evening, but sat in watching TV and eating chocolates, until the excesses of the night before finally caught up with me and I went to bed. She followed soon after, and we went to sleep cuddled into each other's arms.

The week was a rush. I called the agency first thing on Monday to find they wanted me as a stand-in for a pregnant PA in the City. That meant taking the train into Paddington and the Circle Line to Moorgate, and the man I was working for turned out to expect me to have mysteriously acquired his regular assistant's complete body of knowledge on the way into work. He also had a strange and intricate filing system which I had serious trouble getting the hang of. I was actually grateful when he started to come on to me on the Wednesday and I could give him a piece of my mind, making sure he'd ask for a new girl for the following week.

It left me exhausted by the Friday afternoon, and I hadn't had a chance to find out where the place AJ hung out was, or if she'd be there. I couldn't very well ring her up and ask, or Naomi either for that matter. I didn't even dare dial her number. Turning up with one of the other butch girls was going to cause all sorts of problems, so in the end I had to sneak into Soho after work and ask Gina, who worked behind the bar at Whispers.

Naomi, her friend Sam or even AJ might have turned up at any minute, and I didn't hang around, but got the address and made a hasty exit. I got away with it, but had visions of being caught in the street and tickled until I wet myself running through my head all the way to Paddington. Even in the train I was looking out for her black motorbike on the roads outside the rain-streaked windows, which was just plain ridiculous.

The place didn't even have a name, as such, but was known as The Pumps, an ex-filling station turned bike garage just south of Hatfield, on a stretch of what had been the A1 before the motorway was built, or so Gina said. It was not the easiest of places to get to without a car, and I couldn't very well ask Penny for a lift. Penny wasn't even going to know.

Fortunately she was lecturing on the Saturday morning, so I had at least some time to prepare. I bought a map, and the nearest station proved to be a place called Brookman's Park, a mile or more away across fields, but with a convenient footpath going almost directly there. That gave me an idea. Just in case AJ ruined my clothes I could buy some old tat in a charity shop and leave a spare set in a bin bag nearby to change into. Clever Jade, every possibility taken care of.

It took me a while to find a shop, but the clothes were easy. I bought an old pair of jeans, some tatty boots, a pink crop top and a thing like a flashers' mac which was hardly flattering but could cover everything else. Back at Penny's I cut down the jeans and frayed the hems to make a thoroughly indecent pair of shorts, carefully disposed of the bits and put it all on to check my look. It was ideal, turning me into just the sort of baby-dyke biker slut they would expect, with my bum half out of my jeans shorts and my top looking as if it was about to burst. All it needed was a lollipop and pigtails and they'd have me on the spot, AJ or no AJ.

I was dressed normally again by the time Penny got in, with my clothes packed away and her lunch ready. It was quite warm, and we spent a pleasant afternoon walking by the river as far up as Pangbourne, where we had dinner before taking the train back. Our compartment was completely empty, and we were a little drunk and feeling mischievous by then, so we took turns to spank each other, kneeling on the seats with our jeans and panties pulled down at the back.

My bum was OK, with a few lingering bruises but nothing too bad, and the brief and risky spanking left me warm and ready for more. Had it not been for what I had coming to me, I'd have asked for a proper beating from her, but contented myself with a long, loving session across her knee on the bed and having my bottom creamed. I gave her the same treatment before we licked each other to ecstasy, and we went to bed in the best of moods, save for the nagging fear at the back of my mind.

I felt bad in the morning having to lie to her. After a week sleeping together we'd grown more loving than ever and what I really wanted to do was spend the day with her, relaxing in between bouts of good, dirty sex. It had to be done, and I excused myself, saying I had promised to sort my uncle Rupert's house out for him before he got back from Singapore. Penny offered to come and help, then to drive me in, but I politely declined both offers. Fortunately she'd already had to postpone some dinner with her aunt during the week, and didn't make too much of a fuss.

Everything went smoothly. My trains arrived more or less on time, there was no trouble changing my clothes in the loos at King's Cross and I found a good place to hide the bag along the path from Brookman's Park station. I knew I could count on Gina to have tipped off AJ that I would be there and, sure enough, her motorbike was outside a group of dilapidated buildings that could only be The Pumps.

It took a lot of courage to walk over. I was telling myself that if I didn't face the music now it would only mean staying scared and apprehensive until I did. My legs still felt as if they were made of lead as I crossed the road. There were three buildings. One was obviously the old garage office, which was deserted and boarded up. By it was a block with an open front around which a group of tough-looking girls in leathers were drinking coffee and beers. The third was a long, low shed presenting a blank face to the road, presumably a repair shop, and from behind it I could hear voices.

I took my overcoat off and draped it over a low wall as I reached their side of the road and walked forwards. One of the girls wolf whistled at me as I passed the café, and I gave her a smile, not wanting to give any of them a reason to add to my suffering. AJ wasn't with them, and I went around to the back, to find a broad apron of concrete with a thick fringe of scrubby trees hiding it from the new road, two motorbikes propped up with tools spread out around them, and AJ.

She was showing a huge woman with a flat, oriental face how to do something mechanical, her back to me. I tried to speak, but I couldn't, the lump in my throat too big to let the words out. It didn't matter; the other woman had seen me and spoke, nodding in my direction.

'Friend of yours, AJ?'

AJ turned, casually enough, but her expression altered to surprise as she saw me. She stood, slowly, an oily rag and some bits of rubber tubing in one hand, a Stanley knife in the other.

'You have got a fucking nerve turning up here, Jade,' she rasped.

She wasn't calling me Dumplings, and that was bad news, but I stood my ground and even managed to find my voice, my head hanging as I answered her.

'I know. I . . . I wanted to say sorry, and that if you want –'

'Oh, you're going to be fucking sorry, girl, count on it!' she answered. 'I've lost my fucking job because of you, you stupid little bitch!'

'I . . . I . . . sorry, AJ.'

I folded my hands in my lap and hung my head lower still, terrified she would just beat me up and have done with it, and expecting her to slap my face at the very least. She stepped forwards and I felt myself wince as her hand shot out, not to slap me, but to push the oily rag into my face, rubbing it in hard. There was some horrible gritty stuff on it, which went in my mouth, but as I tried to spit it out she pushed the rag in between my lips. I knew better than to spit it out and left it hanging there with my mouth slowly filling with the taste of engine oil.

'You've got no fucking sense at all, have you?' she spat, and her fingers locked into my top, jerking me forwards.

As I saw the knife in her hand I screamed, dropping the rag even as she slit my top. She just laughed, stuck her fingers in the cut and pulled, ripping it wide to flop out my boobs and jamming the torn remnant down around my arms to trap them at my sides. I was shaking hard, the tears already gathering in my eyes. Other women were moving towards us, from the shed and from the café, to watch the fun. Most were butch, hard women in leather and denim, their faces full of amusement or contempt, but not a trace of pity. Even the few femmes among them looked as if they were going to thoroughly enjoy the show.

AJ had picked up the rag, and I opened my mouth obediently as she put it to my face. It was stuffed in, properly this time, nearly all of it in my mouth to leave my cheeks bulging and my throat blocked, with just one oily fold sticking out between my lips. Seeing that I wasn't going to put up any resistance, she sneered, the Stanley knife balanced on the palm of her hand as she decided what to do with me.

I'd left the button of my jeans shorts undone, showing a bit of tummy, and her eyes travelled slowly down my body until she reached it. She nodded, reached out and jerked my zip down. One finger was pushed down the front, into the groove of my pussy. She pulled, bringing me stumbling forward.

'Hold her, someone,' she drawled, and put the knife to my crotch.

Strong, lean arms took my waist and I was held, not daring to breathe as she began to slit the crotch of my jeans. I felt the threads pop, the seam part, then tear as the two halves were hauled wide. My legs came up, lifted clear off the ground by the woman who was holding me, and I was kicking stupidly in the air as AJ wrenched at the denim, tearing them up the back all the way to the waistband.

'No knicks, what a slut!' one of them said and laughed and I was dropped back to the ground, winded, panting through my nose, with the first tears trickling down my face.

My shorts fell down into a ruined mess around my ankles and I was showing everything, nude but for my ruined top, boots and socks, and still held tight. AJ had passed the knife to the Chinese woman, and stepped close, to wipe her hands on my boobs, smearing oil and grit over my skin and scraping my nipples. She began to feel them, lifting them in her hands and running her thumbs over the nipples to bring them erect, and to set me sobbing in helpless frustration and fear.

'Take her in the shed, AJ,' someone advised from behind me.

AJ nodded and I was released, to hobble towards the shed door. Someone kicked me and I broke into a stumbling run, then again, right up my bottom so that I nearly tripped. They were laughing at me, and more kicks followed, most from AJ, booting me in under the big iron roller, which was promptly closed to leave me in a dim space smelling of oil and petrol and leather. AJ's hand gripped my torn top; it was wrenched away and I was nude but for my socks and boots, shivering in the warm, humid air.

'What you need,' AJ stated, as she came to stand in front of me, 'is a lesson. That way, maybe you'll learn to do as you're told. What did I say about the cabaret?'

She reached up to my mouth to jerk the rag out.

'You said hardcore!' I whined. 'It was hardcore, we just –'

She took hold of my face, crushing in my cheeks to force my jaw wide and shut me up.

'Hardcore, yes,' she went on, 'not kinky. Stuff straight blokes are into, blokes like Bob Ryman. Sucking each others' tits and licking cunt, not spanking, and not fucking pissing games!'

I'd meant to keep the other girls out of it, but my nerve had gone, and I was immediately trying to blame Sophie and June, but only a muffling burbling noise came out as she squeezed my face harder still, just about managing to mouth the first name.

'Don't talk, listen,' she hissed, and spat, full in my open mouth. 'Yes, I know that dirty little bitch Sophie Cherwell started all that and, if I catch her, she's going to get it. For now, I've got you. On the ground, now!'

I got down, as fast as I could, grovelling at her feet with my whole body trembling violently. My mouth was full of the taste of oil, and I was sure I was going to be sick, from that, and from fear. I got right down, my head hanging, waiting for the kicks to start, but she drew up a stool in front of me and crossed her legs, lifting one heavy boot to my face.

'Lick it,' she ordered, 'clean.'

It was clean, perfectly clean, the surface so brightly polished I could see my filthy face in it. I looked up, unsure.

'The sole, stupid.' She laughed, and others chuckled in response as they saw what I had to do.

They were army boots, the leather uppers polished to a shining brilliance but the sole was filthy, the grooves choked with soil, bits of leaf, gravel and a large wad of dirty pink chewing gum. Sure she couldn't really mean it, that she was joking in order to get a laugh out of me, I took hold and started to pick bits out with my fingers.

'With your mouth, bitch!' she spat.

She did mean it. I tried to make myself go forwards, but my gorge rose and I ended up looking up at her, trying to plead with my eyes. It was pointless. She couldn't back down, and she didn't.

'Lick – my – fucking – boots,' she ordered. 'What part of that don't you understand?'

'I . . . I . . . sorry, AJ,' I managed. 'I . . . I can't . . .'

She reached down. Her hand locked in my hair, twisting hard. I squeaked in pain as my face was pulled hard against her boot and rubbed into it, smearing dirt over my cheek and lips. I couldn't speak, but I was immediately flapping my hands about in a frantic effort to tell her I'd do it, and the instant she slackened her grip I was. She gave a little harsh laugh as I began to lick at the sole of her boot, my mouth immediately filling with the sour tang of soil and the foul taste of rotting leaves, oil too.

They watched, enjoying themselves as I licked, struggling not to get the horrible oily muck in my mouth. It was no good. Most of it was caught in the grooves and I was forced to winkle it out with my tongue, pushing the tip in and using my teeth to pick out the bits of gravel and old gum. Soon my mouth was clogged with grit and bits of leaf, so I had to spit it out or be sick. I spat, into the rag she'd made me take in my mouth, a gob of black slime. I went back to work, near to puking, with the tears streaming down my face and my body shaking in shame and frustration and an agonising helplessness for the way I was being treated. As my mouth once more began to load with filth my nerve broke, and I found myself looking up at her and whining piteously, barely able to see for my tears.

'Please, AJ, I beg you! I'm going to be sick . . . I'm sorry about your job . . . I really am! And I'm sorry –'

'Fucking baby!' she spat. 'OK, we don't want you puking everywhere, so just get in the pit.'
'The pit?'
'The inspection pit, stupid. Behind you.'
I turned, and the girls moved apart to let me see down into a deep pit in the concrete floor. Chipped and oily steps led down into it and the floor was black and foul. I nodded, not sure what to expect, but certain it could not be worse than eating dirt off the soles of her boots. I didn't stand, but crawled, eager to show them how submissive I was, how willing.
AJ kicked me, and I felt the wet of my spit on my bottom as her boot pulled away. They'd stood aside, to make a corridor of leather- or denim-clad legs and polished boots for me, leading straight to the pit. AJ booted me along as I crawled, as fast as I dared on the rough, dirty concrete, and the others began to lay in too. It wasn't hard, but they aimed for my boobs as well as my thighs and bum, to make them wobble and swing beneath me and smear polish over my skin.
I was really blubbering, and I couldn't stop it, but they just laughed, helping me down into the pit with their boots until I was too far down to be got at. I turned and squatted down in the pool of engine oil and grease and rubbish at the bottom, looking up at them. They moved around the side, grinning down at me, butches and femmes alike, AJ at the top of the steps with her arms folded across her chest. She nodded.
As one their hands went to the front of their clothes, to unfasten leathers and dungarees or lift little skirts. I realised what they were going to do as they pushed their clothes down – give me a piss bath. All I could do was cower in the pit, unable to take my eyes away as they bared themselves, pushing down their panties or pulling the crotches aside,

spreading their pussies. I managed a single, feeble plea not to do it in my hair as they pushed out their hips and started to let go.

I covered my face just in time as the first stream of piss hit me, splashing hot on my back. A second caught my legs, and more, tinkling on the ground around me and on my body. They didn't spare my hair. They didn't spare me at all, each and every one giving me everything she could, over my head, my back, my boobs, my legs, until my entire body was dripping piddle.

It broke me completely. I squatted down in the mess, their urine running down my body, their laughter ringing in my ears, trying to hold onto a last tiny scrap of dignity. One of them managed to aim the full force of her stream right onto the crown of my head and I gave in. My hand went back between my legs, my fingers probed in among the wet folds of my pussy and I was frigging myself, with hot piss cascading down my back and between my open bum cheeks, over my anus and into my hand.

They saw what I was doing and began to jeer and whistle, calling me a slut and a bitch and a dirty tart. It was true, what I am, a filthy little bitch, rubbing myself as they urinated on me, a dirty pig, a shameless slut. My mouth was full of the taste of dirt, my body soiled and bruised, my boobs fat and filthy and naked, my bum bare and spread, piss trickling down between my cheeks. Yet I was frigging over it, rubbing at my pussy with my ecstasy building in my head to blot out everything but the need to be soiled, used, humiliated, hurt . . .

My head came up, and my mouth came open. Piss squirted in my face; I didn't know whose, and I didn't care. I caught the stream, full in my mouth as I started to come. Some went down my throat as I swallowed deliberately, more bubbled out at the sides to run down over my boobs, hot and wet and lovely. I was there, and as my orgasm hit me I was wishing I'd been a better girl for AJ. She was right, I was a baby, unworthy of her, not even worthy to be pissed on. A true bottom would have licked her boots properly, picking out every last bit of dirt with her lips and teeth and tongue and licking the soles until they shone. I began to babble.

'Sorry, AJ . . . sorry . . . I meant to do it . . . I meant to . . . make me do it . . . make me eat it, all of it . . . 'til I'm sick, and throw me back in here and piss on me and kick me and beat me and fuck me and hurt me so, so bad –'

I broke off, screaming, the orgasm exploding in my head. My fingers were snatching at my sex, my bottom bouncing and splashing in the pool of oil and urine beneath me, piss spattering off my body and running from the rat-tails of my hair, dripping from my straining nipples and tickling my bumhole. My eyes stung; I couldn't see or breathe or hear properly, or do anything but frig myself as I revelled in my own degradation.

Only when I started to choke on the piss in my mouth did I stop. I went into a coughing fit, which popped my ears, and when I'd finally recovered I realised that they'd gone silent. All of them were looking down on me, as I discovered when I managed to open one sticky eye, and, if most of the butch ones were trying to be cool, the femmes were in awe. I managed a smile.

'What am I supposed to do with her?' AJ sighed. 'I mean . . . what a fucking slut!'

I didn't know what to say. It was true, and I knew it, but it took a lot to take me where I'd just been, a place in my own head in which I had no control whatsoever over my own actions, save for what gave me the pleasure I craved. She knew too, and she was well pleased with herself, while most of her fellow butches were trying to hide their envy and admiration. For me, I had enough sense not to smirk as I climbed out of the pit.

'Clean that mess up,' AJ ordered, pointing to the lake of pee filmed iridescent with oil at the bottom of the pit. 'There's a pump in the stores, and plenty of rags, your clothes for a start.'

She sent me on my way with a well-placed kick to my bottom and I began to clean up the mess. It was horrible work, and nobody else so much as lifted a finger to help, but she had really got me, and I felt I was where I belonged. I had to do it nude too, pumping and scrubbing and mopping up with my ruined clothes until every square inch of my body was filthy with oil, scratched, bruised and sore. Just cleaning up the mess her friends had made wasn't enough either. I had to scour the pit completely, until I'd got down to the oil-blackened concrete. Even then I wasn't sure if it would pass her inspection, but after a moment she jerked her thumb over her shoulder towards the little washroom I'd been fetching my cleaning things from.

'I suppose that's as good as I can expect from you, Dumplings,' she sighed. 'Get washed.'

I was Dumplings again, which was good.

'Are we OK together then?' I asked.

She paused to consider, then spoke again.

'Yeah, we're OK, just watch what you're doing in future, and count yourself lucky Double-A couriers took me on.'

'Yes, AJ.'

'Good, make sure you remember that. Here, have some water.'

She had a litre bottle of water and I accepted it, drinking nearly the full contents before I took it away from my mouth. For once she didn't use it as an excuse to do something horrible to me, and her voice was quite friendly as she went on.

'There's plenty of soap, and Swarfega to get the oil off; use as much as you like. There are some old overalls in the store, I think, unless you fancy going on the back of my bike in the nude?'

'No, thank you, AJ.'

'I was joking, stupid.'

She cuffed my ear, not hard, and as she walked off I drew a sigh of relief. It was over, and I'd even escaped a whipping, for all that I had plenty of bruises from their boots. I went to the washroom and began to scrub down, which took ages. The rest of them were going about their ordinary business, some working on motorbikes and a couple of cars, more just chatting. After I'd been put in the pit one heavyset butch girl had taken her femme into the storeroom, presumably to be licked, but that was it. Nobody seemed to care that I was nude, much less about the state I was in.

Washing was hell. My hair was a mess, but I'd kept the worst of the muck out of it and was sure a couple of good washes with shampoo and conditioner would see me OK. My skin was worse. The oil had got right into it and I was bruised and scratched all over, which made scrubbing so, so painful. I managed it eventually, inspecting myself in a mirror to find myself bright pink all over except for the bruising, of which there was plenty. I even had the imprint of one of AJ's boots plainly marked on my left bum cheek where she'd landed a kick. She glanced in as I was cleaning my nails and saw, laughing and making me pose with my bum stuck out so that she could show the Chinese girl and one other. I did as I was told, too far gone even to feel resentment.

There were overalls, three pairs, all worn but at least fairly clean. One set was far too big, another too small, the third a bit long and embarrassingly tight over my bum and boobs. I had to roll the legs up, and I couldn't get the zip closed properly at the front at all, so it still left me feeling acutely self-conscious, more so than when I'd been in the nude. I went outside and AJ laughed as soon as she saw me.

'Hitching, are you?' she joked. 'Out to give some lorry driver a thrill? She sucks cock, this one, you know.'

The Chinese girl made a face of utter disgust, as if AJ had told her I was into bestiality or scat. I knew exactly how she felt, and found myself blushing. AJ went on.

'I'd give you a lift, only I don't want piss all over my seat.'

'I won't pee on your seat!' I promised.

'That's not what I meant,' she answered me. 'Watch this, Xiang, this is a laugh.'

I realised what she was going to do immediately, and I was already backing away and begging her not to. It was pointless. She'd told me it was going to happen and it was, but I'd just washed and put on new clothes, and she'd already taken me about as low as I'd ever been, and it just wasn't fair!

'Still not learned your lesson?' she asked. 'Do as I fucking tell you!'

She snatched out, grabbing my arm, twisting even as she tripped me. I went down on my knees and she was on top of me immediately, her legs clamped tight across my waist, her fingers up under my armpits. All I could manage was one despairing howl and then I was giggling stupidly as she began to tickle. Xiang laughed and gave me a solid swat across my bottom.

I fought it, for about a second, but she'd brought me down far too low for me to manage more. Even as I started to squirm in her grip I knew I was going to go in my clothes, and I did, just seconds after she'd started to tickle. I felt my pussy prickling as I struggled to hold myself tight against the helpless twitching of my body and the knowledge that she, AJ, wanted me to piss myself, and then I had.

My scream of frustration as pee squirted out into the seat of my overalls brought a gale of laughter from AJ and a yell of disgust from Xiang. Others were watching too, in revulsion or delight or both, as I jerked and giggled beneath AJ with the piss bubbling out behind me and soaking in across the taut seat of my overalls. Fresh tears burst from my eyes and somebody called me a baby again, but I barely heard, lost in the helpless agony of being tickled and the shame of filling my clothes with piss in front of all of them.

AJ dropped me before I was done, but it was too late to stop myself and I just kneeled there, my head hung low, gasping for breath as the last of my pee came out in a series of little squirts, then a trickle. My whole bottom was soaked, the denim clinging to my flesh, hot and soggy, also my crotch and the insides of both legs, while some had run down over my belly.

They stood watching, AJ a little to one side, her face set in a knowing sneer. When I finally found the strength to get to my feet I turned to her, my head bowed. I knew I'd been stupid to think she wouldn't carry out her threat, but now she had it really was over. Surely what they had done to me in the pit, plus making me piss myself by tickling me was enough?

'Sorry, AJ,' I said meekly. 'I will try to be obedient, but please don't tickle me again, please?'

'Why not?'

'I hate it!'

'Tough. I still owe you one.'

'No! You just did me!'

'No. I said I was going to do you in the street, and I'm going to. This isn't a street, Dumplings, in case you hadn't noticed. But that's just a laugh, yeah? If I were you I'd watch out for Bob Ryman and Ronnie Miles. They are well pissed with you. The Palace has been closed down.'

Five

I was not happy. All the time I'd been thinking how brave I was being, and how clever, and all I'd managed to do was take the edge off AJ's anger. Now I had both Bob Ryman and Ronnie Miles after me, when really it was their own fault for not giving us proper instructions. Ryman at least had some gripe with us, as it wouldn't have been completely unreasonable for us to have realised that adding watersports to the cabaret was going to mean pissing on the heads of his precious celebrities, but Ronnie Miles had nobody to blame but himself.

As I found out from the local paper, the reason the Palace had been closed down had nothing whatever to do with our cabaret, at least, not directly. With the alarm going and the water sprinklers on, the Fire Brigade had turned up in double-quick time, to find that every single one of the fire doors had the handles locked off with plastic tags. Gabrielle had broken ours with a pair of nail scissors from Poppy's make-up bag, but if there really had been a fire it would have been disastrous. Presumably Miles had done it to stop people letting their mates in from outside, but it was an insane thing to do and he had got exactly what he deserved.

If he thought I was going to be held to account for it he was wrong. I may go down for AJ, but not for some seedy old porn baron. I was safe too, because if he tried anything the whole story would come out and he'd be in worse trouble than before. For one thing he probably didn't even have a licence for striptease, and I'm sure there's no such thing as a licence for full-on lesbian sex shows. The council would crucify him.

Neither of them knew my address anyway, and the only possible way they could get it was through AJ. Bob Ryman had already sacked her, so she was hardly going to be doing him any favours, but it was obviously in my best interests to keep her sweet. That was all very well, and easy enough, but it threatened to bring to a head the problems which had been building up for nearly a year.

AJ knew she could do just as she liked with me, or, rather, she thought she knew. I do feel she should have that right. As a submissive my deepest need is to be utterly and unconditionally the property of a strong, dominant woman, but reality keeps getting in the way. Many, many times I'd frigged over the idea of being her property, living in her house with nothing on but a collar and my bottom and boobs permanently welted, tattooed as her property, maybe even branded.

It's just not feasible. What would happen if she chose to get rid of me? If I found I couldn't handle it after all? If, God forbid, she died on her motorbike? In a fantasy scenario I'd be sold off for some yet more degrading fate, or dragged back and tortured until I finally came to understand my true self, or thrown onto her funeral pyre along with the remains of the bike and her leathers. In reality I'd be stuffed, penniless, homeless, jobless and pretty well worthless.

So I'd let her have her way with me when and how she pleased, hoping it would all balance out, and until recently it had. She'd had two others girls in much my position, both of whom had been if anything more focused on her than I was. Unfortunately neither of them had been up for a reality bypass either. One had accepted a job in the States and the other had suffered a sudden change of heart and gone off with a man. That left me, and the way she had treated me at The Pumps made it quite clear to everyone that I was hers.

Then there was Penny. I was in love with Penny in a way I could never be with AJ, as equals, and after our week sleeping together it was leading me to question my whole self-view as a lesbian bottom. AJ didn't approve of her either, mainly because Penny didn't walk the walk, but also because when Penny went down for her it was for the sake of humiliation. AJ wanted worship, for the suffering she gave to be needed for its own sake, not because it brought on feelings of erotic shame.

As a final fly in the ointment, there was the situation with Sophie. She had become so much a regular playmate for Penny and I that we were almost a ménage à trois. Penny was bad enough with men, but Sophie was worse. Sophie meant men, and not just any old men, but outstanding perverts like Fat Jeff, Monty Hartle and Morris Rathwell. AJ thought I had cut off all such ties, and it was very important she didn't find out it wasn't true.

I was going to have to play it all very carefully. For one thing I couldn't go back to Penny's until it was at least a little less obvious that I'd been given a kicking. It was not something I could pretend had happened at my uncle Rupert's, so she'd know I'd lied to her, and guess what had really happened. So I went back to my flat, despite the high probability of Naomi catching up with me.

She can be a vindictive bitch, and it wouldn't have surprised me to find her car parked outside my flat.

It wasn't, only a row of bikes from Pizza Population, which seemed to be taking up more and more room. Several of the delivery boys were there, leering at me as usual, but I ignored them and ordered a deep-pan Hawaiian with extra chilli in the hope of taking the lingering taste of dirt out of my mouth.

I ate it at the computer, knowing that a week's absence would have filled my mailbox with spam. Sure enough, of the 432 messages waiting for me, 426 were complete and utter rubbish. Of the remaining six one was the new menu from the pizza place whose product I was already eating; one was from Poppy asking about the consequences of the cabaret; two were work; one was from Fat Jeff asking if I'd like to go dogging again. The last was from somebody calling himself Romeo Casanova, which I'd have deleted along with the spam if it hadn't been for the subject line – 'big tit schoolgirl jade you will be mine'.

It had to be one of the girls pissing around, probably Sophie, so I clicked it open. A great chunk of text appeared in the new box, and I began to read:

> to jade i love big tits!!!!!!! always i love big tits!!!! your tits biggest roundest fattest fun bags i ever see on girl not mother, not up duff, not fake silikon balls like porno star! like udders on cow!!!!!!!!!!! i want to suc nipples i want to fuk!!!!!!!!!! your nipples best to see best to suck best to rub cock on!!!!!!!!!!!! your fucking gorgeous!!!!!!!!!!!!! i want fuck your tits, yes please???? fuck slow and long not quick like band bang boy! i good lover slow hand lover ten inch rock steel cock fit nice betwean fat tits!!!!!!! my knob stick out between!!! suck it while tit fuck!!! cum in face!!! good yes? you like cum in face??? i like cum in face too! prety face only not ugly face! you pretyist girl in world best tits in

world!!! best for fun bag fuck!! i mean best for real not to make you in bed no lie!!!!!!!!!!! you see when we fuck!! you meet with me yes? you wear school-girl dress? you open shirt!! you get out big fat fun bags!!!!!!! you fold big fat fun bag tits round cock!!!!! we make tit fuck cock in mouth two!!!!! i cum on tits and over face!!! cum on bra!!! cum on shirt!! cum on skirt and nickers maybe!!! i make plenty cum!!!!!!!!! you suck up, swallow good, lick fat tits, lick up cum, swallow good!!!!!!!!!!!!! good yes? we meet saturday night, yes for good tit fuck yes? we meet pally car park 11 at night like before no men just us i fuck tits!!!!!!!!!!!!!!!!!!!!!!!!!!!!!!!!'

Despite my mood I was laughing by the end of it. It was obviously a joke, but I wasn't sure who it was from. Sophie would have made at least some reference to my bottom, I was sure, and she would definitely not have suggested being alone. With Sophie's fantasies there is always an audience. It couldn't be Penny either. It just wasn't her sense of humour. It had to be somebody who knew about the schoolgirl cabaret, and my little dogging expedition too. That meant Penny and the other girls, and Fat Jeff Bellbird.

It was just possibly from Fat Jeff. He had my email address, and he knew about the schoolgirl cabaret, but he hadn't turned up in the end, so might well not know it had ended in disaster. It made sense, and I pulled up the message source in the hope of getting some clues. There weren't any, which just about proved it. Only Jeff, and perhaps Monty too, would have gone to the trouble of covering their tracks so well, even using a distinct ISP. What they didn't know about computers between them wasn't worth knowing, while none of the girls was better than competent.

I had to reply, if only to take my mind off the situation with AJ, while in a funny way flirting with a man made me feel better about how far she'd taken me down. I thought for a little while and then typed back a reply almost as over the top as the original, if in slightly better English, and which I knew would have Jeff steaming:

> Dearest Romeo Casanova, thank you for your beautiful, touching email, you certainly know the way to a girl's heart! Of course you can fuck my tits, darling, how could I refuse? In fact I can't wait to fold them around your lovely ten-inch prick. I'm thinking about it now, all hot and hard between them, pumping away in my cleavage with your knob popping up and down between so I can have a suck too. Oh yes, that would be good, so good. I'm in my school uniform now, because I always wear it when I'm horny, and your email got me so horny I had to change immediately. I keep reading it, and thinking about how you'll fuck my tits and come right in my face. Then I'll suck you and swallow it all down. I've got them out for you, darling now. My school blouse is open and I've undone my bra. They feel so heavy, so big, and my nipples are so hard, and just for you. Oh no, I can't stop myself. My hand is down my panties now, darling, and I'm all wet and ready. I'm going to come, darling, I'm going to come while I think about you on top of me, in the back of your car, with my school blouse open and your lovely cock between my tits. Yes, please, darling, take my tits out and suck my nipples while I do your lovely cock and then fuck me hard so hard really hard til you spunk in my face and i can come then i'Ill lick it all up.

I've come now. That was nice. Thank you, and see you Saturday, big boy.

All my love,

Big tit schoolgirl Jade xxxxxxxxxxxxxxxxxxxxxxx

I read it through, deleted the bit about swallowing his come, because the thought made me feel sick, then put it back in. After all, it was only a joke.

The next priority was a long, slow bath. My skin still smelled of oil and my hair was badly in need of attention, but after three rinses and an hour's soak I felt fully human again. That was another problem with AJ, she just didn't care about the consequences of what she did to me. She'd ruined my chair and the rug I'd had underneath it, and several times she'd left me in the most appalling state. I need to have my control taken away from me, but the person who does it really ought to have some respect, at least for my things, if not for me. Unfortunately, it was exactly that which turned me on so much, and she knew it.

I don't want my top to respect me; I want her to use me, to treat me as a dirty little sex doll whose only function is to provide her pleasure. It might not be practical, but it was still nice to think about it, which is just as well, really. There's something about having really large breasts that makes people react to me that way, as if being busty means that sex is all I'm good for. Often it can be annoying, but when it comes to submissive sex it's great.

The bath left me in a much better mood, very drowsy, just right to let my mind drift to rude things. Not that I have many inhibitions anyway, but what few I do have always seem to melt away when I'm half asleep, and for all my difficulties I had built up an immense amount of sexual tension. As I lay on the bed with only a warm towel covering my body I let it all go, thinking of AJ, and Penny, and how things could have been. In an ideal world, one in which I never had to worry about mundane things and everybody always got on, I could have happily surrendered myself to AJ, permanently. She would have kept me, like a pet, like a dog, naked except for my collar, chained up sometimes . . .

No, the way I wanted to be treated would have landed any dog owner a hefty fine, and rightly so. I wanted her to keep me on a lead, and naked, but to thoroughly abuse me as well. She would feed me dog food out of a bowl on the floor. I'd have to do my business outside in the garden, or in the street, and it wouldn't matter who saw me. She'd beat me frequently, and kick me, and I'd just grovel on the floor, grateful for her attention. I'd have to lick her, and her friends, to order, regardless of my own feelings. Sometimes I'd even be chained in the lavatory and made to lick their pussies and bumholes clean after they'd finished . . .

I made myself comfortable, smiling sleepily as my thighs came up and apart to bare my pussy. My boobs needed attention, and I pushed the towel down, leaving it just over my tummy to take them in hand, stroking my nipples slowly to tease them to erection. I could almost taste it in my mouth as I imagined how it would be, with maybe a couple of hundred girls at a house party, and every one of them using me the same way they would use a piece of loo paper.

A shiver ran the full length of my spine at the thought. My hands went down between my legs, to find my pussy wet and ready, my hole already open. It was going to be good, because there was not the slightest trace of guilt or ill feeling as I started to rub myself, just raw, submissive lust.

Having my face used as loo paper was bad, but I wanted it worse, and more pain. She would mark me, not that she'd have to, because I'd be her property as much as a piece of soap or a can of beans. It would be done just in a moment of idle amusement, her initials tattooed onto my bottom . . . no, branded in, with me tied up good and tight to keep me still, and screaming as the iron bit into my flesh. Afterwards she would slap me in the face for making a fuss over nothing, then piss on the fresh mark just for the fun of it.

I was wishing I had Penny there, to play with my boobs while I attended to my pussy, or stick her tongue up my bottom the way she likes to. She made a nice addition to the fantasy anyway, side by side with me in AJ's back yard, naked and chained to the wall, eating dog food out of our bowls, our bums branded. We'd be made to do all sorts of disgusting things for AJ's amusement, drinking each other's piss the least of it.

My legs came high, rolled up to my chest and spread open, exposing myself completely. I stuck a finger in my mouth and put it to my bumhole, imagining it was Penny doing it as I penetrated the tight little ring and slid up into the warm, wet inside. My thumb went up my pussy, my hole sopping with juice and wide open and I began to squirm on the bed, rubbing myself hard as I came up towards orgasm.

In my fantasy world AJ wouldn't be so prissy about men either. She'd have me covered regularly, despite the fact that I hated it . . . because I hated it. I would be put out in the yard, Penny too, chained at the neck with our hands tied behind our backs. Men like Monty and Fat Jeff Bellbird would be let out to us, with permission to do exactly as they pleased.

They'd fuck our tits, just like Jeff in his dirty email. They'd make us suck their big, ugly cocks. They'd bugger us, taking turns up our bums . . . or there'd be four of them, so we'd have cock in our bumholes and mouths at the same time, roasting us like the pair of dirty little fuck-pigs we are . . .

I screamed out as I started to come, the image fixed in my head, Penny and I on our knees, nude and tied, cocks in our mouths and cocks up our branded bottoms, AJ standing over us, gloating at our utter degradation. It was glorious, long and high and tight, with my fingers wiggling in my twin holes and flicking and nipping at my clitty. Right at the peak a new and awful detail hit me. If I was as much her property as a can of beans, then I would be just as disposable, to be discarded when used. After the four men had used us we'd have become useless to her, not even worth selling. We'd have been slung out with the rubbish, dumped head first into a municipal waste bin with our hands and feet still tied, to be picked up by the first rough sleeper who passed by, if he could be bothered.

I was so tired I went to bed immediately after frigging myself off, and woke to the first light of dawn. As I had anticipated, the man I'd been with the week before wanted a new girl, and I had an assignment in a parcel depot in Ealing, sticking different coloured labels onto packages. It was not the most strenuous job in the world, or the most demanding. I was in a little compartment on my own too, so there was plenty of time to think.

It was easier to get to work from Penny's than my own flat, despite being three times the distance, so once it was marginally less obvious that I'd been kicked up the bum, on the Wednesday, I went to her.

Like me, she'd received a message from Fat Jeff asking if she'd like to go dogging, only in her case he'd stuck to that. Neither of us was particularly keen, but Sophie was going, which made it a great deal more tempting. The alternative was staying in London and waiting for Naomi to catch up with me, or worse, so in the end I accepted.

He'd set it up for the Saturday night, not at the car park we'd visited before, but on a common somewhere off the A3. Monty Hartle was coming too, as I discovered when they picked us up from Penny's flat, and on the way down I was telling myself I would behave and leave the dirty stuff to Penny and Sophie. I knew full well I was likely to crack if it got me horny, and was feeling a bit bad about it, but I needn't have bothered. It started raining as we got to Bagshot, and by the time we reached the dogging spot it was one huge puddle with the rain lashing down so hard that not even the most desperate of dirty old men would have come out. Nor were there any other cars there, and I was left to watch Penny and Sophie suck the boys off with an odd mixture of relief and regret.

I can never quite get used to seeing my girlfriend with a cock in her mouth, any more than I can to taking one myself, and it left me feeling both horny and resentful as we drove in towards London. Monty was being particularly disgusting too, joking about how Penny and Sophie wouldn't need any dinner now they'd been fed and introducing me to the term 'snowballing', where two or more girls share a man's spunk between them after he's come in one's mouth. I couldn't get it out of my head, and was feeling distinctly sick by the time we reached the M25.

Monty suggested a curry, and stopped in New Malden. It felt strange, sitting there in such normal surroundings after what we'd been planning to do, and in view of what we were quite likely to be doing later. Being with other women when the people around us didn't know we were together as sex partners had been the same, before I'd stopped caring, and there was no denying that it was a thrill, and a guilty thrill at that.

It wasn't far to Monty's, and he suggested going there but, according to Jeff, June was going to be at some club in Vauxhall. That seemed to me as good a place to go as any, because if we didn't I knew full well I was going to end up snowballing with Penny and Sophie just as soon as the boys had recharged themselves. Penny, never really one for crowds and noise, preferred Monty's idea, but Sophie was with us and they got outvoted.

So we drove on, Monty's satellite navigation leading unerringly to a seedy pub built in beneath a railway bridge which he promptly refused to park anywhere near. I could see his point, but we made him let us out in the dry under the bridge and left him to sort himself out. The event was at least fetish-oriented, a party for some SM web group June belonged to. Both Monty and Jeff joined in occasionally and knew a few of the people there, but it was straight male dom, so not my thing.

I'd been looking forward to meeting June again, but she was nowhere to be seen. Two men had approached me as I wandered around, both asking if I was with a Master. It was obviously an etiquette thing, and to avoid complicated explanations I simply pointed to Jeff at the bar and said he didn't let me play with other men. He and Penny were getting the drinks in, while Sophie was already chatting enthusiastically to a small, slim girl in nothing but a studded collar, whose pert bottom was decorated with cane welts.

'Doesn't look like June's here yet,' I stated as I joined them.

'If you mean Boots, she's in the loos,' the slim girl answered and raised her eyes heavenwards meaningfully. 'Last cubicle on the left.'

'Ladies?' Sophie asked.

'Gents.'

'This I have to see!' Sophie giggled. 'Catch you later, Nikki. Come on, Jade.'

I'd guessed what June was up to, and the idea of watching did hold a certain awful fascination. Not that it seemed to matter much whether I wanted to or not. Sophie took my hand, grabbed Penny in passing and led us towards a corridor over which a sign showed the way to the toilets. Jeff looked around in surprise as he took the first sip of his pint.

'What are we doing?' Penny asked as we reached the door of the Gents. 'Hey, this is the Men's!'

'June's on a glory hole,' Sophie explained, bumping the door open with her bottom.

The smell of man hit me as soon as I went in, and I saw Penny wince too. Sophie drew in her breath, then pretended to choke. There was a row of urinals, another of sinks, and four cubicles facing each other. Two men were peeing and looked around as we came in, but neither showed any great surprise, until Sophie went up to them, put her arms casually around their shoulders and peered between, to one side, then the other.

'Not bad,' she commented as she came away.

One man looked seriously discomfited, but the other, thick set with striking ginger hair, was grinning as he turned around, his cock still out, with a drop of pee hanging from the tip. Sophie ignored him, went to the end cubicle and gave the door a sharp kick. It swung open, and there was June, seated on the loo, wearing nothing except for black leather knee boots and a pair of white panties, into which she had her hand stuck firmly, down the front. She was looking at us in surprise, her mouth around an erect cock which protruded from a crudely cut hole in the cubicle wall.

For an instant she looked none too pleased, but her expression turned to delight as she realised it was us. She came off the cock, transferring it to her hand and wanking gently at it as she spoke.

'Hi! Great to see you. Coming in?'

Sophie squeezed in, and with the man outside now tugging as his rapidly growing cock shaft I followed, Penny too, forcing the door shut behind her with difficulty. It was hot and clammy, with the smell of male and in particular of cock thick in my nose, but that wasn't all. June had been playing with herself, as shameless as I'd ever been; the front of her panties were damp and I could smell her pussy.

'Hang on, this one's nearly there, I think,' she continued casually, and popped the man's cock back in her mouth.

I couldn't take my eyes off it, watching with mixed arousal and revulsion as she mouthed on the fat white stem. She was so pretty, her black hair pulled up into a ponytail which she'd tied off with a red ribbon, and her sweet face set in pleasure, an awful contrast to the ugly, gnarled penis in her mouth. I thought of my own, limited, cock-sucking experience, the taste and rubbery feel of a man's erection in my mouth, the feel of it sliding in and out between my lips, gagging when he got overexcited and tried to stick it down my throat . . .

She was right about him being nearly there. After just a few moments he started to push into June's mouth. Her cheeks sucked in and bulged out as her eyes came abruptly wide, and sucked in again. I realised he'd come in her mouth, and she'd swallowed it, without spilling a drop. My stomach twitched at the thought of it, the horrible slimy texture of spunk, and the awful salty, male taste.

June didn't seem to mind. She was making a purring sound in her throat as she sat back, and her hand was still busy down her panties. As the cock disappeared her thighs came apart, showing off the full spread of her panty crotch, and below, where the tight white cotton curved down over chubby bum cheeks. Penny took a handful of my bottom and Sophie's arm slid around my waist as we watched the ecstasy build on June's face. One hand went to a plump, coffee-coloured boob, her fingers teasing her nipple, which was just too much for me. I ducked down, to take the other one in my mouth, suckling her as she masturbated.

Sophie giggled and Penny planted a firm swat on my bottom, calling me a slut. I wiggled, wanting the spanking, hard, to punish me, not for being so dirty, but because as I sucked on June I was having trouble keeping the image of the man's erection out of my head. Penny and Sophie obliged, taking me around my waist and smacking away at my bum, the slaps mingling with the wet, fleshy sounds of June frigging. Their grip changed; Sophie's fingers were on the button of my fly, and as June came with a long, low moan my jeans and panties were hauled down, baring me.

I would have stayed down, maybe until they had made me come in turn, only even as Penny once more began to slap at my now bare bottom I saw an eye appear at the glory hole, a male eye. I jumped up, confused and embarrassed, because there was no denying that the thought of being watched by a stranger as they brought me off appealed. It was not what the man, presumably the one who'd been outside before, had in mind. His eye disappeared and his cock was thrust through the hole, long and skinny and white, except for the head, which was a glossy red colour. A voice sounded from beyond the partition, harsh and full of passion.

'I want the blonde.'

Sophie giggled and got straight down, seating herself as June moved aside for her. The man thrust his cock further out, a bristle of ginger pubic hair pushing through the hole. Sophie began to play with him, using her nails to tickle his shaft and the meaty mass of his rolled-back foreskin. He moaned in pleasure and she giggled, her eyes bright with excitement and laughter as she continued to tease him.

Penny's hand was on my bottom, stroking and kneading gently. It seemed silly to pull up my jeans and panties, and I let her do it, with my sense of arousal rising slowly, guilt too. I'd tried so hard to make myself exclusive to girls, to live the lifestyle, but here I was, getting horny as I watched a cock teased in a men's lavatory, even if it was my girlfriend's hand on my bum.

I shut my eyes, telling myself I would have fun with the girls but would not go down on a man. They were being submissive, in a sense, making themselves available for cock sucking by any man who chose to stick his erection through the glory hole. My place was obvious. I would be on my knees, my tongue ready for their pleasure as they sat on the open loo, a slave to slaves, surely an appropriate place for me? Maybe they'd even want to use the loo while I was doing it, to pee in my mouth, to have me lick them clean . . .

To think was to act. I got down, pushing out my bare bottom as I kneeled between Sophie's legs, looking up at her. She gave a squeak of delight and let go of the man's cock, to stand up and quickly push her jeans and panties down to her ankles, sitting back down with her thighs wide and her pussy pressed forwards for my attention. I buried my face, licking at her with my guilt and sense of self-betrayal fading quickly as the taste of pussy filled my senses.

She took the cock in her mouth, sucking eagerly as I licked her, Penny and June watching bright-eyed, their backs to the door and their arms around each other. Nobody could get in with them there. I was safe, a grovelling slut for the girls but unavailable to the men, as I wanted to be. After pulling my jumper and top up, I took my boobs in my hands, playing with them through my bra for a moment before pulling it off to let them swing free.

Something touched my bottom – Penny's toe, her tights tickling my flesh to make my muscles tense. For one awful moment I thought I was going to wet myself, but as she found my pussy my pleasure rose up over the awful tickling sensation. She began to tease me, stroking my lips and mound, amusing herself with my spread bottom. I wiggled, encouraging her, and June, to do just as they pleased with me.

A hand locked in my hair and Sophie was pulling me in, her pussy already tightening in my face as I licked, her mouth now working hard on the erect cock in it. She didn't even know who he was, and she was sucking his erection through a hole in a toilet wall, so dirty, and with me at her feet, on the floor, near nude and licking pussy. It was where I belonged, a naked slut to be used for my friend's amusement, but I couldn't help thinking of the man Sophie was sucking, and his lewd red face as he'd flourished his cock at us, the tip still wet with piss.

What if they made me suck? Not for the pleasure, but because it amused them to see me with a cock in my mouth. I'd have to do it, whether I liked it or not, to take that big, ugly erection in my mouth, to suck on it, perhaps with my head held by the hair, forcing me, until I started to gag on it, until he spunked down my throat . . .

I pushed the thought away. They could do as they pleased with me, but they were not dominant, not cruel, no more than mischievous. Perhaps they would make me, perhaps they wouldn't, but I would do as I was told, my right to self-determination given away, and my guilt with it. For the moment, I had to concentrate on making Sophie come.

She was at the edge, her thighs tight around my head, her pussy twitching as I licked at her clitty. I stopped playing with my boobs, a selfish act, and took hold of hers, feeling them through her top. She abruptly pulled it up, bra and all, and I had a pair of plump little titties in my hands, bare and warm, her nipples erect. I heard her gulp and realised the man must have come in her mouth, and suddenly she was there too, her hand twisting in my hair and her body squirming on the toilet seat as it went through her even as she was swallowing down her slimy mouthful.

I stopped licking only when she pulled my head back. She was smiling, her face set in drowsy pleasure, with a froth of spit and come hanging from her lower lip. The man withdrew his cock and an eyeball appeared once again, swivelling round to take in the sight of Sophie's bare tits, and mine. It was a new man, the dark brown skin quite clearly not that of the ginger-headed one Sophie had just sucked. She saw, and opened her mouth, showing the contents, and I realised she hadn't swallowed at all. The ginger man's come was still in her mouth, a thick clot of white lying on her tongue with bubbles in it where it had mixed with her saliva.

'Wobba spoeball?' she managed.

June giggled, but it was Penny who bent down, after just a moment's hesitation, to open her mouth against Sophie's. I watched in disgust, yet wishing I'd been ordered to do it myself, as they shared the spunk, rolling it between their tongues and sucking it in to make more bubbles. Some escaped, to make a thick white streamer, hanging from Penny's chin, which broke, to land on Sophie's tit and roll slowly down her flesh.

The eye disappeared from the hole. I heard a grunt, the rasp of a zip and his cock was thrust through for our attention, already erect, a thick brown pole of meat with a plump head of a rich purple colour. He was big, a lot bigger than either of the others, and heavily veined along the trunk, with a thick foreskin stretched tight below the neck. I stayed down, wondering if they would order me to suck the terrifying, compelling thing, and as Penny and Sophie finally broke apart and swallowed their mouthfuls he spoke.

'Come on, June.'

'I've had one.' She giggled. 'I mustn't be greedy. Who d'you want?'

'Jade,' he answered, 'and wrap your titties round me first, yeah, love?'

I didn't answer. I couldn't. He wanted me to take his cock between my boobs, then suck it. The idea made my stomach crawl, and I looked up to Penny, waiting for her to take the responsibility out of my hands. She understood, and immediately pointed to the huge cock sticking out from the glory hole.

'Go on, Jade, do as the man says, between your breasts first, then suck him. That's an order.'

Sophie was giggling as she rose to leave the loo vacant for me. I sat down and the others moved back, except for Penny. She alone fully understood how I was feeling, and what to do. Taking me firmly but gently by the hair, she pushed me close to the man's cock. I was staring at the huge erection in front of me, wondering how it would feel between my breasts, and in my mouth, also how he knew my name, something that made it that much more personal, and harder to do.

'Take your breasts in your hands, Jade,' Penny ordered. 'That's right, now fold them around his cock.'

I'd lifted them as she gave the order, splaying my fingers to pick up each and feel that wonderful sense of weight and roundness that is so much a part of who I am, and of my urge for submission. The man looked fit to burst, and I hesitated for a moment before plucking up my courage and pressing my boobs together around his erection. It felt hot, and hard, and very much alive as he sighed and began to fuck my tits, pushing himself in and out through the glory hole.

Penny held me close, soothing me by stroking my hair and telling me it would be all right, that I should just relax and let my feelings take over. I wanted her to take over, to force me to do it, and worse. There was a wonderful firmness in the way she was behaving, a no-nonsense manner it was very easy to give in to, if not the cruelty I so often crave. I imagined the way AJ would have done it, if she'd ever let herself near a man's cock, calling me a bitch and a slut as she forced me to perform. I thought of Fat Jeff's dirty email, telling me I was going to be titty fucked on the Saturday night, and wished the girls had stripped me and held me down in the car while he did it to me. I considered how it would feel if they tied me in the cubicle and let the men queue to use me, one after another fucking in my slimy cleavage, maybe at fifty pence a time, or twenty pence . . .

'Time you sucked, darling,' Penny said gently, and pulled his cock free from between my boobs.

My mouth came open. I was shaking hard, unable to do it of my own accord, and then it had been done for me, Penny taking him in hand and feeding me, the head in my mouth as she began to tug on his shaft. I could taste him, strong and salty and so, so male, and before I really knew it I had closed my mouth, sucking on the thick, rubbery head as she began to tug harder.

'All the way, darling, I think,' she said.

She was going to wank him off, into my mouth, and I found myself shaking my head, but it was more than I could do to pull back. I heard June giggle. Sophie took me in her arms, soft, subtle fingers slid beneath me, to cup my pussy and fan out into my bum crease, and I was lost. My head was a jumble of thoughts as I waited for it to happen, my own orgasm, and his, in my mouth. I tried to focus on what I ought to, the girls' cool, easy control of my body, and my reaction. I tried not to focus on the wilful act of sucking a man's cock, and knowing he was going to come in my mouth, and that I could stop, if I wanted to, if only I wanted to . . .

He grunted, Penny gave a sudden, sharp flurry of tugs on his shaft, and it was too late. His come was spurting into my mouth, eruption after eruption of slime, to make my eyes pop in disgust and my cheeks bulge as I struggled not to be sick on the spot. I kept my head there, still sucking on the fat knob of brown cock meat in my mouth, unable to stop myself even as my mouth filled.

Sophie was rubbing hard, her fingers working me up, so skilfully, but it was just enough to make me take my mouthful, not enough to get me there while he was doing it. He pulled back, a last strand of saliva and spunk joining his cockhead to my lip, stretching and breaking to leave me open gasping, his come pooled in my mouth.

'Next!' Sophie called, and an instant later a fat white cock had been thrust through the hole and into my mouth, Jeff's, I was sure.

I began to suck, too far gone even to think of stopping myself. They had me, as surely as if I'd been tied and my mouth clamped wide, the girls' caresses making it impossible to stop myself. Sophie had two fingers deep in my pussy, and was using a third to tease my bumhole open, all the while with her thumb flicking on my clitty, over and over. June pushed close, her hands finding my boobs, her fingers closing on one nipple, and I was there, sucking on Jeff's erection, as eager and wanton as any of them, a complete and utter slut, a dirty, filthy little cock-sucker . . .

They were laughing as my body jerked and shook in orgasm, and I heard Jeff mutter something about putting him off. I sucked all the harder, hoping he'd fill my mouth with spunk and add one more awful touch to my helpless ecstasy before I'd finished coming. I already had one man's come in my mouth, and to make it two would be all the better, or four, or eight, or a hundred, pumped into every orifice in my body until I was bloated with it.

I got it, right at the top, a great mouthful of sticky, slimy muck exploding down my throat, more as I struggled to swallow, wanting my belly full of it, and more, in my face as Jeff pulled back to finish himself off in his hand. Sophie gave a squeal of laughter, but Penny bent low, her mouth to mine, opening wide to snowball with me as I came slowly down from my orgasm, the two of us rolling a thick wad of bubbly come between our mouths. An eye appeared at the glory hole, watching us, and I was sobbing as my ecstasy faded to shame, but still kissing, with mess dribbling down over my tits and plopping on the floor beneath me.

Sophie and June were in no mood to stop, or even pause. Penny was pulled off me, squealing and laughing in mock protest as she was quickly stripped for action, her top and jumper jerked off over her head and her jeans and panties pulled quickly down. They put her on the seat, bare bottom, just as soon as I'd vacated it, and I was pushed to my knees in front of her. She already had a cock to suck, maybe Monty's, maybe not, and took it in her mouth even as I began to lick her.

I knew what would be going through her head, the humiliation of being stripped and made to suck a stranger's cock, of doing it in a lavatory. So many times she and I had lain together, exploring each other's fantasies, and I knew just what she'd want. I took hold of her bottom, slipping one hand beneath, found her bumhole and slid a finger in. Her ring was already slippery with her juice. She began to wriggle as her rectum was penetrated, and to suck harder on the cock in her mouth, holding it too, and tugging on his shaft.

He came, Penny pulling back at the last instant to get it in her face, milking him out over her cheeks and nose and lips. I kept on licking, and fingering her bottom as she soiled herself, waiting until at last her bumhole began to pulse on my finger before I pulled it free and stuck it into her open mouth. She sucked greedily as she came, to the sound of Sophie and Jade squealing and clapping in delight and disgust. It took her a while too, long enough to allow Monty to get his eye to the glory hole and see what she was doing.

Penny was still coming down when Monty moved away and yet another cock was stuck through the glory hole. June began to tug on it half-heartedly, but the rest of us had had enough and quickly made ourselves decent while she finished him off in her hand. There was quite a queue outside, and for a moment I thought it might get nasty, but everybody seemed to know June, and accept it when she said that Monty and Jeff were our Masters. At least with Jeff and Monty we were safe, and I stuck close to them, so we escaped with nothing worse than a few pinches to our bums.

Our drinks were untouched on the bar where Jeff had left them. I badly needed mine, because I hadn't dared pause in the Gents long enough to wash my mouth out and I wasn't sure that the Ladies would be any better. I took most of it down in one, and nearly choked as I finished it. A man was coming towards us, a black man bigger than Jeff, bigger than anyone else in the place, and shockingly familiar – the bouncer who had let us in at the back door of Bolero's. I was desperately trying to find the right words to say as he came up to us, but nothing would come out.

June spoke first, calm and friendly. 'All right, Teo? Good, wasn't it?'

'Great,' he answered, exposing a broad row of white teeth, one of which had a diamond set in it. 'Nice one, Jade.'

'N–nice?' I managed. 'You mean . . . you don't mind . . . about the cabaret?'

He looked puzzled.

'Not the cabaret, silly,' June cut in. 'Who do you think you just sucked off?'

Six

In the first few minutes after being introduced to Teo I could cheerfully have strangled June. I knew she'd fancied him, but not that she'd taken his business card when they'd spoken at the door. Even then, given what had happened, I'd have expected her not to follow the contact up, but the little slut had called him for a date the very next day. She'd started taking him to clubs, SM clubs, not the sort he was used to working at, and he had quickly got into it.

He'd also got into her, fortunately, so that he was quite happy to compromise what loyalty he had to Bob Ryman in order to keep her sweet and playful. Not that Ryman was all that angry, apparently, having cooled down when he realised that, by using a different venue and putting somebody else in as front man, he could not only continue running Bolero's but take advantage of the publicity we'd gained him. He still wanted to see us, but apparently only to get an apology, and Teo was hoping to fix it so that in the end everything was above board.

I was not convinced, especially as there was nothing to stop Ryman bringing Ronnie Miles along, and Miles was apparently furious. June thought I should do it, arguing that it was best to bring it to closure, and pointing out that Ryman was probably just looking for an excuse to squeeze a blow job out of me. When I pointed out that it was all very well for her she just laughed, but she also promised to come with me and stand in for me if it came down to having to suck cock.

Penny was against it, Sophie unsure. Neither felt it was wise to trust Ryman, but Sophie didn't want to be looking over her shoulder every time she went out on the town, which didn't bother Penny as she never goes to straight clubs if she can help it. Jeff refused to take it seriously, making impractical suggestions such as blowing up Ryman's office, while Monty had gone off to try and persuade June's friend Nikki to take a spanking. In the end I agreed to do it, but only if Teo and June came with me and we turned up at Ryman's office unexpectedly.

One other interesting thing came out of the evening. We were messing about at the very end, all rather drunk, when Monty came up behind me as I was kissing June goodbye and tickled me under the armpits. I came within an ace of wetting my panties, only saving myself by dropping down quickly to press my heel between my pussy and bumhole, which often works if I have a chance to do it. Although I could see that the idea of me peeing myself appealed to him, he was very apologetic, and suggested that I should have a word with Poppy's girlfriend Gabrielle, who was a therapist but apparently had a pretty good medical background. She was also into nappies, so there would be no embarrassment whatsoever about talking to her.

I had no desire to make a formal appointment and end up paying her outrageous fees, so I was sneaky and rang Poppy to ask if they'd like to come out with Penny and me for a drink and maybe a little play at the weekend. She was full of enthusiasm, and that was that, except for bringing it up in conversation, which could hardly be difficult with a girl whose idea of a good time is to wet herself anyway.

Ryman needed to be dealt with in the week, and by good fortune my assignment was with a firm of accountants in Marylebone, a short bus ride from his office. Being a student, June had no real difficulty making time, and Teo's only stipulation was that the meeting should be in the evening, when he would be up and about. We agreed on Thursday, and, while I trusted June, I wasn't taking any chances with Teo.

I said I would be leaving work at six and would meet them in a café in Mortimer Street almost directly across the road from Ryman's offices. I actually finished at five, and took my place in a different café some way down the street at half past, to watch. Teo arrived, then June, but there was no sign of anyone else. Feeling pleased with myself but more than a little nervous, I waited until a quarter past six and then joined them.

We drank a coffee and went over our story before crossing the road, and Teo had us buzzed up to Ryman's office. Everybody else seemed to have gone home, and we found him behind a large and untidy desk, as smarmy as ever in his sharp suit and shades. Teo was supposed to have met us in a club he was working at and persuaded us to come and apologise, and gave his opening line as Ryman looked up in surprise to see who he had with him.

'Found them at Transition, Mr Ryman. Said they owed you an apology, I did.'

'Good man, Teo, good man,' Ryman answered, fingering his chin as he turned to look me up and down.

Just to be in the same room as him made my skin crawl, but I hung my head meekly, as if scared to meet his eyes. June had stayed back, next to Teo beside the door, and I felt very vulnerable indeed, but not close to how I'd have felt on my own.

'Sorry, Mr Ryman,' I said after a pause.

He didn't answer immediately, just looking at me and shaking his head. 'You're a dirty little tart, aren't you?' he asked finally. 'I mean, just what the fuck did you think you were doing?'

'What . . . what we were told to do,' I managed.

'What you were told to do?' he echoed. 'Told to do by whom? By that mad dyke bitch, AJ?'

'No,' I answered quickly, determined that whatever I did I was not going to drop AJ any deeper in it. 'She just said you wanted hardcore, and . . . and that's what we . . . what we thought we did.'

'Nah,' he answered, 'you didn't think. More than thirty years I've been in and out of the sex trade. I was running a dirty bookshop when I was eighteen, me. I've been in shops. I've been in clubs. I've been in strip bars. If there's one thing I've learned, it's that the girls don't think. They want money, and they want their money as easy as it comes. That's the way it is, so don't go giving me any of your bullshit about how it was all your idea!'

His voice had risen, and I didn't reply, despite the urge to tell him that he was a prat and that it was no surprise at all if in thirty years no woman had ever confided her true thoughts in him. I didn't know what he was getting at either, because I couldn't see why it made any difference who had decided what we did unless it was AJ, and, if it hadn't been AJ, it had to be me and the other girls.

'I know who put you up to it,' he went on, calm again, and with his voice oozing arrogant certainty. 'I ain't stupid, you know. It was that bastard Rathwell, wasn't it?'

It was completely and utterly unexpected, and he must have mistaken my look of surprise for shock, because he laughed and went on, more confident than ever. 'You see, you silly little cows don't think I know a thing, but I do. I know, that your little blonde friend, the one who started the pissing business, she works for Rathwell, don't she?'

'Yes, but . . .'

'And she's a hostess at his clubs too, ain't she?'

'Yes, but . . .'

'So that's the story, ain't it? Our AJ asks you to get a cabaret up, and naturally you choose the dirtiest little lezzer tarts you can lay your hands on, and they don't come no dirtier than little Sophie, do they? So old Morris gets wind of it and he sees a way to fuck over the opposition, 'cause he don't like other people treading on his toes, does he?'

I shrugged, not knowing what to say. For all that I wanted to deny it I knew it was possible. Sophie would certainly have told Morris about the cabaret, there was no reason she shouldn't have done, and she had been the first one to suggest pissing games. Only it didn't make sense. We hadn't known we'd be on the balcony, or that it had a perforated steel floor, or about the fire doors. For that matter I couldn't see a large and pretty much mainstream club as a rival to Morris's strictly kinky affairs, or Sophie behaving that way.

What it did mean, as I quickly realised, was that I was off the hook. His little piece of logic might be wrong, but it deflected the blame away from me. He obviously didn't think of Sophie as anything more than a pawn, while Morris was well able to take care of himself. Better still, if his version of events got back to Ronnie Miles I would be completely in the clear. I said nothing, but hung my head lower still, playing the stupid little girl for all that I was worth.

He said nothing for a long while, just looking at me until I had begun to wonder if he was going to demand his cock sucked after all. I knew I couldn't accept it, and was glad that June was there, yet if he didn't want her, if he had some power trip about making me do it . . .

Then I'd refuse.

When he spat a final, condescending 'get out' I was so relieved I felt weak at the knees. I was shaking as we went back down to the street, and it wasn't until I'd got a couple of breezers down my neck that I started to feel even close to normal. June and Teo were as pleased as I was, both having got the result they wanted, and June without even having to go down on Ryman. I was going to have to tell Sophie what had been said about Morris, but otherwise it was all over.

They wanted to celebrate, but I just wasn't up for it. It had been a long day, and a long week, and the interview with Ryman had left me feeling drained. So I left them to it and took the tube home, grabbing a deep pan Mexican Hots at Pizza Population and eating it in the bath. My stress slowly melted away as I filled up with pizza, and by the time I'd finished I was feeling thoroughly pleased with myself and looking forward to the weekend, with just Friday to get out of the way.

Penny arrived late on the Saturday afternoon and we drove over to Victoria together. Poppy was eager to play, and had put on a little maid's uniform with a short flounced skirt supported by a layered gauze petticoat to show off her bum, or rather her nappy, which was what she had on underneath, along with stockings and suspenders. It was a proper adult baby-girl nappy, white with pink hearts around the rim, and very puffy. She looked cute and she knew it, wiggling her bum for us as she went about making coffee. Gabrielle had been working, and was in a smart two-piece suit of pale yellow wool, which made Poppy's outfit seem all the more indecent.

It was easy to relax, with Poppy flirting and quite obviously keen to play, and no harder to bring the conversation round to my little wetting problem. As we drank our coffee, Poppy was happily describing how she'd handcuffed Gabrielle to the bathroom pipes and left her until she did it in her panties, and Penny chimed in right on cue.

'You wouldn't have to bother restraining Jade, just tickle her. She'll wet herself on the spot.'

Poppy's interest was immediate, and Gabrielle's too, but professional as well as sexual.

'I'd love to be like that!' Poppy chimed in. 'Imagine, so helpless!'

'No you wouldn't,' I assured her, 'not all the time anyway. AJ says she's going to do it to me in the street, a crowded street. I wouldn't mind so much in private, or even with a group of girls who understand submission, so long as I was in the mood, but she's going to make it a punishment.'

'Sometimes you just have to take it,' Poppy advised, 'but, if you really can't handle it, tell her to fuck off.'

'That's what I keep saying,' Penny put in.

'Do you have no control whatever?' Gabrielle asked. 'The emission is entirely involuntary?'

'Yes,' I confirmed. 'It just comes out, all at once. I can't help it, and knowing it's going to happen only makes it worse.'

'I see. It is not really my field, but I think I can explain what is happening, if that would be of interest?'

'Yes.'

She paused, steepling her fingers in her lap, her delicate face completely earnest, then went on. 'To start at the beginning, urination is primarily under the control of the detrusor, a large muscle which expands as urine builds up in the bladder, and squeezes to empty it. Most incontinence problems are related to detrusor control, either physical when this muscle contracts more often than normal or at inappropriate times, or due to the formation of a psychosomatic link between detrusor contraction and some other stimulus. The urge to urinate, or less frequently involuntary urination, when a hand is placed in cold water is perhaps the commonest example, but it might be anything. In one case I remember a client, a middle-aged man, had become conditioned to want to urinate at the sound of a bell, this being the way time was called in his local pub, where it had been his invariable habit to visit the loo before closing time. In your case, you are suffering from what is called giggle micturition, when laughter stimulates the relevant control centre in the brain to completely empty the bladder with no warning. Does it happen when you laugh at any time, or only when you are tickled?'

'When I'm tickled, usually, but if I'm really laughing hard, then sometimes, yes.'

'And do you sometimes find yourself adopting a particular posture to stop it happening, a low curtsey with your heel pressed to your perineum?'

'What's a perineum when it's at home?'

'The area between your vagina and anus.'

'Yes, that has saved me many, many times.'

'It is called Vincent's Curtsey, and is a common sign of giggle micturition.'

'Who was Vincent? An incontinent transvestite?'

She smiled, then went on. 'A learned urologist, I expect. I know about it because one school of thought contends that it is primarily a psychological condition, and I agree. There is a drug, propantheline, which can be used to prevent this sort of thing, but it does have unpleasant side effects, including blurred vision and high light sensitivity. It would be on prescription, of course. It is probably unnecessary anyway. In my view, what you need to do is break the link you have built up in your mind between being tickled and wetting yourself.'

'Easier said than done!'

'Put her in incontinence pants,' Poppy remarked casually.

'Very funny, Poppy,' I answered her. 'I'm serious!'

'So am I,' she went on. 'Just make sure you're wearing a pair of plastic pants when this AJ woman catches you. That way nobody will notice you've wet yourself, and if it doesn't work she'll quickly get bored with it.'

'A sensible short-term solution at the very least,' Gabrielle agreed.

'You want to put me in incontinence pants?' I queried.

'Only temporarily.'

'There's a problem. What if she decides to spank me or something?'

'Do not let her spank you.'

'She doesn't usually bother to ask.'

'You have a stop word, surely?'

'AJ thinks stop words are for people who're only dabbling. She did let me off when I broke down over cleaning the soles of her boots with my mouth, but nothing I could say would stop her getting me bare for a punishment. After all, if it was that easy I could stop her tickling me.'

Penny sighed. 'You mustn't allow yourself to be bullied, Jade. Consent must be –'

'But I like to be bullied!' I answered her. 'Just like you like to be humiliated.'

'Yes, but I always retain the final control . . .'

'Which makes it all the more humiliating, because you know you could stop it. It doesn't work that way for me. I need my control taken away from me, completely, and I can only do that within a framework of rules, so that I can ultimately trust those who are dominating me.'

'Like AJ making you wet yourself in the street?'

'It's a punishment. She has that right. I've given it to her, and I can't take it away, not without losing her respect, and some times I need full-on domination.'

Penny made a face but she didn't answer. We'd had the argument before, many times, and she knew it was pointless. Gabrielle nodded thoughtfully, but Poppy shook her head. I knew why. Penny had explained Poppy's history, with several years living as the lifestyle submissive to Anna Vale. Anna was a legend, even to AJ, for all that she called her a mad bitch and worse. For absolute devotion to the lifestyle there was nobody to touch Anna Vale.

'It's up to you,' Poppy said, biting her lip, 'but I wouldn't recommend it, not twenty-four seven.'

'I'm not going for it twenty-four seven,' I assured her. 'I know I couldn't handle it.'

'Not many can,' Poppy answered. 'You met June? Her friend Nicola and my ex, Anna, lasted all of two months, and she wanted it so badly.'

'Nikki? Very slim girl, hair right down to her bum? She was at a club we went to last Saturday night, on her own, and stark naked except for a collar.'

'Sure, she didn't lose it completely; she just

couldn't handle Anna. Anyway, how about we get you in those incontinence pants?'

'What, now?'

'Why not? You'll have to get used to them. We've got some.'

She was grinning all over her face, and it was quite obvious she wanted me in them. I nodded, feeling more than a little embarrassed but determined not to be pathetic about it. It was a good idea. I had more or less implied I wanted to play when I rang her. She had already disappeared into their bedroom anyway, and returned a moment later with a garment that sent the blood straight to my cheeks.

I'd been expecting something medical, made of that horrid brownish-coloured rubber you see on the TV sometimes, and strictly utilitarian. They weren't; they were pink, and completely see-through, and had frills around the leg holes, more like a pair of little rubber bloomers than anything medical.

'They're made for me, so they might be a bit tight for you,' she said casually as she tossed them to me.

'Cheek!' I answered, but it was true. Her bum is fleshy enough, but nothing like as big as mine.

'Put them on,' she urged.

I shrugged. All three of them were looking at me, Poppy with unconcealed relish, Gabrielle coolly, Penny with the little quiet smile she always wears when somebody else is about to be comprehensively humiliated instead of her. I made a face as I started to undo my boots.

'So come on, what am I supposed to do if AJ takes my jeans down and catches me in these things?'

'It's more fun with a nappy on underneath,' Poppy stated, ignoring my question completely.

'You just need to make sure she can't get your jeans down,' Penny put in.

'How?' I demanded as I pushed my clothes down. 'We've been through that, she'll just do it. Do these things go over my panties or under them, Poppy?'

'Over them is more comfortable, but it really is best in a nappy.'

'It would bulge! Everybody would know I was wearing one!'

'Not necessarily,' Gabrielle answered. 'If you wear a thick woollen skirt and use a towelling nappy it is really quite discreet, especially with a coat on. Otherwise, for comfort, you should wear your panties underneath. Remember you will only wet yourself when AJ makes you.'

'My bet is she can't wait that long!' Poppy laughed.

'Speak for yourself,' I answered as I began to pull the awful things up my legs. They clung to my skin, which made it difficult, and, while Poppy was watching with delight, Penny was struggling not to giggle.

I promised myself that she would get her bottom warmed before the morning, at the least, and stood to tug the pants up my thighs and over my hips. They were not comfortable. For a start they were too small, squashing my bottom and my tummy, as they came right up to my waist. They were already beginning to feel hot and sticky too, even as I pulled my jeans back up over them. It was a solution though, a little discomfort a small price to pay for not having half of Soho or wherever it happened watch me wet myself.

'What you do,' Penny said suddenly, 'is this. You wear tight jeans, not in a modern style, but high waisted, with a chain belt padlocked at the front. With your figure it will be impossible to get them down, your jumper will conceal the lock, and if AJ does get you then you can explain that another dominant woman has made you wear it. She'll respect that, even if she does figure out that the key has to be in your pocket.'

'Nice one,' I admitted, 'only she's marked me as hers, and none of the others would touch me without her permission . . . no, you're right. We'll say it was Melody Rathwell.'

'She'll have to know,' Penny pointed out, 'and that probably means playing hostess at one of Morris's parties.'

'I can handle that. It's worth it.'

It was well worth it. AJ was tough, and with any other butch dyke she would have felt obliged to face them down. Not Melody Rathwell. Mel was bigger than her, stronger than her, and would think nothing of giving AJ a panties-down spanking if the occasion seemed to demand it. AJ knew it too, and steered well clear of Mel. Nothing, but nothing would be worse for AJ's status than having her bum bared for an OTK spanking from another woman. The odds were good AJ wouldn't even question my claim, and Penny could easily square it with Mel if she did. OK, so Mel was likely to want to top me herself in return for the favour, which was just fine, and I might end up performing for Morris, but I'd just have to put up with it.

'I'll do it,' I said, 'we'll find a DIY store first thing tomorrow.'

As I sat down the rubber pants made an embarrassing squeaking noise, something I hadn't anticipated. They felt very odd too, tighter still, to keep me acutely aware that I had them on as I went back to my coffee. Poppy was watching bright-eyed, and I could tell she was hoping I'd put the pants to the test, but it meant wet panties.

'You can go home in a pair of mine,' she said happily, as if she'd read my mind.

'Thanks,' I answered, not bothering to keep the sarcasm out of my voice, but she just laughed and stood up.

'You must treat me as the maid, anyway,' she went on as she started for the kitchen. 'I'm going to cook you all a lovely dinner, and you're to be as bossy and cruel to me as you like. The slightest bit of lip or bad service, and over I go, OK?'

'What about us, you greedy slut?' Penny demanded.

'It is her turn,' Gabrielle explained, 'after chaining me to the pipes. I will be in charge this evening, if you would like? Do you wish to be spanked?'

She didn't wait for an answer, but leaned over to take Penny firmly by the shoulders. Penny gave a little squeak of surprise, but she went, eased down across Gabrielle's knees, bottom up, with the taut blue denim of her jeans providing an excellent target. She was spanked, coolly and methodically, her jeans undone and pulled down, her panties inverted around her thighs and her bare bottom given several dozen hard swats. As usual she made a fuss over it, kicking and wriggling about on Gabrielle's lap with her fists clenched and her face alternately screwed up or open-mouthed, and it left her pink bottomed and trembling.

'Now,' Gabrielle ordered as she finished, 'you will go into my bedroom and find some more appropriate clothes. You too, Jade.'

For all that she was into nappies and adult baby-girl play it would have been hard not to obey. Dressed the way she was, and with her height and slender figure, not to mention the slightly Germanic tone to her accent, it was easy to see her as a dominant. I went, following Penny into the special bedroom, which could not have been more different to the black leather and steel and glass of the rest of her flat. Everything was pink for one thing, and she had the most enormous collection of cuddly toys, all very girlie and innocent until you started investigating the drawers and found such things as rectal thermometers and huge syringes for giving enemas. To her it was a playroom, to Penny and me a temple to humiliation and sexual torture.

We stripped off, Penny nude, me down to my rubber pants and the cotton ones underneath. I liked the way Poppy was dressed, and chose a pink tutu that left my pants on show, and big pink ribbons for my hair. Poppy was in a corset under her uniform, making the best of her boobs, but with the way she was behaving I wanted to go one better. I remembered something Penny had once said while explaining the fetish, that an adult baby-girl doesn't need a top because she has nothing to be embarrassed about, so I went bare. So did she, completely, save for a little powder for her smacked bum and a dummy. She also took one of the thermometers and a tube of lube.

Poppy gave us an arch look as we came out of the bedroom, but she was already preparing dinner and didn't say anything. I felt a little silly, but vulnerable too, and extremely submissive. I don't revel in my own humiliation the way Penny does, but I understand it, and it was getting to me. She was the same, and wanted more, going straight back across Gabrielle's knee to have the thermometer inserted again. I watched as her cheeks were pulled open and her anus lubricated, then the bulb of the thermometer eased in up her bottom.

It showed between her cheeks when she stood up, and of course she couldn't sit down properly, but had to curl up on the settee with her head in Gabrielle's lap, sucking her dummy. I felt I needed to be a little more horny to really appreciate what I was doing, maybe restrained or punished in some way, but I wasn't sure what, and asked Gabrielle.

'I . . . I think I need something to perk me up a bit, like Penny's thermometer or . . . or maybe something a bit more painful?'

She nodded, gently removed Penny's head from her lap and walked into the special bedroom. A moment later she was back, holding a strange ring-shaped object of chrome-plated steel with various screws and plates attached.

'Will this do?' she asked casually, holding it up. 'It is a jaw brace, designed to hold the mouth wide, and –'

'I know,' I answered, my eyes glued to the horrible thing. 'OK.'

It was much more my style, and I was shaking immediately, just at the thought of being unable to hold my mouth closed. I'd seen one in use, in a picture I'd stumbled across while looking for girl-on-girl domination pics on the net. The victim had been tied, her hands lashed tight behind her back, kneeling and held by the hair, with the jaw brace in as two men masturbated into her open mouth. I'd come over the thought of AJ putting me in the same painful and helpless condition, then peeing down my throat.

Gabrielle was looking deadly serious as she adjusted the brace and I waited with my mouth open. She was good for such heavy play, sensible and safety-conscious, for all that she lacked the cruel streak I look for in women. It didn't stop her pushing the right buttons, intentionally or not.

'You must never put anything in your mouth with this on,' she advised. 'It is impossible to swallow and you would risk choking. A patient with such a device in place would have to be fed intravenously, or possibly via a tube.'

I hastily dismissed the idea of AJ pissing in my mouth and replaced it with one of her force-feeding me, with a tube down my throat as she poured some vile but nutritious substance down my neck. Gabrielle put it in my mouth and I tasted the sharp tang of the metal on my tongue as the plastic pads met my teeth. I stayed perfectly still, mouth agape, as she pulled the ring down over my head and adjusted it, locking it off, then twisting the screws until my mouth was as wide open as it would go.

It hurt, and I felt utterly helpless, bringing my sense of submission quickly up. My hands were already behind my back, and she took the hint without having to be asked, returning to her bedroom for some cuffs, which she clipped into place. She had a second pair too, larger, which I thought were for my ankles until she led me into the kitchen, sat me down at the table and casually clipped my leg off to the bar underneath. I was genuinely helpless, unable to escape, unable to speak, which was going to make wetting into my incontinence pants so much easier, and so much more pleasurable.

Poppy giggled at my plight, but carried on with her cooking preparations, sparing me only the occasional glance. Gabrielle pulled my tutu off as it was getting in the way, and left. A moment later I heard the smack of palm on bottom and Penny's squeals as she was given another spanking, then the bang of a door as Gabrielle took her into the bedroom.

'I expect Gabby will put her in nappies now,' Poppy remarked. 'This isn't very fair, you know. I wanted some attention.'

I tried to answer, but only managed a muffled gargling noise. She went on.

'Oh well, I expect I'll get my share. For now, I suppose I'd better make the best of it, and try to earn a decent punishment.'

She'd been putting together some complicated dish in a roasting pan, and paused to slide it into the oven. When she stood up again it was to reach up to one of the cupboards and take out a small bottle of some red substance with a label showing a man with a bright red face and flames coming out of his mouth and ears. She was grinning as she turned to me, and a nasty suspicion became a certainty as she unscrewed the bottle and very carefully poured a blob of it out onto the tip of one finger.

I closed my eyes, shaking hard as she reached out, to rub the chilli sauce onto one of my nipples, cool and soothing for one instant, and then starting to burn. She chuckled as I gasped, and anointed my other nipple, rubbing the sauce well in, until I was squirming in the chair and shaking my head from side to side in pain. Both my nipples had popped out, agonisingly stiff and burning hot. She just giggled, casually returned the bottle to its place and swayed out of the room, speaking as she left.

'I'm going to see what they're up to, might be fun.'

All I could manage was a gurgle of protest and then I was alone. My nipples felt as if they were going to burst, and I was cursing her for being such a bitch. If she wanted to torture me she could have done, bringing me off with a hand down my pants as I wriggled in agony on the chair, but to leave me was worse by far. I couldn't frig myself; I couldn't get the sauce off or the jaw brace out; all I could do was squirm in pain and wait until one of them took pity on me.

I never even realised she was behind me until her fingers jabbed into my armpits, tickling. My whole body jerked in shock; my teeth jammed down on the jaw brace, and my bladder burst, painfully hard. Piss squirted out into my panties, and through them, bulging out the front of my rubber knickers. I was kicking and struggling immediately, but still she tickled, giggling madly and peering down over my shoulder to watch my pants fill.

She only stopped when I'd done it all, by which time there was a fat bulge of piss-filled rubber over my pussy. My skin was prickling with sweat; my jaw was in agony and I was shaking, with the muscles of my belly and one leg still twitching involuntarily. The pants had held, but pee was seeping down between my bum cheeks, hot and wet against my anus and in my crease.

Poppy chuckled and her hands came around my waist, pausing to cup my boobs, then sliding lower. She cupped the bulge of pee, sighing as she felt what I'd done in my incontinence pants, then pulled out the front as my throat contracted in a single, mute sob. Her hand went down, into the front of my sodden knickers, under the pee. She gave a little disgusted giggle and she was exploring the folds of my pussy, one finger slipping inside, and a second to stretch me wide and let the pee run in. I groaned as my vagina filled, and I was pushing my hips out, desperate for her touch, to be brought off in my pain and humiliation.

For once she took mercy and began to frig me, rubbing my pussy to make the bulge in my pants wobble. I spread my legs as far as they would go, concentrating on the awful feeling of helplessness, and the pain I could do nothing to stop, my aching jaw, my burning nipples, the memory of how my muscles had jumped and twitched as she tickled me, how my bladder had just burst at a touch . . .

I would have screamed as my orgasm hit me, but I couldn't, my jaw clamped wide to send my throat into a series of agonising spasms instead, too much for me, but I couldn't stop it. Every muscle in my body seemed to be pulling in different directions. My pussy was in contraction, sucking pee in and out with a lewd gurgling noise. I couldn't breathe and my stomach was twisting itself into knots. The leg Gabrielle had cuffed to the table had started to kick uncontrollably, and for one awful moment I thought I was going to pass out in reaction, and then it was over. I was sucking in air through my open mouth, my chest heaving.

Poppy pulled her fingers out and took me in her arms, cuddling me as I came down, stroking my hair and whispering to me. I just burst into tears, shaking with emotion, completely surrendered to her, and knowing she understood, because she accepted the same herself. Only with Penny had I ever let myself go so completely, to a depth I could only ever share with another submissive woman, because no dominant could ever fully understand.

There is no such thing as perfection when it comes to sexual pleasure; there are only different ideals. AJ offered one; Poppy and Nicola in turn had hoped to achieve that same ideal with Anna. Their experiences proved just how hard it was to realise, and even then there would be drawbacks. It could not be perfection, and to think it could be was self-delusion. Penny offered another ideal, a balanced, loving relationship as equals, each catering for the other's needs. Again there were drawbacks, but it was a lot easier to realise than full-on lifestyle submission.

What I really wanted, perhaps a third ideal, was a bit of both, but it was taking a lot of juggling to achieve. I'd been feeling bad about going to The Pumps and not telling Penny ever since it had happened, and I confessed over dinner with Gabrielle and Poppy. She had guessed something had happened, and simply thanked me for being honest. Again, she was like me, so she understood, at least in part.

We stayed the night, after playing until the early hours, Penny and I sharing the ordinary bedroom, Gabrielle and Poppy the special one. Gabrielle had stayed in charge until after dinner, giving Poppy an absolutely blistering spanking with a hairbrush for what she'd done to me. She was then made to stand in the corner with her nappy pulled down at the back to show her bare red bottom until it was time to put the vegetables on.

Penny had been given a long session of anal play, ending with her coming while held over Gabrielle's lap while her bumhole and pussy were creamed, which left her thoroughly content. It was only fair to give Gabrielle her turn, so we dealt with her after dinner, bathing her, applying powder and cream, and sending her to bed in just a nappy, where Poppy brought her gently to orgasm in the quiet and darkness of the special bedroom. By then Penny and I were kissing on the settee, and so it went, until we were simply too exhausted to do more.

I woke late, to the feel of Gabrielle shaking my shoulder and the smell of freshly ground coffee. My jaw ached and I'd had my bottom smacked, but I felt surprisingly fresh, and we were out of the house before noon, intent on finding a DIY store on the way.

Measuring me up for the chain earned us a few strange looks, with Penny carefully considering the merits of each different sort before selecting welded steel links intended for a security lock. Neither of us could cut them, which had to be a good sign, and it took two of the store assistants pulling on the lever with all their force to do it. We chose a padlock to match and left, confident that, short of using power tools, AJ would be unable to break it.

Penny rather spoiled my sense of satisfaction by pointing out that it would be easy enough to cut the tabs on my jeans, but it didn't seem likely that AJ would be prepared to cross Melody so openly. We were in Kilburn, so we drove up over the Heath and called in on the Rathwells. Morris wasn't there, but according to Melody he hadn't been too bothered by Ryman and Miles, but simply thankful to me for passing the information on. Mel was happy to play the game, insisting only that we help out at one of their parties in return. That meant a spanking in front of men, but I was prepared to put up with it as long as they didn't get to touch, and they would be kinky after all. Penny had just about got over having her head depilated, so agreed.

I was teasing her the rest of the way, and got my bottom smacked again at the flat, which led to us spending the rest of the afternoon in bed together. She had to get back, but I wanted her help with my computer, and we sat down with some fish-finger sandwiches to sort it out. I'd managed to get my system infected with a virus, something called a Welchia, which made the Internet connection crash every few minutes and was therefore extremely difficult to get rid of. Penny managed to remove it by carefully keeping the pages we needed up, with me praying as the removal tool downloaded. It worked, leaving her feeling pleased with herself, and me with just under 400 emails in my box, mostly spam.

Not all spam, not by a long way. No less than fifteen were from the supposed Romeo Casanova, more than two a day on average. Evidently Jeff had decided to squeeze every last drop out of the joke. I went to make coffee and clicked the first one open as I began to sip:

> to jade why was you not at pally car park Saturday night 11????? three hours i wait in rain, bad rain!!!!!!!!!!!!!! you stupid fat bich!!!!!!!!!! i not fuck tits now!!! i not fuck at all!!!!!!!!!!!!!!!!!!!!!!!!!!!!!!!!!

I was left staring at the screen. It seemed a bit much, considering that at eleven, more or less, I'd been sucking his cock through a glory hole, unless . . .

Unless it wasn't Jeff after all. In fact it couldn't be Jeff, not unless he'd done something very complicated. The message had been sent shortly before three o'clock on the Sunday morning, at which time we'd still been at the club. As I clicked open the next one a nasty suspicion was dawning on me, and I was wishing fervently that I hadn't sent my mock-enthusiastic reply. He'd changed his tone, but it was not a great deal more reassuring:

> jade i am sorry, true sorry but you make me very angry last night. i wait and wait and you dont come. Cock is hard in my pants very hard hard for you for your tits biggest roundest tits and you dont come!! i cum in pants thinking of big tits jade with tits like big green melons from cyprus tits like udders on cow!!!!! you dont come! i am very wet!! i am angery!!! now i am not angery!! i am sad! you should send mail to say you dont come you should!!!! it rain hard not nice for big tits jade maybe?? OK you don't come but you come next time yes??? tonight you come pally car park midnight for big cock tit fuck with romeo!!!!!!!!!!!!!!!!!!!!!!!!

I hadn't replied because I hadn't seen the message, but that didn't seem to have occurred to him. The next message was berating me for not turning up, the one after apologetic once more and demanding a date in no uncertain terms, and so on, in ever greater desperation. I would have been laughing my head off by the end had it not been for the growing suspicion that it was not a joke after all, but real. Twice he said that he had seen me but not been able to talk, explaining that his family would not approve, and I was left feeling more than a little uneasy, wondering if I'd managed to pick up a stalker with a serious boob fetish.

The fact that he claimed only to be able to meet me in secret seemed a bit convenient, making me wonder if it was a joker after all, but if so, it was no longer funny. Joke or not, there were only so many people it could be and, after putting the security catch up on my door we sat down to think about it.

He knew my name, he had my email address and he knew I'd been in school uniform on the night of the cabaret, and that I'd been naughty in the car park. That narrowed it down to the girls, Jeff and Monty, or just possibly somebody at the club. It couldn't be AJ or Naomi, the idea was ridiculous. None of the other girls seemed likely either, and Penny, Sophie and June could safely be eliminated along with Monty and Jeff because they'd been with me at the club when the first email was sent. Zoe seemed highly unlikely, which left the pizza boy and the cab driver, Dough Boy and Lardo.

Both of them could never keep their eyes off my boobs; both of them had seen me dressed as a schoolgirl; both of them might have been among the doggers in the car park. I thought back to the night, and the man who'd spunked up against the window.

All I could remember was that he'd been fat, hairy and had pasty skin, and that didn't help. They were both fat and hairy and they both had pasty skin.

Penny thought it was more likely to be Lardo, as he was older and seemed more confident. I was more inclined to go for Dough Boy, who always had an air of sexual desperation about him. We both agreed that there was only one thing to be done. I was going to have to be strong about it, strong but sensible. One was innocent, so I could hardly accost both, and they might just deny it anyway. I needed proof, and that meant catching him in the act. He finished his final email with yet another plea to meet, that night. It wasn't going to happen, but I would meet him, and point out that what he was doing was completely unacceptable. I wouldn't be alone, either, I'd be with Teo.

Seven

It was typical. Just when I'd got rid of Ryman and Miles, another one had to turn up. I wasn't surprised. It always seems to be the way with me. Whatever I do, there always seems to be a man with an issue over me somewhere in the background. When I should have been trying to balance my relationships with Penny and AJ, I was wasting my time with an idiot who seemed to think that just because I have large breasts it gave him some sort of right over me.

To make matters worse, I couldn't get hold of June, and eventually discovered through Sophie that she and Teo had taken off for a week in Kos. I could have waited, but on the Monday morning there was yet another email from Romeo Casanova, and I just wanted the problem to go away. So I rang Fat Jeff, who gleefully agreed to escort me. I then replied to the email, promising to meet on the Saturday afternoon in the car park. Jeff wasn't quite as physically awe-inspiring as Teo, but he was the best I could get. He was also nice enough not to try and take advantage of me, or not too badly. At worst I would probably end up having to hold my panties down for him while he tossed off, which wasn't too bad.

With the date made, I put it from my mind. I was in Ealing again, and spent the week shuffling between

Penny's flat and my own. My belly was swollen, as it always is just before my period, which made the rubber pants even more uncomfortable than before, but I started on the Tuesday, and it got slowly better over the week. I was determined to keep them on anyway, because it would have been just my luck for AJ to catch me on the one day I'd left them off.

By the Saturday I was getting quite used to them, so that having them on made me feel secure rather than irritable. The chain I barely noticed, and I always have to buy my jumpers a little too big for me anyway, because of the size of my bust, so the hems came down far enough to keep it concealed. I even thought about giving somebody else the key, so I would be genuinely in restraint, but it wasn't practical during the week.

Penny had to take some students on a field trip to Wales for the weekend, so couldn't come with me, but I felt confident enough as it was. Fat Jeff was already there by the time I got to my flat, munching on a Meat Feast directly outside Pizza Population, which I thought was a bit tactless, although there was no sign of Dough Boy. We had a bit of time to go, so I let him come up to my flat. I'm not often on my own with a man, and I knew he was quite capable of asking for some sexual favour in return for his help, so I was more than a little nervous. If I refused it would cause bad feeling, and I needed him on my side, so I more or less had to do it. He didn't seem bothered, fortunately, content to eat a whole packet of custard creams with his coffee and tell me about camouflage and surveillance techniques.

There was a purpose to it, as he suspected that if Romeo Casanova saw that I was not on my own he might not approach. I had to agree, and readily accepted his suggestion that I wear bright colours and sit in the car park in plain view, while he lurked in the bushes until Romeo, who Jeff referred to as our 'mark', was actually talking to me. Jeff had worked it all out in advance, and was even wearing combats patterned in the browns and dull yellows of autumn, so it was easy to let him make the choices.

We drove over, only not to the dogging car park, but to one at the top of the hill. Jeff disappeared in among the bushes and I was left to walk down the hill on my own, feeling nervous but determined. I walked along the edge of the wood, so that I could see the car park clearly as I walked down, and the bushes around it where the doggers hid to watch. There were people about, walking their dogs or cycling along the track at the bottom of the park, but nobody who might have been either Dough Boy or Lardo.

I nearly walked into him, Dough Boy, still in his red and white striped Pizza Population uniform, complete with hat. He was behind a clump of holly, seated on a bench, right next to where the path came out. It left my heart hammering, and I was extremely grateful to see the bear-like bulk of Jeff as he emerged from some bushes further down. It was working, but I had a little conversation to get through before Jeff arrived.

'Hi,' I managed.

'You came,' he answered, standing to give a little respectful bow, which was the last thing I'd have expected of a man who'd more or less told me he was going to fuck my boobs whether I liked it or not. He was more embarrassed than I was.

'Yes,' I answered, my confidence growing. 'Look, er . . . sorry, I don't know your name . . .'

'My name is Romeo. You know.'

'What, really? OK . . . so anyway, I think there's been a bit of a misunderstanding between us . . .'

'You want to be with me, yes?'

'No. I mean . . . I know when I replied to your first email I sounded as if I did, but . . . but you see, I thought you were . . . somebody else –'

I'd stopped just before claiming that Fat Jeff was my boyfriend, which was asking for trouble. Dough Boy – or Romeo if that really was his name – worked so close to me he would know I was lying. Jeff was not a frequent visitor at my flat.

'– I didn't mean to come on to you,' I finished.

He was looking at me, his expression like one of those little boys with unreasonably large heads and huge blue eyes you see on Valentine cards. There was no anger, no aggression, nothing but hurt and disappointment. I realised that he wasn't more than eighteen or nineteen. I shrugged and smiled, feeling pretty foolish. Jeff had come up to us, and spoke.

'All sorted then?' he asked.

I was about to speak, but Romeo beat me to it, addressing Jeff.

'You are Jade's friend, yes? From the car. I know your beard.'

He was the dogger. An image of his pasty white belly and erect cock pressed to the glass of Jeff's car rose up in my mind, complete with spunk, then of how I had been, bent over for a bare-bum spanking as Jeff fingered me. I knew my face was going red with embarrassment, but there was nothing I could do about it.

'Yeah, that's me,' Jeff answered.

'You are a lucky man,' Romeo went on, 'but not her boyfriend, I do not think?'

'Er . . . no,' Jeff admitted, stopped, glanced at me and then went on. 'The thing is with our Jade, is that she prefers girls. It's nothing personal –'

'She gave you a hand job, I saw,' Romeo broke in accusingly. 'So why not me?'

He was ignoring me completely, which I was beginning to find insulting, as if there was no point in talking to a woman if her man was around. Jeff didn't answer for a moment, perhaps as taken aback by the question as I was. Dough Boy just looked at us, waiting. I was trying to find a really pithy explanation for why I couldn't be expected to have casual sex with any man who happened to ask, but Jeff beat me to it.

'What you've got to learn about girls,' he said carefully, 'is that you need to be nice, make friends and, most of all, don't be a threat. Then, if you ask nicely, they probably will go for it . . . give you a hand job, maybe, or at least show you their tits while you jack off.'

I nodded, not entirely happy with the explanation, but keen to back Jeff up.

Dough Boy turned to me. 'I will be your friend. We have fun, yes?'

'No!' I answered indignantly.

'Why not?' he asked, giving his hurt look again. 'In the car you showed what you like, with –' He broke off, looking at Jeff, from whom he seemed to expect support. 'I apologise,' he said, 'I do not know your name. Mr?'

'Bellbird,' Jeff answered, once again taken aback. 'Jeff Bellbird.'

'You come here, where men come to watch,' Dough Boy went on, addressing me again. 'You know this, and you take Mr Bellbird cock in hand, and you are rude with your dirty girls. You dress as schoolgirls for Bolero, and you show it all. You are English, yes? So why will you not do it with me?'

What he meant was that I was a slut, and therefore shouldn't be too particular about who I had sex with. It was not easy to answer. I've always been proud of being sexually liberated, as any modern girl should be, but it wasn't hard to guess that in his culture things didn't work that way. To him I was easy, and therefore he had every right to approach me.

'No!' I managed after a moment. 'It . . . it just doesn't work that way! Look, OK, so I'm a . . . a bad girl, whatever, but, like Jeff said, that's between friends, and I prefer girls anyway!'

Dough Boy nodded. He didn't look best pleased, his small, fat mouth set in a stiff line and his eyes downcast. He sighed. 'I am not good enough for you.'

I thought he would go, but he made no move, and I looked to Jeff for some support. He spoke. 'I reckon you ought to take him in the bushes for a quick toss, Jade. I mean, you don't want him spitting in your pizzas or something, do you? They're good pizzas, they are. Pays to be friendly.'

My mouth had come open, but no sound emerged. I was staring at Jeff, but he merely shrugged. Dough Boy spoke up. 'You are a clever man, Mr Bellbird, this is good advice.'

'The way I see it,' Jeff went on, addressing me, 'is that Romeo wants a bit of titty action, or whatever, and you want peace. I can tell him to fuck off if you like, but he'll be pissed with you. Much better to toss him off, which won't take a minute, and then he's as happy as Larry and you don't have to worry.'

'You're supposed to be helping me!' I protested.

'I am,' he answered. 'Makes sense, yeah?'

'Makes sense,' Dough Boy agreed.

'Men!' I answered, and took Dough Boy by the hand.

Jeff was right, it was mercifully quick, but it was also seriously gross. I began to lead Dough Boy in among the bushes, but I had no idea where I was going, and he did. In fact he seemed to know every single one of the muddy little paths of a maze which

I could only assume had been made by voyeurs, flashers and other dirty old men. It did mean he knew a safe place, behind a redbrick hut that must have had something to do with the sewage works at the bottom of the hill and provided excellent cover. Jeff had followed, and kept watch as Dough Boy propped himself against the wall, lifted his red and white striped apron and pulled down his red and white striped trousers, to reveal a pair of grubby underpants, plain white for once, or grey, really.

'Big titties bare, yes?' he asked happily as he flopped his cock out.

'No, it's too cold!'

'I show you my cock. You show me your tits.'

'No, Dough – Romeo, that's not how it . . . oh, to hell with it!'

I pulled up my jumper, top and bra as one, flopping my tits out. It was cold, and my nipples were erect even before I'd made my dishevelled clothes comfortable. I was wondering what to say if he asked why my jeans were chained up, but I needn't have bothered. His eyes were fixed on my boobs, and looked as if they were about to pop out of his head.

'I have nice cock, yes?' he asked, holding it up for my inspection.

'Very nice,' I answered, not wanting to go into explanations of just how ugly I found the thing I was about to take in my hand. 'No touching, OK?'

'You must touch.'

'No, not me, Romeo, you. Leave my boobs alone. You can look, but not touch.'

'Boobs are tits? Nice word, fat word. Fun bags, knockers, melons, bazookas! Boobs is best. I like English. I like English girls.'

He gave me a dirty grin. I sighed, swallowed my pride and my revulsion, and took him in hand. His cock felt hot, and sweaty, and rubbery. I began to tug, and he began to grow, his eyes never once leaving my boobs. He was hard in no time, a pole of dirty brown meat, dark against his pale, hairy belly. I tugged faster, keen to make him come and aware of the submissive feelings having to do it was triggering in me. He took his balls in hand, feeling them, his mouth coming open to release a blob of saliva that rolled down his chin, and off, hanging by a strand, and breaking as his body jerked in orgasm.

His spit landed in my cleavage, and so did about half his spunk, a huge amount, sprayed high to spatter my boobs and my belly, my jeans too. I let go, jumping back, and he snatched his cock, jerking frantically at it to eject spurt after spurt of thick white spunk, most of it down my legs and over my shoes before I could get clear.

'Thanks!' I managed, looking down at myself in utter disgust. 'Did you have –'

'No problem!' he gasped. 'Any time. Good, yes?'

All I could manage was a sigh of resignation. One of the main reasons I gave up on men was that so few of them have any idea that a woman can take pleasure in anything other than giving it. He was obviously a prime example, a male chauvinist pig right out of the oldest sty, for all his youth. Fortunately I had a tissue in my pocket, and I was just mopping up when Jeff's head appeared around the corner of the shed.

'All sorted then?' he asked for the second time as he made a leisurely inspection of my boobs. 'You are fucking horny, Jade, you know that?'

I stuck my tongue out at him. Romeo carried on as he smoothed out his apron.

'You come here again, yes? In the car. We have fun. Now I must go back. I will be late for work soon.'

With that he leaned forwards, kissed my cheek, took a last look at my naked, soiled chest, and left. I carried on mopping up, wondering if Jeff was going to want his cock seen to, and if I was piqued enough to refuse.

'Not a bad lad, all in,' Jeff remarked as Romeo disappeared from view. 'Say, this is a good place, isn't it? Nice and tucked away. Why are your jeans chained up?'

'To . . . it's a long story.'

'Got the key?'

'No, I have not!' I lied.

'What happens when you need the loo then?'

'I . . . never mind what happens!'

'Bit of humiliation, is it? Nice one! If you're going to piss yourself, can I watch?'

'No you cannot! I mean, no I am not going to piss myself!'

'What then? You're not into panty pooping, are you?'

'No!'

'Shame, that I would love to see.'

'Look, Jeff, if you want to come, fine, but I am not up for anything heavy, or gross.'

'I only asked. All right, if you fancy it. Shall I fuck your tits, or do you want a suck, or what? You tell me what you want.'

'I don't . . .' I sighed. 'Oh, never mind. Get it out.'

I made myself as comfortable as I could against a tree and he pulled up his belly to get his cock free, his balls too. He was bigger than Dough Boy, and uglier, but I took my boobs in my hands, playing with them as he began to wank. My nipples were stiff and sensitive in the cool air, and it was impossible not to think dirty thoughts as he grew slowly erect over my body. I'd just wanked a man off, and I was holding my breasts out for another to do the same. It was a submissive thing to do, no question, to give them their pleasure simply because they wanted me. My feelings didn't matter; I was just there to be wanked over, a dirty little slut fit only for their amusement.

Some of the girls should have been there, to put me under orders, maybe to beat me for my behaviour, maybe just to laugh at me as I degraded myself, and then make me lick them, one by one. My body would be common property, to be used for the pleasure of men, of women, anyone, my boobs especially, but not only my boobs. They'd make me suck, lick, fuck, hold my bottom cheeks open for the little hole between to be violated. I'd end up naked, my body scratched and bruised and dirty, plastered with pussy juice and spunk . . .

I got down, squatting in the mud and leaves at Fat Jeff's feet, to fold his cock between my breasts. He began to fuck them, his bloated helmet popping up and down between, then in my mouth as the last thread of my resistance snapped. He groaned as I began to suck him, and took hold of my hair. My hands went down, to the plump divide of my pussy, my lips hot and sensitive even through the layers of denim, rubber and cotton. I began to rub, masturbating as I sucked, a dirty, wanton little slut, my boobs out for fucking, my jaw straining wide to take a man's penis. I wanted to pleasure him, for him to use me, to feed me his big ugly cock and the fat, wrinkled sack of his scrotum too, especially that.

Jeff moaned and filled my mouth with thick, salty come, pushing his cock in right to the back at the last instant, to leave me coughing and blowing spunk bubbles out of my nose. It barely slowed me down. For some reason the idea of sucking his balls had fixed itself in my mind, and the instant I'd got my breath back I had taken them in my mouth. He gasped as I began to roll them over my tongue, and took hold of his cock, to milk the last of his spunk into my hair.

The rest was down my throat, trickling into my belly, hanging from my nose or splattered over my naked boobs. I was soiled with two men's spunk, a thought I held as I started to come, imagining myself forced to service not two, but hundreds, until I was drowning in it. I'd have slimy white mess coming from every orifice. My belly would be bloated with it, my mouth full, my hair caked and my eyes closed. It would be running from my well-fucked pussy and oozing from my buggered bottom hole, and with every single one of their girlfriends laughing at me for what I'd become, a receptacle for their boyfriends' excess spunk . . .

I came, long and tight, still mouthing on Jeff's balls, with my fingers rubbing hard against my crotch to get enough friction to my clitty. There wasn't much, but enough, and it really drew it out, with the same filthy detail of my fantasy running over and over in my head. Fluid was squirting into my panties with every contraction, wetting me, but I didn't care how much mess it made, I just wanted the pleasure to go on for ever. Only at an unexpected sound nearby did my pleasure break, to be replaced with shame and the old familiar sense of betrayal. I let Jeff's balls free and stood quickly, my hands fumbling for my jumper, because I was sure somebody was going to catch us.

They already had. There was a man standing there, watching, not ten feet away, his erect cock in his hand.

He spoke as he stepped forwards. 'Between the titties for me, love.'

'No!' I protested. 'I am not . . .'
'Why not?' he asked, looking hurt.
'Just no! No! No! No! No! No!'

The day had not gone the way I'd planned it. It had started well enough, but I'd ended up tossing off Dough Boy the pizza delivery man in the bushes, followed by Fat Jeff. If I'd refused the complete stranger who had expected just to join in without so much as introducing himself, then I knew it was only because I'd just come.

I felt thoroughly ashamed of myself, not so much because I'd done it, as because I'd wanted to do it. Not only that, but, had it been less cold, less uncomfortable, less fraught, I knew full well that I'd have been up for more, men and women too, regardless of how often I'd come. I hadn't even managed to get rid of Dough Boy, or not completely anyway.

Jeff was not long on tact, ordering a family-sized Mexicana with extra chillies and garlic bread the moment we got back. Inevitably, Dough Boy himself brought it up, simpering and making suggestive movements of his hands as Jeff paid him. I ate a slice anyway, because it was good and, as Jeff said, I could at least be sure it wouldn't be contaminated.

I had nothing to do, and I didn't really want to go out for the evening with Jeff. He'd tried to help, in his own way, and, if he'd made a right pig's ear of it, he obviously didn't see it that way. From his point of view we'd had a good day. He'd enjoyed the encounter with Dough Boy, who was no longer a threat, and there was no reason we shouldn't carry on. For me, I'd had quite enough cocks for one day, or for one lifetime, and even the pizza hadn't entirely taken the flavour of man out of my mouth. So I declined his suggestion that we go dogging and tried to explain to him that I was trying to get my life straight and express myself as a submissive lesbian. He didn't understand at all, arguing that as I so obviously enjoyed showing myself off and playing with cocks I should do so. As I'd frigged myself off while sucking him I could hardly deny it, but I tried to explain that the pleasure had come from having my control taken away from me.

He just laughed, pointing out that I could have stopped it at any time, and I was still trying to explain when the doorbell went. I wasn't expecting anyone, but went to the window hoping it would be Sophie, who would have been just the right person to defuse what was threatening to become an awkward situation. It wasn't, it was Naomi – exactly the wrong person – looking up at me from below my window with an expression of confident cruelty. She snapped her fingers.

'Keys, Dumplings, now. Payback time.'

I hesitated. Being caught with Jeff in my flat was bad, but she wasn't going to do me in front of him. I could refuse to let her in, but it would be worse when she caught up with me – and she would. Yet I knew her, and she lacked AJ's calculated sadism. Whatever she did to me it would be in private, or at worst in front of other kinky women, for her pleasure, and so ultimately for mine. A delay meant it would be stronger; to let her up with Jeff in my flat meant yet another blow to my credibility as a lifestyler.

'Make me!' I called down, and her expression changed to surprise, and affront.

'Who is it?' Jeff asked from behind me.

'Sh!' I hissed, turning too fast and banging my head on the window. 'Ow! Shit!'

'Who's in there?' Naomi demanded.

'Nobody . . . just a friend . . . not one you know,' I answered quickly. 'Look, Naomi, another time, yeah?'

She was staring at me, her mouth wide, amazed that I had the nerve to refuse her. I was going to be put on the cross in Whispers, hung upside down in chains in AJ's garage, taken to The Pumps and put in the pit, whipped and kicked and beaten . . .

Inspiration hit me.

'OK, it's Mel . . . Melody Rathwell,' I called down.

'Oh,' Naomi answered, biting her lip as she stepped back towards her car. 'I'll be back, Jade, soon. Say hi to Mel, yeah?'

I was laughing as I closed the window. Unlike AJ, she already knew what it felt like to take a trip over Melody's knee, and she couldn't be sure it wouldn't happen again. She would tell AJ too, which would add substance to the story of Mel having decided to take me as hers.

'Naomi,' I explained to Jeff as I sat down again, 'she wants to get even with me for what we did to her at Bolero's.'

'What, when you pissed all over her? Nice! Why didn't you let her up? I love a good lessie show.'

'She wouldn't have done it in front of you, Jeff, and . . . well, it was awkward.'

'So you pretended I was Mel Rathwell?'

'Yes. Sorry, it's nothing personal, but if she found out there was a man in my flat . . .'

'Yeah, I know. I still don't get it. You coming out then, or what?'

'Um . . . no . . . yes . . . maybe. Let me give Sophie a ring.'

I went back to the window, in time to see Naomi's old blue BMW pull away from the lights and make a right turn down Green Lanes. She was gone, but she was likely to be back, maybe with AJ and others. I was not going to be there, and definitely not with Jeff.

Sophie was in, bored and keen to see us. She also wanted to go dogging, but I managed to dissuade her without Jeff realising what I was talking about. We agreed to meet in Highgate instead, a good place for a pub crawl and not somewhere we were likely to run into Naomi or AJ. It was the best choice, a few pubs in good company, and, if Jeff and Sophie wanted to get down to anything, that was up to them.

I was feeling sticky in my knickers, so changed and abandoned the rubber pants and the chain, sure I wouldn't need either, not in Jeff's company. He wanted to drink, so we took a cab, meeting Sophie as agreed. We told her about Dough Boy, which she thought was hilarious, and that set the tone for the evening. It was hard to feel bad about something she just found funny, and in no time we were joking about male desperation for sex.

Jeff held his peace, concentrating on sampling each of the selection of real ales on offer, and ignoring our teasing remarks. We drank bottled cider, then breezers, quickly getting drunk, and by the time the bell rang for last orders my head was spinning and my bladder was beginning to twinge dangerously every time Sophie made me laugh. Jeff headed for the bar and I headed for the loo, leaving Sophie at the table to mind our coats.

The pub was packed, and it was a real fight to get to the Ladies. There was a queue too, inevitably, and I joined it, already biting my lip and holding my tummy against the growing strain. Four women were ahead of me, and that was just in the corridor, but I hung on, and had just reached the door when a voice spoke from behind me.

'I see Melody's put on a bit of weight, Dumplings,

and had a sex change. I don't think the beard suits her at all, do you?'

I spun round, but I'd already recognised the accent – Naomi.

The shock nearly made me wet myself on the spot, and my first thought was that she was going to tickle me. I cringed away. I was having enough trouble holding my bladder as it was, and it would have happened on the spot, right into my panties, and soaking into the red low-rise slacks I'd put on in place of my jeans. Everyone would see the wet patch spreading up my pussy and over my bum, down my legs, the pee dribbling into my boots . . .

She just stood there looking smug. It wasn't going to happen, but that was only so much consolation.

'How?' I began, but it was obvious.

She'd gone around the block and waited, expecting Mel to leave so that she could get to me. There had been no Mel, only Fat Jeff Bellbird.

'Don't tell AJ, Naomi, please?' I begged as her mouth curved up into a self-satisfied little smile.

'Of course not,' she answered, 'just so long as you're a good girl.'

'I will be, I promise,' I sighed.

She took my hand, leading me towards the door at the end of the passage. I had to speak. After all, if she didn't let me pee it was likely to happen anyway, whether she tickled me or not.

'Could . . . could I use the loo first?' I asked.

'Do it on the Heath,' she answered as she drew me through the door.

'Is that where we're going?' I asked. 'What are you going to do to me?'

'I'm not sure.'

'Well, could I get my coat, please? It's cold!'

'What, and have you take shelter behind Fat Jeff? Do you think I'm stupid?'

'No, but –'

'But nothing. We're going on the Heath.'

'OK, but can we hurry, please? I need to go!'

'Not my problem. So, what were you up to with Fat Jeff?'

'Nothing!'

'Sure, at the least you and Sophie were going to get down to it for him. I know Sophie, and I know you.'

'No! I swear! We were going to meet up for a drink, that's all, and he came round to me first.'

'Yeah, sure. Why so guilty then? Why pretend it was Melody? You'd probably already had his cock in your mouth, you dirty little bitch.'

'No! I don't suck cock . . . not any more.'

'No? Maybe I should make you, then. Maybe we can find some gay guys out cruising? I dare say some of the older ones and uglier ones would put up with having a bitch instead of another guy.'

'No, please, Naomi! Don't make me do that!'

'No? OK, you get a choice. You ask ten guys if they fancy a blow job. If all ten refuse, you get away with it. That, or you lick my cunt, after a punishment.'

'I'll lick you, of course I'll lick you, you know that! Spank me too . . . or whip me, you can do it hard if you like.'

'I can do what I fucking please, but I'm not sure I will. Maybe you're too much of a pain slut to make it a real punishment?'

'No . . .'

'That's why I ought to make you suck some men, but if you're willing to suck Fat Jeff –'

'I didn't! Please, Naomi, use me any way you like, but –'

'Shut up!'

'Yes, Naomi.'

'You pissed on me, you little bitch, you and your friends. You have a major lesson to learn, believe me.'

'I know. I deserve it, whatever you want to do to me, but no men, please.'

Her hand lashed out, catching me hard across my face.

'Shut it, slut! You do as I tell you, and, if that means sucking cock, you suck cock. Not that any self-respecting gay guy is going to let a fat little tart like you put her mouth around his prick. Maybe they'd let you ream them out, eh?'

'No, Naomi, please! That's not funny!'

'Sounds funny to me, even funnier than it will be watching you piss yourself . . .'

'No, not that either!'

'Demanding little bitch, aren't you? You get what you're given, and it's going to happen. AJ's going to get you, but only when it suits her. She reckons Oxford Street might be funny, just before Christmas, or maybe in a store. I just hope I get to see it!'

'But . . . but you're not going to do it, not now?'

'Nah, she's made everyone promise they'll leave you to her.'

She went quiet as the pavement narrowed to force us to walk single file, with a high redbrick wall to one side and the road on the other. Only when there was enough space to walk two abreast did she speak again.

'You don't want AJ to know about this evening, do you?'

'No!'

'Fair enough. I won't tell, and you won't either, will you?'

'No, of course not!'

She laughed, and took my hand, to pull me to a stop and press me to the wall. I realised she was going to kiss me, and let my mouth open to hers as her arms came around me. Our tongues met, only for her to pull away, still holding me.

'Sorry, Dumplings, tickle time!'

I squealed in protest, even as her fingers dug in under my armpits, but the next instant I was in helpless hysterics and my overfull bladder was twitching. I couldn't hold it. My toes were wriggling frantically, my bum cheeks and belly muscles squeezing, but to no avail. Pee was leaking from my hole, and then gushing, filling my panties, my slacks, and bubbling from the crease of my pussy to patter on the ground at my feet. Even as I went into my stupid little tickle dance, with my arms batting at her body in futile protest and my feet kicking up and down, I could feel the wet patch spreading out over my bum and up around my belly, warm and squashy and sticky . . .

She stopped and stood away, laughing at me and pointing as I sank down into my Vincent's Curtsey by instinct. It was too late: most of my piss was already in my panties and slacks, or running down the hill in a golden dribble, glittering in the headlights of the passing cars, every occupant of which was going to see what I'd done. I ran, but the instant I got out of position the pee came again, spurting out to run down my legs and into my boots. Again I stopped, and again got into Vincent's Curtsey, sobbing my heart out with the tears streaming down my face.

It was hopeless. I'd done it and everyone was going to see anyway. After a moment I stood and walked on, praying for a turning so that I could duck out of sight, with the damp patch spreading slowly across the seat of my slacks and over my tummy. Naomi caught up, and took me firmly by the hand, leading me down the hill. I didn't even try and resist, following her and wiping at my eyes, acutely aware of my wet bottom behind, visible to every single car as they came down the hill, one after the other, each driver, each passenger knowing that I'd pissed in my panties.

There was a turning, just a few yards further along. Naomi led me down it, along an alley lit bright with streetlamps. There were no cars any more, but anyone who passed was going to see, and there was nowhere I could squat down and let out what was left inside me. I had to plod on, the pee squelching in my boots, and soon sticking to my skin. The moment we reached a bit of shade I squatted, pushing my slacks and panties down to empty myself into the gutter.

Naomi watched with an expression of cruel satisfaction and lust. I knew she was going to have me, and it didn't surprise me at all when, instead of turning back, she led me further down the alley and through an old gate, onto the Heath. It was dark, rough underfoot, and I was shaking with emotion. I was soaking, and I smelled of pee, and now she was going to make me lick her, maybe make me take some hard-up bisexual businessman in my mouth as I squatted in my wet clothes, sucking until he'd added a mouthful of spunk to my woes.

When the first man passed I would have wet myself if I hadn't already done it. I didn't even see him until he brushed past Naomi, and then he was only a darker shape among the shadows, and a smell, aftershave and fresh spunk. He'd come, but there would be others, like Dough Boy, like Jeff, like the man I'd refused, lurking in the bushes with their cocks ready to thrust into my mouth, between my boobs, up my pussy, in my bumhole . . .

'Here,' Naomi said quietly, and she was pulling me through a gap in a hedge, up a slope and out onto a meadow, cold and dull silver in the light of a half-moon.

I knew better than to speak. It would just get me into trouble. She led me into the middle of the meadow, well off the track, to where a low copse hid us from view, and stopped, listening. A bird called somewhere off on the Heath, nothing more, but I was thinking of men in the bushes, cocks in each other's mouths, or alone, waiting their turn.

'Strip!' Naomi hissed.

'It's cold!'

'OK, don't. Lie down, tits out. I'm going to piss on you.'

'I'll strip! I'll strip!'

I began to hurry my clothes off, boots first, and my wet socks, peeling the sticky slacks and panties off my skin and down, tugging my jumper, top and bra off as one. If I'd been wishing I'd worn my rubber pants and the chain before, now the regret was twice as strong as I stood nude and shivering, hugging myself with my skin covered in goose pimples and my nipples like little corks. Naomi had taken her trousers off too, and her thong, leaving her lower body bare in the dim light, but for her boots.

'On the ground,' she ordered as she took off her coat, 'face up, I'm going to do it in your mouth.'

My teeth were chattering as I obeyed, laying myself down in the long, damp grass. She threw a leg across my body immediately, straddling my waist, and pushed out her hips. I could see the shape of her pussy, thrust out, and her belly, a pale bulge beneath the hem of her top, distended with pee.

'Open wide, Dumplings.' She chuckled, and let go.

I shut my eyes just in time, as her pee hit me, between them and in my hair, splashing over my face and chest too. My face had screwed up in disgust, but I was struggling to make myself open my mouth even as she snapped the order out once more.

'Open it, bitch! Wide!'

My mouth was already open, and filling, with hot, sour piss. I knew she'd want me to drink it, and tried, swallowing frantically, only to get her stream up one nostril as my mouth closed. It burned like mad, and sent me into a coughing fit, blowing snot and piss out of my nose as I turned my head aside. She kicked me and I forced myself to turn my face back, mouth open, to take her stream again, and to hold it in my mouth. It overflowed in seconds, running out at the sides, down my neck and into my hair.

She shuffled back a little to soil my boobs, my belly and the mound of my pussy, making sure I got a good covering of piss. I swallowed what was in my mouth and gaped for more, getting it as she moved back up my body. She had me, broken down just the way I need to be, my clothes soiled, my body soiled, stripped and pissed on in the long grass, her slut to be used as she pleased, degraded, ruined . . .

My hands went down between my legs as she gave a long, contented sigh, emptying what was left in her bladder into my mouth as I began to frig, my fingers working in the warm, pissy folds of my sex. I swallowed it down and spread my thighs, offering myself to her in total surrender. She realised what I was doing as I began to moan, and lifted one booted foot, to press it to my belly, cold and muddy, marking me.

'What am I supposed to do with you, Dumplings?' she drawled. 'I piss on you, and you're rubbing your dirty cunt!'

I spread my thighs wider still, hoping she'd keep talking as I came, tell me what she'd done, insult me, anything to keep me in my place.

'Slut!' she spat, and kicked me.

'Please, yes,' I moaned. 'Hurt me, Naomi, kick me again . . . slap my face . . . hurt me . . . beat me up while I frig for you . . . please . . . please . . .'

'Stop it, you fucking little dirty bitch!' she snapped, and kicked again, only at my arm, to knock my hand away from my pussy. 'You're not the one who gets to come, I am!'

I was babbling immediately, my hands on my head, my body arched beneath her. 'Sorry . . . yes, Naomi . . . please . . . I'm sorry . . . do as you like with me . . . make me lick . . . queen me . . . yes, queen me, please . . .'

Her answer was a grunt, but she went down, onto her knees, and lower, to settle her pert little bottom right in my face, her cheeks spread. I caught her scent, rich and feminine, pee and pussy juice, then stronger still as she sat her weight down, pressing the tip of my nose into the slippery dimple of her bumhole.

'No touching yourself,' she ordered. 'Now, lick me.'

I poked my tongue out, lapping up under her bumhole, between her cheeks. She moved up, pussy to mouth and I was licking her properly, in her hole and between her lips, eagerly, keen to make her come as she wanted. I felt her thighs tighten as she squeezed a little more pee out into my mouth, then relax as I swallowed it. She was going to come, right in my face, and then I would be allowed to frig off, lying dirty and used at her feet as I masturbated over what she'd done to me. Only now I had to keep my hands on my head, her obedient little slut, doing as I was told for her pleasure.

She reached down after a moment, to take a firm grip in my hair and pull my face into her sex. My mouth slipped from her clitty and she was rubbing herself on my nose, using my face to masturbate on. I tried to lick, lapping at her hole and in the crease of her bottom, to taste her sweat and the acrid tang between her cheeks. She squatted down a little lower and her bumhole was against my mouth. I stuck my tongue straight in, privileged to lick her clean as my mouth filled with her taste. She gasped as I penetrated her, then spoke, her voice hoarse with pleasure.

'Yes, that's right, clean me up, you little bitch, get your tongue in . . . right in. How does it feel, Dumplings, with your tongue up my arse? Good, I bet, you filthy little –'

She broke off with a grunt and she was coming, wriggling her pussy against my nose as I struggled to finish cleaning her, my tongue pushed deep up her bottom, licking for all I was worth and wishing she would fill my mouth then and there. If she had I swear I'd have kept it in until she'd finished, and frigged off like that, swallowing as I came, and as it was my hands went straight to my pussy as she climbed off my face.

I was frigging immediately, and hoping she'd do something horrid to me, anything. She just watched, silent above me, dark against the orange sky as I brought myself up, one arm under my boobs, my hand cupping sticky, rounded, heavy flesh, my fingers teasing my nipple as I flicked at my clit. Naomi spoke.

'So you're going to come, are you?'

'Yes,' I panted, 'help me, please, do something, anything. Let me lick you again . . .'

'No. I meant to punish you, Dumplings, and I'm going to. Slow down.'

I'd been on the edge, but I obeyed, letting my body relax and starting to stroke my pussy mound and down between my cheeks, feeling the cool skin where my bum cheeks bulged out and the little sensitive star of my anus. Naomi didn't move, but gave a little sigh after a moment, then a grunt. The urge to touch my clitty was close to unbearable, but I held back, unsure if she was teasing me, or . . .

She moved abruptly, swinging one long leg over my body, to squat across me, her bum spread just inches over my boobs. I heard her grunt; I realised what she was going to do, and I was masturbating again, as hard as I could, rubbing frantically on my clitty, and I was there. Fluid squirted from my pee hole even as I felt the first moist touch in my cleavage, and I was screaming, my feet hammering in the long grass, my nails digging into my flesh, my mind focused completely on the hot, heavy mound growing in my cleavage as Naomi casually, contemptuously, dumped on me.

Eight

What had happened on Hampstead Heath was not something I was going to admit to anybody, not even Sophie, and certainly not Jeff. I rang them on Naomi's phone, to say she had taken me for punishment and not to worry. Sophie just giggled and told me to have fun, which was typical, but even she would have been shocked if she'd known how far it had gone. I had trouble accepting it myself, and Naomi was apologetic as soon as she'd come down from her dominant high.

Cleaning up was a nightmare, but we ended up giggling guiltily together as we fled the Heath, and she stuck me in the boot of the BMW to get back to her place, which fortunately wasn't too far. We both went straight into the shower, me with my clothes still on, so that I could strip with the water running down me and wring them out ready for the washing machine. We spent the night together, cuddled close and both feeling too drained for sex, until she woke me in the early hours so that we could masturbate together, hands on each other's pussies as we talked over what we'd done.

We agreed it was our secret, and I for one intended to keep it. For popular consumption, especially AJ, Naomi had simply taken me on the Heath, pissed on me and queened me. That was enough to placate AJ, who hadn't been best pleased about Naomi letting herself get done by us, for all that she did it herself quite often. Naomi had even been spanked for it, in front of quite a few other girls at The Pumps, as she admitted in the morning.

I needed my coat, so she drove me right down to Fat Jeff's place in Lewisham, where they'd ended up. They'd got pretty rude too, as I discovered when I had a chance to speak to Sophie alone. Both of them had been very drunk, and he'd dressed her up in an obscene clown costume that left her tits and bum bare, and buggered her. Listening to her giggling as she described how he'd used margarine to lubricate her bottom hole made me feel that maybe I wasn't quite such a dirty girl after all, but I didn't tell.

We were all worn out, and I went back with Naomi, via a supermarket so that she could get some petrol and I could buy her a box of chocolates for the trouble she had taken over me. After all, if she'd really wanted to punish me she could have left me on the Heath. She was also very frank about the situation with AJ, advising me to accept my punishment for what it was, a gesture of dominance from the woman I had accepted as having the right to do it.

I didn't say anything, but I was not willing to accept what she was saying. AJ could do as she liked with me if it was in private, or at somewhere like The Pumps where everybody knew the score, even in Whispers. Doing it in front of straights was another matter, especially making me wet myself by tickling me, which is something I'm especially sensitive about. Penny's plan was better, so I was straight back in my rubber pants and chain on the Monday morning. As a courier, AJ's job overlapped with mine quite frequently, she being called on to deliver things to offices all over London and me likely to be doing just about anything vaguely clerical just about anywhere. I wasn't taking any chances.

It was just as well. I was back at Ealing, the same tedious job as before, only with the Christmas rush starting to pick up there was a lot more to do. We had lorries coming and going all day, and it was just about all I could do to get the right labels on the right parcels, never mind helping to stack them up for loading. I was either in my little room or on a raised part of the loading bay, which allowed the parcels to be wheeled straight into the lorries on trolleys. That was fine, until we had three lorries turn up at once and the third to arrive began to unload outside without waiting for the others to go. The driver was a complete pig about it, and my supervisor ordered me to come down and help shift the parcels, along with everyone else. We were still doing it when a motorbike courier pulled up at the security office, an unusually slim motorbike courier on a black bike – AJ.

She'd seen me, and the instant she took off her helmet I knew she was going to do me, then and there, in front of fifty men and women – men and women I worked with, but who knew nothing about my private life. Her mouth was set in a smile that would really have been quite sweet if it wasn't for her shaved head, piercings and black leather. As it was it just looked sinister, or certainly to me as I backed quickly in the direction of the Ladies, only to be told to get back to work by my supervisor. I hesitated, and it was too late. AJ was blocking my only escape route unless I simply fled down the street. She would catch me easily but it was still tempting, and had I not had my rubber pants on I'd have done it.

As it was I tried to bluff it out, smiling at her in the

vain hope she would be too embarrassed to tickle me in front of them. It was vain, completely. She greeted me cheerfully, gave me a friendly hug, pushed her hands up under my jumper and stuck her fingers deep in at my sides, holding me tight and tickling at the same time. I went straight into my stupid, squirming dance, stamping up and down and giggling, my control lost in a matter of seconds. I wasn't that full, but it still happened, my bladder bursting and hot pee squirting out into my panties, through them, and into the rubber pants. She was still tickling me, and I was still writhing in her grip as they filled, as helpless as ever, but protected from the final disgrace of having it show.

When she finally let go and stood back there was a happy grin on her face, but it quickly changed to disappointment as she saw that I was dry. She had been right about people's reaction though. Most of them were looking at us, but nobody looked shocked or even surprised. After all, they'd only seen a couple of friends messing about together. If I had wet myself, it would have been hideously embarrassing. They'd all have seen, and they'd all have known who to blame for the accident – me.

After a moment AJ shrugged, and leaned close. 'Nothing to drink at lunch today?' she whispered. 'No big deal, there'll be a next time, and I'll make sure.'

She kissed my cheek and walked away, as cool as you please, even allowing her hips to sway slightly, which showed just how cocky she was feeling. I didn't know what to feel. I'd done it, sort of, or at least taken a step in the right direction, but it was still embarrassing. I try to keep my sexual orientation private when at work, but AJ makes no secret, as butch as hell and not caring who knows. She'd cuddled me, tickled me and kissed me, fairly innocent perhaps, but enough to raise a few eyebrows.

Also, I might have fooled AJ, but I'd still wet myself. My rubber panties were bulging with pee, around my pussy and under the tuck of my bum, and around the leg holes too, which I wasn't at all sure would hold, especially if I sat down. I was going to get sore pretty quickly too, so there was nothing for it but to duck into the Ladies and peel off in a cubicle, cleaning myself up as best I could with loo roll. At least I had had the sense to put a fresh pair of panties in my bag, so it wasn't too bad.

Unfortunately, while she might not have figured it out, from what she'd said she was obviously going to try again. I was going to have to keep wearing the rubber pants, but I risked the journey home without them. I got away with it, and collapsed gratefully into a bath as soon as I got home. How many times she would do me before she got bored and gave up I didn't know, but I could obviously help myself by telling her I'd been cured of my tickling problem. No, not telling her, because she would think I was just trying to get out of it, but getting the information to her in such a way that she didn't know it had come from me.

I couldn't use Naomi, despite our new intimacy, because after Saturday night she would know I was lying. She wouldn't pass on the lie for me, as she felt I should submit myself completely to AJ. Penny was much better, as she knew what was going on and would support me, while she wasn't in the lifestyle and had the courage to stand up to AJ if she had to. If she told AJ that I was getting therapy, AJ would believe it, assuming it was with Gabrielle, whom she only knew by reputation.

The problem was getting Penny and AJ into the same place without looking suspicious. Penny never goes to Whispers, or any other dyke hangouts without me, so it was going to look pretty odd if she suddenly turned up at one. It was a problem, but one AJ managed to solve for us. Penny and Sophie were coming down for the weekend, and Sophie arrived first. She'd only been there an hour or so when we heard the gruff roar of a motorbike right outside. It was AJ, but fortunately Sophie was nearer the window than I was and I'd already told her what I needed.

I scrambled into my bedroom, hissing instructions to her even as she threw the window up. Under the bed was the only place I could hide, and I did, biting my lip as I listened to the outer door, my flat door, and Sophie's voice asking AJ if she'd like a coffee.

'Sure,' AJ answered. 'Where's Dumplings?'

'Therapy,' Sophie answered, with just the right hint of accusation in her voice.

'Therapy?' AJ queried. 'What does the silly tart want to go to therapy for?'

'Giggle micturition,' Sophie answered, from the kitchen.

'You what?' AJ demanded.

'Giggle micturition,' Sophie explained. 'Wetting herself when she laughs or, more often, when you tickle her.'

'What's she want to stop that for? She loves it!'

'She –'

'And don't start any bullshit. I've got her with slippery knickers twenty-four seven, just thinking about when it's going to happen to her. She told you I got her at work, yeah? She didn't have anything to piss. Shame.'

'No, she managed to resist. The therapist is working on breaking down the mental link Jade had formed between being tickled and wetting herself. It's working.'

AJ didn't answer immediately, but when she did she sounded pretty hostile. 'Who told her to do this? Not you? Muffet, it was Muffet, wasn't it?'

'No, she –'

'Bullshit, Sophie. Muffet made her, didn't she? You two can't handle Jade being my girl, can you?'

'No. Jade made her own choice, because you are threatening to break her right of consent by taking her outside her personal boundaries.'

'More bullshit. You just don't understand, do you? Jade wants to be mine, completely, but she's scared. She knows just how good it can get, and the only way she's going to get it is to go down to me, one hundred per cent.'

'I know, blanket consent, total fulfilment as a bottom, I've heard it all before, AJ, and, yes, Jade fantasises over complete surrender to you, but you've got to let her set her own boundaries.'

'No. I set the boundaries.' AJ sounded cross. I'd have been grovelling on the floor at her feet, babbling apologies and begging to be punished.

Not Sophie. She went on. 'No, AJ, you do not set the boundaries. Ultimate control must rest with the submissive partner. That is Jade's right.'

'Yes, her right to accept me as her top. That's what she needs, Sophie.'

'Within boundaries agreed between you. Sugar?'

I caught the chink of metal against china. They were on the edge of a real argument, and Sophie was calmly making coffee. It wasn't going quite as I'd hoped. If Sophie didn't watch herself, she was going to get a slapping. I'd decided I would come out and take it in her place, or try to, but when AJ spoke again she sounded a lot more reasonable.

'I've seen you in action, Sophie, and Miss Muffet and all. You're the real thing, both of you. So what's the problem? You're scared you'll lose Jade, aren't you? Don't worry about it. I let my sluts play together when –'

'You don't let them play with men.'

I was biting my lips, terrified Sophie was going to admit that I still sucked the occasional cock. She didn't, and once again AJ held herself in. If it had been me saying the same things I'd have been on the floor at that moment, where I'd have been slapped, kicked and then pissed on. She had more respect for Sophie, or something, because she sounded really quite calm as she went on. 'There have to be rules. Rule one is: no men.'

'What about me? I like men. You'd play with me, wouldn't you? You play with Penny, and she goes with men.'

'Oh yeah, I'd play with you. Can you even begin to think what I'd like to do to you, right now?'

'No. Beat me up maybe? Pee on me? Wash my head down the toilet? Do tell.'

Sophie was going to get it. She was taunting AJ, and no subbie girl gets away with that, ever. AJ must have been as shocked as I was, because it was Sophie who went on.

'You can do it, anything you like, and the more painful and humiliating the better, but no marks on my face or hands, nothing that leaves permanent marks or risks long-term injury. Those are my limits, AJ, and you have to respect them.'

'And what if I just do as I fucking please with you?'

'You won't. Now, how about starting with a nice long spanking across your knee? Start on my jeans, until I'm nice and warm, and, when you take them down, do it really slowly, so I can feel every second of my exposure. The same with my panties, and –'

'Nobody tells me how to do it, bitch!' AJ snapped suddenly. 'Do you want it? Do you really want it?'

Sophie's answer was a muffled squeak, and I realised AJ had her, probably by the face. There was no question that Sophie was asking for it, but she did not know what she was going to get. I couldn't just leave her, but if AJ found I'd been there all the time I was really for it. Slowly and carefully I slid myself out from beneath the bed, walked quietly to the door, opened it with agonising care, and shut it with a bang.

'Jade?' AJ's voice rang out and I caught the smack of wood on flesh and Sophie's squeal, quickly muffled.

'Yes. Hi, AJ,' I answered, pausing as if taking off my coat.

'In here,' she ordered, 'come and watch your little bitch friend eat her lunch.'

I did as I was told. Sophie's head was in the kitchen bin, held tight by the hair, her face well down in the contents. Her skirt was up and her tights down, her panties too, leaving her bottom bare. AJ stood over her, urging her on with a kitchen spoon to feed from the contents of the bin.

'Eat it!' AJ ordered, and laid in another hard smack to Sophie's bum. 'What's this crap I hear about therapy, Dumplings?'

'I . . . er . . . I went to see Gabrielle Salinger . . . about my wetting problem,' I answered, my eyes fixed on Sophie and the red marks on her bottom.

'Don't,' she answered me. 'Are you ready?'

'Ready?'

'To piss, stupid.'

'No . . . I . . . I, er –'

'Then get drinking, now!'

I was nodding immediately, and crossed to the sink, filling Sophie's empty coffee mug with water and draining it quickly.

'More,' AJ demanded, 'keep going until I say otherwise, and watch your friend.'

'Yes, AJ,' I answered, filling the mug once more as Sophie's face was pulled out of the bin.

She was a mess, her whole face plastered in tealeaves and bits of eggshell, with a smear of reddish grease from the kebab I'd failed to finish the night before. There was mess in the fringe of her hair too, tealeaves and a long, curly piece of bacon rind hanging down over one eye. She was gasping, her mouth half-open, but empty.

'Eat it, I said!' AJ snapped and thrust Sophie's face back in the mess, rubbing it in.

The spanking started again, AJ bringing the spoon down hard on Sophie's bum, again, and again, hard and faster, until suddenly Sophie's jaws had begun to work and she was gobbling down rubbish. AJ laughed and paused in the beating to let Sophie swallow a mouthful of the half-eaten kebab, then began again, harder still. Sophie began to kick and wriggle, gasping into the bin as she struggled to eat, then speaking as she forced her head up.

'Ow! Not so hard, AJ, please! We've got to do a spanking party tomorrow!'

AJ's response was to force Sophie's head back down into the bin, right down, squashing the mess against her face and getting more of it in her hair. She didn't stop spanking either, and it got harder, until Sophie was kicking like mad and flailing around with her hands in a pathetic and useless attempt to defend herself. I was shaking, thinking of what I'd get myself and praying AJ didn't find out that I was going to be at the party too. Suddenly AJ pulled Sophie's head back up, revealing her face, filthier than before, her open mouth half-filled with bits of egg white and rotting salad from the kebab.

'We? Who's we?' AJ demanded.

'Sophie and Penny,' I said quickly. 'The party's at the Rathwells'.'

'Muffet coming, is she?' AJ answered as she thrust Sophie's head back in the bin. 'Now?'

'Sometime today,' I admitted.

AJ nodded and went back to beating Sophie, laying in three smacks before pausing once more and pulling her head up a little to leave her mouth and nose just in the rubbish. I couldn't really see, because a paper butter wrapper had stuck over one eye, but her mouth was shut and she wasn't chewing.

'You don't want bruises? Then eat!' AJ ordered and laid in one more heavy smack.

Sophie squealed, but her mouth came open and her tongue poked out. She was trembling hard, and trying to take the least horrible things from the rubbish, but she was eating, filling her mouth with bits of salad and pitta bread. AJ tightened her grip, turned the spoon in her hand and put the handle between Sophie's thighs, easing it up into her pussy. It was left sticking out between Sophie's reddened cheeks.

'More water, Dumplings,' AJ ordered, 'and give some to the pig . . . that's a good name for you, Sophie, isn't it? The Pig.'

I swallowed the water in my mug and filled it again for Sophie. Her eyes met mine as her face was pulled out of the bin for her to drink, hazy with reaction to her beating and being forced to eat rubbish. I gave her a smile, hoping she could cope, and held the mug to her lips. She drank, swallowed and her head was pushed back down. She began to eat, properly, mouthing up bits of egg and kebab, and I knew her resistance had gone. I'd have been the same.

AJ realised and let go of Sophie's hair. Sophie went on eating, the spoon wiggling behind her as she fed on the contents of the bin, her head well in, just like a pig, a pig with its face in a bucket of swill. I poured another cup of water and drank it, wondering if I'd have a chance to get into the bedroom and take my chain and the rubber pants off without AJ noticing. It was not likely, but as the doorbell went I realised I had a chance.

'That'll be Penny,' I said.

'Get the little slut up then,' AJ ordered.

She'd put my keys down on the side, and I took them quickly. I went to the window and, sure enough, Penny was below. I threw the keys down, signalling frantically to indicate an A and a J. She nodded and I pulled myself back in, already scrabbling for the padlock key in my pocket. For what seemed like an age I couldn't find it, then I had it and I was pulling up my top as I nipped quickly into my bedroom, praying AJ would keep herself interested in degrading Sophie. My jumper came up, the key slid into the hole, and I stopped, frantically tugging my jumper back down as I heard AJ's voice.

'Back in the kitchen, Dumplings, now! What are you doing?'

I turned, to find her right behind me, in the doorway, looking puzzled. My face had gone red with blushes, a dead giveaway. She stepped closer.

'Hands on your head.'

I obeyed. My jumper was tugged up, high up, over my boobs. AJ's expression changed from curiosity to annoyance as she saw my chain.

'So what's this?' she demanded, taking the padlock in her fingers.

'I . . . I –' I answered, wondering if I dared tell the story. 'Mel put it on me, Melody Rathwell. Sorry, AJ, but you –'

'She did, did she? And just who the fuck does she think she is?'

'Well . . . I . . . you . . . I mean –'

'It's about time we got this straight, Dumplings. Who do you belong to?'

I hung my head. It was not working out as we'd planned. She might be scared of Mel, face to face, but she wasn't going to admit it, not to me.

'You, AJ,' I said meekly.

'Yeah, me, so take it off, now!'

'I . . . I can't, it's padlocked on,' I answered, and immediately wished I hadn't.

'I can see that. Use the key, you must have it.'

'No! I mean . . . I can't! I'm . . . I'm not allowed . . . Mel says –'

'I don't give a fuck what Mel says. Open it!'

I nodded miserably, praying I would still have the chance to take off my rubber pants. She watched, her hands on her hips as I opened the padlock, just as the door banged behind Penny as she let herself in.

'In the kitchen, Muffet,' AJ ordered. 'Get it off, Dumplings.'

Reluctantly, I pulled the chain free. Penny appeared behind her.

'What's Sophie doing?'

'What I told her to,' AJ answered. 'D'you want some?'

Penny shook her head. She'd seen what I was doing.

'Didn't Melody order you to keep that on?' she asked.

'And I'm ordering her to take it off,' AJ answered her. 'No shit from you, Muffet, or you'll end up sharing with your little friend, The Pig. Now go and sit quietly out of the way like a good girl while I sort my bitch. Strip, Dumplings, you are on for one fuck of a spanking!'

'But, AJ –'

'Are you all right, Jade?' Penny asked.

I nodded. It was too late; the whole thing had failed miserably, and all I could do was take my medicine. I was close to tears as I hung my head, surrendering myself to AJ and fully aware that it would have been the sensible thing to do in the first place. Penny hesitated, then left. AJ stepped forwards, took hold of my ear and pulled hard, making me squeal in pain as I stumbled across the room. She sat down on the bed, pulling me straight down across her lap. I hung my head in utter defeat, waiting for the spanking to start, knowing it was going to be hard, and shameful, and knowing I deserved every smack.

'Right, you little brat,' she hissed, her hand burrowing under my tummy, 'you are going to get it, and good.'

My jeans button popped; her thumbs went into my waistband and they were coming down, my eyes squeezed tight in humiliation as what was underneath came on show, not the simple cotton of panties, but pink, frilly rubber stretched taught over my bottom, which felt impossibly big.

'What the fuck are these?' AJ demanded, stopping with my jeans held down at the level of my thighs.

'Incontinence pants,' I admitted miserably.

'What, so this is part of your therapy, is it? I know that Gabrielle's weird, but . . . Hang on, you didn't have these on at work the other day, did you? Did you? Because if –'

'No!' I wailed. 'She fitted me this morning! I swear!'

'Oh she did, did she? And I suppose Melody Rathwell just happened to be there as well, did she?'

'No . . . I mean . . . Mel told me I should –'

'Wrong answer, Dumplings. Mel didn't tell you to put a chain on, did she? Since when did she give a fuck who plays with you? She's got Annabelle, hasn't she?'

'She . . . she . . . she –'

'Bullshit, Dumplings. Now shut up before you make it any worse.'

She leaned out, reaching for something, and I realised she had taken the long-handled hairbrush from my bedside table. I heard a whimper of fear escape my throat, even as the hem of my incontinence pants were taken firmly in her fingers and drawn down, over my bottom, exposing my panty seat and quite a lot of flesh. She adjusted them, well down, inverted around my thighs. My panties followed, peeled off my bum and down, to leave me bare and ready, my whole body trembling. She called out as she patted the hairbrush on my skin.

'I've work to do, Pig, so just keep eating, and you, Miss Muffet, you stay out of this if you know what's good for you.'

'Jade?' Penny asked, and I realised she was standing in the doorway.

I looked around, my vision hazy with the first of my tears. She was looking at me, scared but determined. I shook my head.

'No, Penny. I deserve this.'

'If you're sure,' Penny answered.

'Some sense at last!' AJ joked. 'Shame it's too late.'

As she spoke she had lifted the hairbrush. It came down, landing across my bottom with a sharp crack. I screamed out at the sudden pain, but clenched my teeth as the second one landed, determined to take it well, to accept it and not make a fuss. I was talking though, babbling my apologies to AJ as she beat me, hard and firm, putting me in my place, as she had every right to do, my voice breaking each time the hairbrush whacked down on my bottom.

My eyes were full of tears, my head full of remorse for my stupid, stupid behaviour. I knew I should never have done it, that she was absolutely right to spank me, to punish me, to bring me to her feet, grovelling and apologetic. It was right, and it was exactly what I needed, but I couldn't keep still, the pain too great, for all I knew I should take my punishment. When I nearly fell off her lap, she took my arm, twisting it up into the small of my back, and the spanking began again, harder than ever.

Even with the pain stabbing into my twisted arm I felt a great surge of gratitude go through me. She was holding me, keeping me in place for the beating I so richly deserved, as I wanted to be held afterwards, warm in her forgiveness with my bottom a blazing ball of pain behind me. I didn't deserve it, but she would, I knew, because she wanted me, for all my faults. Not that I deserved it. I deserved to be left on the floor and pissed on, kicked out in the street and made to walk with my fat, bruised bottom wobbling naked behind me, tied hand and foot and slung out with the rubbish.

I just came. She'd been laying in really hard, right on my sweet spot, the fattest part of my bum, right over my pussy. Every smack had been sending a jolt right through me, taking me through pain to pleasure, and ecstasy as I squirmed on her lap, writhing and kicking and bucking in orgasm as I imagined myself stuck head first in a huge litter bin, my bare bottom and legs sticking up in the air.

Fluid squirted from my pussy, all over her leg and the bed. I heard her grunt in disgust and the spanking stopped abruptly, but I was still coming, and I couldn't stop myself. I cocked one thigh out, spreading my sex on her leg, to bring myself to a final, glorious peak as I rubbed on the slimy leather that covered the smooth muscle beneath.

I just made it before she pushed me off, and then I was on the ground, sprawled at her feet, and grovelling as I found my balance. Her hand lashed out, catching me across my face, a hard, open-handed slap, and another, knocking me away even as I tried to snuggle in to her. She spat in my face as I came close again, catching me in the eye, and her hand had locked in my hair. I was pulled in, but not to her crotch, onto the slimy mess I'd made on her leg.

'Lick your filth up, you dirty little bitch!' she sneered and pulled my face in hard.

My tongue went straight into it, lapping up my own pee-hole juice. I was where I belonged, at her feet, and I held on to her leg as I licked. Only when I had lapped it all up and swallowed did I let go, pulling my bra up to polish the wet patch away from the leather of her trousers. She watched me, and gave a thoughtful nod as I sat back on my heels, kneeling, my head hung down.

I could feel the strain in my bladder from all the water I'd drunk, and I was sure she'd tickle me, to make me piss in my panties and jeans and all over the bedroom floor. If she did, I was going to be masturbating again just as soon as I'd got control of my body. She didn't, but stood to undo her trousers and push them low, exposing the barbed-wire tattoo and her pussy, the neat pinks folds and her rings glistening with moisture.

She had no panties, and as she sat back down on the bed she pushed her trousers to her ankles. Again she took hold of my hair; I was pulled in and I began to lick. As I took my boobs out for her she made herself comfortable, and settled back as my tongue worked on her pussy, licking her mound and her lips, then between, on the taut bud of her clit. She kept her grip in my hair, watching and stroking one breast through her top. I did my best, trying to be dutiful despite the pain of my welted bottom and the rising sense of urgency in my bladder.

I've have wet myself if she'd told me to, or anything else. She had really put me in my place, delivering a firm punishment spanking to remind me exactly who I was, and what I was: her girl, to be used as she pleased. Now I was licking her, and that meant she had forgiven me, and as she came in my face with her hand twisted painfully hard in my hair I felt only gratitude and love.

The moment she had come down from her orgasm she stood up, pulling her trousers up and immediately taking me by the hair once more. I followed, crawling awkwardly along behind her, showing everything, my boobs hanging heavy beneath me, my spanked bottom bare behind. I knew I was bruised, badly, and sure enough, as I briefly caught sight of myself in the mirror, I realised she'd given me enough to make it painful to sit for maybe a week.

AJ took me into the kitchen, where the others were. Sophie still had her knickers down, and looked extremely sorry for herself with her pretty blonde hair full of bits of rubbish and her face plastered, especially her lips. She wasn't in the bin any more though, but sitting on the floor, splay legged with a carrot up her pussy as she toyed with her boobs. Penny was watching, still fully dressed but bright-eyed with arousal. Neither had heard us coming, and they looked around in surprise. AJ gave an amused grunt as she saw the state Sophie was in.

'Had plenty, Pig?' she asked, peering into the bin Sophie had been feeding from.

'Yes . . . my tummy . . . so full . . .' Sophie answered, the words coming out as a sigh.

She had her top up, and her belly showed, a round, hard ball, as if she was a few months pregnant. AJ chuckled, let go of me, picked up the bin and upended it over Sophie's head, pouring what remained of nearly a week's worth of kitchen waste onto her. Sophie just moaned, still cupping her boobs as some slimy black substance ran slowly down over her face and began to drip onto one nipple.

'Help her, Dumplings,' AJ ordered. 'Lick her cunt.'

I crawled quickly over, to bury my face in Sophie's pussy. She slid forwards, and I realised she'd penetrated her bumhole too, her little pink ring gaping around the head of a second carrot. I began to lick, leaving her free to play with her boobs and soil herself with the contents of the bin. It was all over her: tealeaves and bits of egg and bacon rind, pizza crusts and takeaway cartons, potato peelings and cabbage leaves. Some of it was on top of her head, some on her body, some around her on the floor.

She had fat I'd scraped from the grill in her hair and on her belly too, which she snatched up and plastered over her boobs, rubbing it into her nipples. The decaying end of a cucumber had landed by her leg and she stuck it in her mouth, sucking on it as if it was a cock, her eyes closed in bliss. Her thighs came up for me and I took hold of the carrots and began to fuck her, bum and pussy, easing them in and out of her slimy holes. I moved down to lick between her pussy and bottom, but she took my hair in her greasy fingers, putting me firmly on her clitty, and went back to massaging muck into her boobs. She was about to come, and I started to lick firm and fast. Immediately she spat the cucumber out and began to squeal. She was there, coming in my face. Something squashy fell on my head, but I didn't stop, licking at her sex as she clutched at herself, her thighs tight around my head, her pussy and bumhole pulsing on the carrots inside as I fucked her.

All the time she was squealing, making AJ laugh and call her a pig again, which took her to one final peak. When she came down, it was with a long, pleased sigh, but it didn't stop me licking. I wanted her, and I wanted to come again, with Sophie, tangled together as we licked each other and AJ looked down on us, cool and aloof as we grovelled in rubbish at her feet.

I climbed on Sophie and her arms came open to take me in. Our mouths met, and opened together, snogging as I rubbed my boobs on hers, feeling the slippery muck on her skin and revelling in it. She took my bottom, hauling my cheeks wide and her fingers found my bumhole, tickling . . .

It was too much. I wanted to do it anyway, and as my straining bladder twitched I just let go. Sophie gasped in surprise as hot pee squirted out over her belly, her rucked-up skirt and onto her pussy. Her arms closed tighter, holding me as I relieved myself over her body, the tip of her finger now up my bottom hole. She was whimpering into my mouth all the while, her body shaking, and mine too. I could hear the hiss of my pee, and feel the warmth and wetness of it on my knees as the pool spread out beneath us.

I heard AJ laugh, but I didn't realise why until I felt Penny's hands touch my waist. She'd given in, too turned on to hold back, AJ or no AJ. The last of my pee squirted up in a little fountain as I rolled off Sophie to take Penny in. She was nude, her clothes discarded on the worktop, her body dry and clean, but not for long. We moved to let her between us, on all fours, and even as I planted a firm smack on her bottom Sophie had gathered up a handful of mess from the floor and pushed it into her face.

She fought back, giggling as we collapsed in a tangle of limbs, wrestling together in the slippery mess on the floor. Penny got the worst of it, because she was between us and started off clean, with handfuls of muck plastered in her face and over her bottom in seconds. She'd gone straight in the pee pool too, and was slipping on the floor as she struggled to get at us in turn, so she'd have really got it if Sophie hadn't turned traitor and unexpectedly stuck the cucumber end she'd been sucking up my pussy hole.

After that it was every girl for herself, clutching and slapping at each others' bodies, each doing her best to get the others as filthy as possible and not really caring what she got herself. I'm heaviest, and I was soon starting to get the best of it, mounted on Penny's back as I rubbed her face in the mess. Sophie had wriggled free, but came straight back in, snatching up a handful of muck and slapping it between Penny's bum cheeks. Penny could do nothing, only wriggle and kick as Sophie began to finger her, then to stuff her, feeding in bits of bacon rind and anything else that would go.

As she started to fill, Penny's struggles began to die down. Sophie went right on, pushing more of the bacon rind into Penny's hole until it was a gaping pink ring, then using a finger to stuff it up properly. Penny's bottom came up, her thighs opened and she had given in completely. Sophie laughed and slipped a hand under Penny's sex, her thumb sliding into the sopping, greasy pussy hole, her fingers slipping in among wet pink flesh, frigging her. I'd twisted around and began to spank, slapping at Penny's bare bum and telling her what a slut she was, to want to be brought off as she was stuffed with kitchen waste. She began to beg for more, and she got it, Sophie forcing a whole mouldering salad potato up into the already packed cavity as Penny started to come.

She really thrashed, her bum cheeks clenching and her thigh muscles twitching as she was brought off. Her hole was still open enough to show the end of the potato inside, and it was pulsing, the fleshy pink ring contracting and expanding on the potato, her bum-hole too as if she was trying to blow kisses at the wrong end. It made Sophie laugh, and me, which must have given Penny a huge hit of the humiliation she adores, as her whole body went tense for a long moment before she finally went limp.

I was up for more, my own orgasm, or Sophie's, and leaned forwards to kiss her. She took me in her arms, only to suddenly throw me sideways, off Penny and onto the floor, my boobs squashing in the muck, my hands slithering on the floor as I struggled to right myself, but too late. She got on top of me, and as Penny joined in I knew I was going to get it whether I liked it or not.

They dealt with me thoroughly. I got my own face pushed into the floor, Sophie holding me by the hair and rubbing my lips and nose into the mixture of piss and rubbish. I got my head sat on, Penny mounting me as I was rolled over, to stick her dirty bottom right in my face and rub. I got spanked, Penny still on my face as Sophie rolled me up and laid into my bottom, each slap spraying us with droplets from my slimy skin.

Sophie was slapping me right on my sweet spot, and for all my bruising I knew I would come. I took hold of Penny, licking her pussy and her bumhole as Sophie slapped at my cheeks and thighs. She was getting my sex lips too, and I could feel myself coming, the stinging pain turning to ecstasy as the orgasm built in my head, only to break as Penny lifted, depriving me of having her lovely bottom in my face.

I gave a grunt of protest, but it came out as shock as she reached back to spread her cheeks and I realised what she was going to do. Her hole began to open, the potato showing inside, and my mouth came wide of its own accord, eager to be filled. I heard her tell Sophie she was going to do it in my mouth and the slaps got harder, right on my pussy lips and blending with their giggles. Penny's pussy hole distended; the potato emerged, and fell, right into my open mouth, and more, a ball of greasy bacon rind, and yet more.

My orgasm hit me, engulfing my entire body, my feet hammering on the floor, my nails scratching at Penny's thighs, my bum and pussy on fire, fluid squirting from my pee hole. My mouth was as wide as it would go to make absolutely certain I got my filling. I did, with a vengeance, all of it, until my mouth was piled high, when she let go of her bladder. Her pee burst out, all over my boobs and belly, down my neck, then full in my face as she moved back to add a final, exquisite touch to my utter degradation.

I was done, my muscles going limp the instant Sophie stopped slapping at my pussy lips. Penny finished off in my face, and I let it happen, too far gone to care. They'd really gone to town on me, and with AJ watching, and, if Penny had come, Sophie deserved more, but I needed the bathroom, badly. I ran for it, a sight which had AJ clutching her sides with laughter, but she was undoing her trousers as I left.

By the time I got back they had Sophie close to orgasm, with Penny holding her head in the rubbish bin and frigging her. AJ stood over them, the kitchen spoon in her hand, beating Sophie even as she held her pussy spread, ready to pee. My immediate reaction was jealousy, wishing they'd put my head in the bin, as it was something I'd come over so often. I'd got mine though, hard, and I bit the bad emotion down, watching as AJ let go, urinating over Sophie's head and back, on Penny too. Sophie started to come, her thighs twitching and her bumhole pulsing, pee dripping from her hair and her nipples too, her bum cheeks jumping to the hard spoon smacks. The carrots were no longer up her pussy and bum, but it was only when she was finally allowed to take her head out of the bin and I saw the orange mess around her lips that I realised AJ had made her eat them.

Whatever they'd done, she had enjoyed it. The moment she had recovered she jumped to her feet and kissed AJ, then ran for the bathroom. Penny followed her, casting a look at AJ as they passed, half wary, half devoted. I stayed put, wondering if AJ would want to come again, and eager for the opportunity to show how obedient I could be, but she simply pulled up her trousers and settled against the worktop. As the hiss of my shower began to mask any conversation between us, she spoke.

'It was Penny who set up that little business with the chain, wasn't it?'

My face must have given me away, because she nodded immediately.

'Do you think I should punish her?' she asked. 'And what should I do, when she's as bad as you?'

I hesitated. The answer was that AJ should do as she pleased, but to give it was to betray Penny, whether it happened or not. I'd been done, by her and in front of her, my bottom spanked, covered in rubbish from my kitchen bin, utterly humiliated. Anything else she wanted and I'd have done it, but not that.

'P–perhaps if you found something . . . something really strong but not outside her limits?' I suggested in a feeble whisper, never taking my eyes from the floor.

AJ sighed. 'For fuck's sake, Jade, what am I going to do with you?'

'Sorry, AJ,' I managed.

Again she sighed. 'What does it take to break you, Jade?'

'I am broken, for you,' I answered, forcing myself to meet her eyes.

'No you're not, you just think you are,' she said. 'I want your submission, Jade, and I'm going to get it. That's why I'm going to make you wet yourself in public, because it's just about the only thing that won't leave you rubbing your dirty little cunt five minutes later.'

Even as I hung my head back to the floor I realised something. Just so long as AJ did not own me completely, she would always want me. I might end up in a litter bin literally, but not figuratively.

Nine

The rest of Saturday was spent cleaning up and resting. It came naturally to the three of us to defer to AJ, and we did all the mopping up, in the nude, made coffee and later dinner. Sophie and I creamed each other's bums, and, while we were both delighted with what we'd done, we both knew it was going to be a problem the next day. Melody had asked us to be pristine, and we were both colourful to say the least, with blotchy bruises all over our cheeks and our thighs too.

AJ didn't care, or she said she didn't, and Sophie didn't make an issue of it, still in a submissive mood and not keen to pick an argument. She didn't even bother to dress, save for putting a pinny on while she helped me cook. AJ lapped it all up, sitting fully dressed while three naked girls served her. She had come over because she was bored and wanted to torture me to pass the time, and so left well pleased with herself after having me go down on her in front of them for a second orgasm.

We were tired and went to bed early, Sophie and I sleeping face down to save our bruises. Even in my dreams I was running around with a smacked bum, and in the morning I had to give up any last hope of arriving at the Rathwells' in a fit condition to take a spanking. The rich reds and purples of the night before had dulled to blue-black and coronas of dirty yellow, along with blood-coloured crescents where the end of the hairbrush had caught me hardest. Sophie wasn't much better.

As the party was at the Rathwells' house, it would be discreet and strictly for wealthy perverts. Most or even all the guests would be men, and they would expect to watch some spankings, and to do it too. Mel had agreed to make a display of me rather than hand me to them, but even that was going to be difficult.

We were also expected to go in school uniform, and that at least was easy. The same outfits we'd worn for the cabaret at Bolero's would do, and, if there were sure to be men who wanted longer skirts, navy knickers and other such 'real' touches, that was just tough. I was glad to be able to wear a pair of loose white cotton panties that spared my bruises.

Penny drove us up to Highgate after we'd had a sandwich each for lunch, and we were admitted to the Rathwells' mansion, a huge place with a Greek portico and an entrance hall bigger than my entire flat. Morris was there, greeting guests on the steps, nearly all of them wealthy old men, but none the less dirty for that. Melody was there too, gorgeous in a red silk dress set off with scarlet flowers in her hair and spike heels in the same vivid tone, but the effect was somewhat spoiled by the clipboard in her hand and the expression of annoyance on her face. She came towards us as we got out of the car.

'Hi, you three,' she greeted us. 'Thanks for coming. Sophie, if you could help Annabelle maid for a while, and you're in the kitchen, Penny, helping Harmony. Jade, we're on first, just a straightforward schoolgirl spanking scene to warm things up. OK?'

'I'm a bit bruised, I'm afraid,' I admitted.

'Bruised?' she queried. 'Let me see.'

I turned, lifted my school skirt and pulled the back of my panties down, showing off the mess AJ had made of my bum.

'Shit!' she swore. 'I did ask you, Jade, you know we need –'

'She didn't get a lot of choice,' Penny broke in. 'It was AJ.'

'AJ?' Mel responded. 'Didn't you tell her? Couldn't she wait?'

'She just did it,' I answered. 'She . . . she punished me for that belt business, and I have given her the right to do it when she likes.'

'Fine,' Melody sighed, 'we'll just have to work around it. I take it you're OK, Penny?'

'Pristine,' she answered.

'Er . . . I'm a bit bruised too,' Sophie admitted.

'How come?' Mel demanded. 'You of all people, Sophie! You should know the score.'

'She used a spoon,' Sophie answered. 'I didn't even know she had it, and I did ask, but she wouldn't stop, or do it gently. She had my face in a bin, and –'

'Who? AJ?'

'AJ.'

'I am going to kill her, I am! Jade, I don't mind, that's fair enough, but not you, Sophie. Who the fuck does she think she is? I'll do you, then Penny. You two, get in the kitchen. Sophie, you're maid. Jade, tell my sister to get a uniform on. Shit!'

I shrugged, an apology on my lips, but she had already turned away, walking towards where Morris was talking to a plump woman in a fur coat who had just got out of a Bentley. She was dripping jewels, and everything about her shouted expensive taste and self-importance, but it didn't bother Melody, who interrupted them to explain things to Morris.

We went inside, Penny disappearing upstairs while Sophie and I made for the kitchen. Melody's sister, Harmony, was there, in an abbreviated cook's outfit complete with hat but cut low at the front and with a short, flared skirt that showed frilly knickers beneath, typical of Morris's taste. She was making prawn vol-au-vents, and didn't take too kindly to the sudden change of role, like her sister demanding a display of our bums before she would accept it.

Melody's slave, Annabelle, was there too, in a maid's uniform with a tray chained to one wrist, onto which she was loading glasses of champagne. Sophie went to help her, leaving me to fill the rest of the vol-au-vents. Playing cook was fine, because the idea of being spanked in front of twenty or more dirty old men was making my stomach crawl, so I was feeling more than a little grateful to AJ for putting me out of commission. Penny was going to get it instead, true, but public humiliation in front of men is right up her street.

Unfortunately I'd only just finished the vol-au-vents when Mel appeared, looking more harassed than ever. She was still carrying the clipboard, and waved me over with it, speaking as I came.

'Come with me, Jade, we've got a new job for you.'

'What?' I asked. 'Not men, because –'

'No men, just being companion to Joannie Lang.'

'Who?'

'Joannie Lang. She was a big porno star in the late sixties and early seventies, mags and films. She worked as a Mistress, and had some crap pop record out too, Morris says. For goodness sake, don't admit you've never heard of her; she has an ego the size of a house.'

I just nodded, because we'd entered the hall and the plump woman I'd seen earlier was standing beneath the huge chandelier. She'd had something done to her face, creating a look I found rather horrible, and which her bright red lipstick and vivid blue eye-shadow only made worse. She still had the fur coat on, but it was open, revealing an electric-blue dress beneath, short and tight over her swelling curves. We were heading right for her, and she could only be Joannie Lang.

'This is Jade,' Melody announced, propelling me forwards.

The woman turned to look at me, her gaze haughty, a touch cruel. She had been beautiful, once, but now she was just plain scary, and I was wondering just what would be expected of me. She spoke, not addressing me, but Melody.

'Ah, yes, that's the one I meant. I do like the little fat ones.'

I have a twenty-inch waist in a corset. Hers had to be nearer forty. I bridled and blushed but held my peace.

'My, but you do blush prettily, my dear,' she went on, turning to me, 'but are you well trained, I wonder?'

'I . . . I suppose so,' I managed, not sure if she meant as a maid or as a slave, and not at all sure how I should respond to her, or how I wanted to.

'Not well,' she sighed, 'now if I had had you when I was younger, Jade, you would have been up on the wall for twenty cuts of the whip, in front of a paying audience of men. How would you like that?'

'I . . . I wouldn't,' I answered, and quickly corrected myself. 'I wouldn't, Mistress, I'd hate it.'

'That's better,' she went on, 'so you do know how you should address a domina. You may go, Melody.'

For one moment I really thought Mel was going to lose it and spank the old bat then and there, but the battle light only flared for an instant before dying. Obviously Morris had some good reason for buttering up Joannie Lang, and I determined to be on best behaviour. A grateful Morris tends to give out fifty-pound notes; an ungrateful Morris tends to have Melody give out whippings.

'May I fetch you a glass of champagne, Mistress?' I offered.

'Do, yes,' she answered, and I was forced to go to the trouble of reaching out and taking one from Annabelle's tray as she passed.

Joannie Lang accepted it and as I gave a curtsey she was absolutely simpering, not at me, but at the others in the hall. It looked as though all I would have to do was pamper my companion's ego for the evening. That was easy. A dozen men were already looking at us with jealous eyes as she took my arm and steered me towards the main party room.

It was set out for spanking cabaret, as I had expected, with a clear area in the middle and a ring of chairs facing inwards. There were tables between the chairs, each laden with goodies, both edible and for spanking girls' bottoms, canapés and canes, so to speak. As Joannie Lang seated herself and pulled me down onto her lap I was counting the chairs. There were 27, which meant very, very sore bottoms for the girls due to be spanked. Just thinking about it made me nervous, for all that I was exempt.

Morris was nowhere to be seen, nor Mel. Annabelle was serving, and the only other faces I recognised were those of the Rathwells' lawyer, Mr Montague, a distinguished-looking man who occasionally spanked Penny, and the flabby Mr Protheroe, who had a nasty habit of washing girls' mouths out with soap during punishment. Not one of the men was under fifty.

They were drinking and chatting, all having a good time and looking expectant, as well they might have done, and there was a buzz of excitement as Melody appeared, leading Penny by the hand. Penny looked a little nervous and a little sulky, but Mel looked very nervous and very sulky, which was odd as she was going to be the one doing the spanking.

She didn't waste time either, going through the briefest of preliminaries and then sitting down on a chair to whip Penny smartly over her knee. Penny's blouse and bra were hauled up to free her tits; her school skirt was lifted, her panties taken down and she was spanked, with a speed and fury that looked more like a genuine punishment than something designed to warm up a party. Not surprisingly she absolutely howled, screaming and thrashing about over Mel's lap, kicking wildly so that her pussy and bumhole got a good airing, and in tears by the time it had finished. It left her gasping and clutching her red bottom, but she was sent to stand by the mantelpiece without so much as a kiss better.

I was surprised, as it wasn't Mel's usual style, but the men liked it, clapping and passing remarks between themselves. Penny's panties fell down as she went to her place, right to her ankles so that she nearly tripped over them, which made the men laugh. She was blushing furiously and badly tearstained as she tucked her skirt up to make sure her bum showed properly and put her hands on her head. I tried to catch her eye to show sympathy, but at that moment Morris himself appeared, along with another man I recognised – Ronnie Miles.

For a moment I could only stare, wondering what was going on, only to realise that Morris would find it a lot easier to keep Miles sweet than have him being a pain in the arse. An invitation to one of the guests-only spanking parties was doubtless just the thing, and it would probably be with perks. That meant some unfortunate girl or other would end up with Miles's cock in her mouth before the evening was out. That was if she was lucky. It might be up her pussy or even her bumhole if she wasn't.

I snuggled into Joannie Lang, suddenly glad that the worst I was likely to be called on to do was lick pussy. She responded with a little pat to my bottom where I was nestled on her lap, and as Miles sat down Morris began to speak.

'Gentlemen, and ah . . . lady, as the wonderful Joannie Lang is the only female here deserving of that title tonight, I trust you enjoyed our little schoolgirl spanking display and are now keen for more. Well, you're going to get it, and in style. We have a pair of pretty maids to serve our needs, and there'll be none of that look-but-don't-touch business either. Grope 'em all you like, just so long as you don't keep them from their work.'

A ripple of laughter spread across the room and, as Annabelle and Sophie appeared with fresh trays, Morris's offer was quickly taken advantage of. Sophie had changed and, like Annabelle, was in a black and white maid's outfit, her boobs sitting bare in lacy cups, the flounced skirt supported on trimmed petticoats to show frilly panties beneath. The very first man she came to slid a hand up one stocking-clad leg to feel her bum as she bent to offer a drink, while one of those standing made a point of tweaking Annabelle's nipples before he took his glass. Morris looked on indulgently for a moment, cleared his throat and went on.

'There has, however, been a slight change of programme. Most of you know little Sophie and, as you see, she is a maid. Pull down her knickers, would you, Mr Judd?'

Judd, a nondescript-looking man with a bald patch and greasy hair, promptly did as he was asked, taking hold of Sophie's frillies as she bent to serve another man and jerking them down at the back. She squeaked but stayed down, her bruises on plain show as Judd and several others bent to examine her, with those who couldn't see demanding that she be made to turn around.

They got their wish, Sophie managing a slow turn to show off her bum to the full circle of men. Not that she had needed to, because with the tray chained to her wrists and loaded with full glasses she couldn't pull her knickers up anyway, and the men weren't about to do it. There was nothing for it but to go on serving with her bum bare, and she did, hobbling carefully along with her frilly panties at thigh level.

'Spoiled goods, as you see,' Rathwell went on, raising another laugh. 'So no Sophie in the raffle this time, but fortunately for us my own darling wife has agreed to take her place.'

I turned to Mel, instantly realising why she had looked so unhappy, and why she'd given poor Penny such a hard and perfunctory spanking. She was trying to smile, but it looked more like a scowl, making me wonder if any of the men would actually have the guts to smack her bottom for her. I knew she went down, but it had been getting ever rarer, and even then only with those few women who could take her on in the wrestling ring.

'. . . without further do,' Morris was saying, 'the raffle, with the prizes now as follows. Third, to take little Penny, whose red bottom now adorns the mantelpiece so prettily, and add to her sorrows with six strokes of the school cane. Second, to put Melody through her paces in any style you see fit, for a period of one half hour. First, the exclusive pleasure of her delectable sister, Harmony, for the remainder of the evening.'

There was a murmur of appreciation as Harmony entered the room. She was in school uniform, half in anyway. Her blouse was only just holding in the full bulk of her ample breasts, with one straining button the only thing that stopped them bursting free. Her tummy was bare, and her legs, with white panties showing beneath the hem of her indecently short skirt, tight around the plump fig of her sex and her well-fleshed bottom behind. Unlike her sister she didn't seem to mind what was coming, and strode boldly to the centre of the carpet, where she gave the men a twirl.

Morris joined in the clapping and then raised his hands for silence. A hush immediately fell over the room, with most of the men inspecting pink raffle tickets. Joannie had drawn several from her bag, and I was wondering what would happen if she won, and if I would end up performing in front of the men after all. Morris gave another signal and Penny came away from the mantelpiece with a squat blue urn, holding it out to him. He plunged his hand in and quickly drew it out again, with a ticket, his eyebrows rising as he read out the number.

'Thirty-eight, we have number thirty-eight?'

Penny was biting her lip as her eyes flicked across the faces of the assembled men. I knew she'd want Montague, who she liked, and who spanked her with a good blend of tenderness and severity. She got a man I'd never see before – old, with heavy jowls and a black skullcap perched on the bald and liver-spotted dome of his head. He was not in good health, using a stick to rise from his chair, but he was grinning as he beckoned Penny forwards with a peremptory cock of his finger.

'Congratulations, Uncle Isaac!' Morris called out, which drew a few suspicious looks from the audience.

I would have been mortified. Penny tried to be helpful, but it was a mistake. As Isaac hobbled forwards she went to move the chair she was to bend over nearer, but he mumbled something about being quite capable of looking after himself and sat down on it, then took a grip on her arm. She squeaked something about another spanking not being part of the deal, but he took no notice whatsoever, taking her over his knee despite her half-hearted efforts to stop him.

Her skirt had fallen, but Isaac turned it up to bare her and set to work, spanking steadily with his eyes fixed on her rounded cheeks as they bounced and quivered to the slaps. He was in no hurry, spanking merrily away and pausing occasionally to grope Penny's bottom and pull her cheeks apart to show off the rear view of her pussy and the pinkish-brown spot of her anus. The third time he did it he touched, using one long nail to tickle her bumhole as if to see what the effect would be.

If it had been me the effect would have been to make me wet myself all over his leg, which would have served the dirty old bastard right. Penny burst into tears of frustration and shame, but he carried on quite happily, telling her not to be self-centred, of all things. As soon as he'd had his fill of her bumhole he went back to spanking her, stopping only when Morris finally tapped him on the shoulder to attract his attention to a vicious-looking cane Annabelle was holding out on her tray.

Isaac made a gesture to Morris and went back to spanking Penny, but only for another twenty or so slaps. Stopping at last, he told her to rise and bend over, to open her legs to make sure her pussy showed to everyone, and to pull in her back to make her cheeks spread and flaunt her bumhole. She obeyed each order, snivelling all the while and finally losing her panties completely as she set her feet apart.

He spent a moment admiring her bum, maybe for the hell of it, maybe to let the full humiliation of her position sink in. Then he whacked her, six hard ones in quick succession that left her shaking and flexing one leg in a futile effort to dull the pain. I'd seen harder canings, and longer canings, but it left her in a fine state, tearstained and shaking as she got up and came to give me a cuddle. Joannie immediately took it upon herself to take Penny on her other knee, but she didn't resist. She'd been spanked and she wanted comfort, and it didn't much matter who it came from.

Morris was beaming as he went back to where he'd put the urn down on the table. Melody was looking more sorry for herself than ever as he plunged his hand in, and I saw her swallow as he took out a ticket. I'd have had my head in my hands, considering the choice of men she might be given too, but above all I'd have been praying it wasn't Ronnie Miles.

'Twenty-two,' Morris announced.

It wasn't Miles, but it was the flabby and red-faced Mr Protheroe, who was rubbing his hands in unconcealed glee the instant Morris read out his number. For one moment Mel's face showed her true emotions, shock and disgust, and then she was forcing herself to smile as she rose. Protheroe didn't go to meet her by the spanking chair, as I'd expected, but crossed to Morris instead, to whisper into his ear. Morris nodded and passed whatever the message was to Harmony, who answered him back, got a swat on her bottom for her trouble and skipped quickly out of the room.

Melody was waiting by the chair, trying to feign unconcern and not really succeeding. Protheroe went to her, and as he sat down she nodded to the clock on the mantelpiece. Morris lifted a glass of champagne to acknowledge her as Protheroe patted his lap.

'A little spanking to warm you up, first, I think, my dear,' he said happily, and his hands went to the hem of her dress.

I would quite simply never, ever have dared take Mel across my knee, especially if she'd been giving me the sort of black look she had on her face as her beautiful silk dress was eased gently up her thigh and over her bottom. She had hold-ups on, leaving twin slices of rich-brown thigh on show first, and then the full spread of her glorious bottom, the dark, muscular globes naked, with a scarlet thong just visible where it covered her pussy mound and in the cleft of her bum.

Even bent across a man's knee for spanking the sight of her bottom made me want to get down on my knees and kiss her feet, her cheeks, her bumhole, before licking her to ecstasy with my head held firmly in place by the hair. Not Protheroe. As far as Protheroe was concerned her obvious dominance meant nothing. She was a girl, and girls got their bottoms spanked.

They got their bottoms spanked bare too, and he was going to do it. As he took hold of her thong I felt a sense of outrage, of impropriety, that must have been a faint echo of hers, and it got worse, far worse, as the tiny thong was peeled down and out from between her cheeks. He took it right down, to leave the plump, black swell of her pussy on show, and I felt the knot in my stomach draw tighter.

I couldn't imagine him doing worse. He'd seen the look on her face, and he knew how she felt. She wasn't even fighting, but he had her bum bare and he was going to spank her, surely that was enough? Surely he had some decency? He didn't. With his horrid piglike eyes fixed on her bottom, he took hold of one full black cheek in each hand and spread them, showing off the jet-black, glistening dimple of her anus to every single one of the leering old goats who were watching.

Just watching it made me feel sick, and I was shaking badly as he made a lingering inspection of her bottom. She didn't even clench her cheeks, but let him do it, her face set in mute, miserable resignation as her anus was given a public inspection. I promised myself I would try and make it up – it was my fault, in a way – perhaps offering to lick her beautiful bottom for her in the toilet to let her restore her pride.

Protheroe was well pleased with himself, grinning stupidly as he began to spank, his fat red hand walloping down on Mel's bottom to send slaps echoing around the room. She took it well, her face set in determination, her muscles jumping at each impact, but with none of the babyish display Penny had made. Her stoicism only encouraged Protheroe, who paused to pull her panties further down, and right off, then cocked a leg around one of hers, forcing her thighs apart. Every eye was on her, and a murmur of appreciation ran around the room as her pussy came fully on show, her plump black lips neatly shaved, with the pink centre open and embarrassingly moist.

The man nearest me made a remark, pointing out how wet she was to his neighbour, who laughed. I bit back the urge to point out that just because a girl's been made wet doesn't mean she's keen for what's being done to her. Melody was responding as any kinky girl would to being bared and spanked, but that didn't mean she wanted to be over Protheroe's knee.

He'd gone back to spanking her, low now, over her pussy, perhaps hoping to make her really disgrace herself by coming during punishment. She was beginning to wiggle too, adding to my sympathy for her, but Protheroe stopped as Harmony came back. She was holding a basinful of water and a towel. She put both on the floor beside the spanking chair, and I saw that there was bar of soggy-looking green soap in the water. Mel had seen too and, as Protheroe paused in the spanking, she turned to look at Morris. There was pleading in her eyes, but he shook his head.

Protheroe appeared not to notice, and simply took a firm grip on Mel's waist as he bent sideways to retrieve the soap. I knew exactly what he was doing, but I hadn't realised just how coarse he could be. Instead of making her take the soap straight in her mouth, he made a horrible joke about having to wash her bum, and did it, rubbing the bar between her cheeks until her crease was full of bubbles, then wiping her bottom with the towel. I could see her shaking, and was praying that, having inflicted one degradation on her, he would spare her a second. No, the moment he was satisfied that her bum crease was clean he took the soap once more and pressed it to her lips, telling her it was what happened to girls who swore.

In it went, stuck into her open mouth to leave her looking absolutely furious as the spanking commenced once again. A purple blush had begun to suffuse the rich-brown skin of her bottom, and I knew a white girl in her place would have been bright red behind. It must have been as tender as anything, but it was getting to her, her pussy now leaking white juice for all the anger in her eyes.

Still Protheroe spanked, with a mechanical firmness, and as hard as ever, to make her bum bounce and set her boobs quivering in her dress. It was making her gasp too, despite herself, and soon a froth of bubbles had begun to show between her full lips, then from her nose as a volley of extra hard slaps caught her right over her sex. He stopped; his hands went to her dress and he gave a sharp command. She lifted her body, a clot of bubbles falling to the floor from her half-open mouth, and her dress was tugged up, spilling her boobs out to hang black and heavy against his trouser leg as she was settled back into spanking position.

Again Protheroe began to smack her, faster now, slap after slap after slap delivered over her soaking pussy, until at last she began to wriggle her hips on his lap. Her thighs came wider and she was rubbing herself on his leg as he spanked her, her pussy spread wide, her boobs jiggling. Her face was set in utter misery, then ecstasy as her body betrayed her completely and she came on Protheroe's leg, as wanton and dirty as any submissive little slut.

The men were laughing and clapping as Melody squirmed over Protheroe's knee, the smacks still landing on her upturned bum even as she shook and bucked in orgasm. I could imagine the feelings going through her head, or at least begin to, and I felt sick and nervous. Without my bruises I would have been in Melody's place, red-bottomed and sorry for myself, but so horny, smacked up to submissive ecstasy, and perhaps only too willing to be put under orders. If it could happen to Melody, it could happen to me.

Her head was bowed as she was finally allowed up from Protheroe's lap, and she kept the soap in her mouth until he told her she could remove it. He also told her to strip, and she did, nude. It had taken under twenty minutes by the clock to reduce her from a proud and dominant woman to a spanked and contrite girl, a girl prepared to rub herself off in front of a roomful of men as her bare bottom was spanked. It had got to me, and I wasn't the only one.

'Very appropriate,' Joannie said quietly, as Protheroe began to put Mel through a series of exercises. 'I do like to see a well-built black girl get a good spanking. They always used to seem to need it the most.'

I didn't bother to ask what she was talking about, but stood in response to a gentle pat to my bottom. Penny got the same treatment, and Joannie rose too, chivvying us towards the door with more pats to our bums. Protheroe had Mel jumping on the spot, with her boobs bouncing up and down to the delight of the audience. For all that I felt for her, I wanted to watch, but Joannie had other ideas, and I followed meekly as she led me from the room and up the stairs. Penny had made to follow, but had been taken aside by Harmony at the door.

There was no denying that watching Penny and Mel get it had turned me on, but it was still a struggle to try and see Joannie as a senior and dominant figure rather than a self-obsessed old bat. I'd been given to her though, and I was shortly going to be put down between her thighs, so I did my best, concentrating on my submissive feelings as she led me into one of the playrooms.

It wasn't a dungeon, as such, but there were a few punishment implements laid out on a table for the guests' use, just as someone might have laid out a flannel or some towels. Joannie shut the door behind us and let the catch fall into place, to my relief. Going down for her was one thing. Doing it in front of a load of leering men was quite another.

'Let me see you,' she ordered as she turned to me, and her voice was rich with arousal.

I nodded and put my fingers to the buttons of my school blouse, undoing them as she sat down in a chair, watching. It felt odd, for all the times I've shown my breasts to the command of dominant women, and I didn't know why. I did it properly too, not just flopping them out but undoing my bra catch and taking it off down my sleeve to let myself open the blouse to bare myself. She nodded in appreciation at the act, her gaze fixed to my chest as I took the weight of my boobs in my hands and held them up for her inspection.

'My, you are a big girl, aren't you?' she purred. 'And so pretty. I would have had you in the magazines quick enough. Now take your pants down.'

I nodded and swallowed. After lifting the hem of my school skirt, I tucked it up to show the front of my panties, then pushed them a little way down, baring my pussy. Again she gave her little pleased nod.

'Very trim. You have good hips too, which is just as well for a fat girl. Now show me your bottom, show it off, if you know how.'

'I –' I began, and choked off my protest.

It wasn't fair to call me fat, just because my bum and boobs are big, especially when she had to be twice my weight herself.

'– I'm afraid I'm a little bruised,' I finished, trying to hide my resentment.

I tucked up my skirt at the back as I turned, and pushed my panties the rest of the way down, off my bum, which inevitably felt enormous under her gaze after what she'd said. She'd told to make a display of myself, so I put my hands on my knees and stuck it out a little, just enough to be sure my pussy lips would show between my thighs.

'So you have, you poor little thing!' she said. 'What brute did that to you?'

The tone of her voice gave the lie to her words, her sympathy false, or at least insincere. She liked the idea of me getting a good beating, no question.

'My girlfriend . . . my top,' I answered, not sure if she'd understand what AJ was to me.

'Morris warned me you had been spoiled,' she went on, 'but never mind, there are other ways to enjoy a fat little thing like you. Turn around, and put your hands on your head.'

She was going to torture my tits, and I was already shaking as I obeyed her, also wondering if I should admit just how ticklish I am. If I didn't and she tickled my boobs I was going to pee myself, but if I did she might make me anyway, but surely not on the carpet . . .

'I . . . I'm very ticklish,' I said as I faced front with my boobs pushed out and my hands on my head. 'Very ticklish. I . . . I can't always hold myself.'

'Well you shall just have to,' she answered as she picked up a thin chrome steel chain from the table.

'I really mean it,' I tried, only to be cut off as she raised a finger to her lips.

'Sh!' she ordered. 'I have no time for wet games, or your little lies to make the sex go your own way. Believe me, I have handled girls far, far cleverer than you.'

'But . . .'

'Be quiet, Jade, remember who you are with.'

I shut up, biting my lip and wondering who would get it if I peed on the floor. The answer was obvious – me. For whatever reason, Morris wanted to suck up to Joannie Lang. Fortunately my bladder wasn't that full, and I braced myself as she stepped close with the thing she'd picked up, a pair of nipple clamps like little bulldog clips joined by a chain. I bit my lip and closed my eyes, wishing my nipples hadn't popped out quite so invitingly the instant I'd realised what was going to be done to me.

Cold steel touched my flesh; the jaws eased onto one stiff bud, then the other, and let close, drawing a hiss of pain from between my clenched teeth. Both my nipples were clamped, and both began to burn on the instant, leaving me shaking as she began a leisurely exploration of my boobs, stroking, pinching, tickling . . .

I nearly burst, my teeth gritted hard and my toes wriggling as I struggled not to give in to the agonising sensation. It would have happened too, right into my half-lowered panties, but she stopped just in time, and slid a finger into the crease of my pussy and up the hole.

'Just as wet as I would have imagined,' she remarked. 'Do your nipples hurt, Jade?'

'Yes,' I answered, 'a lot.'

'Good,' she answered. 'I shall think of your pain as I come. Now, on the bed with you.'

I went, scrambling on quickly. Not just my nipples, but the whole of both my boobs felt painfully swollen and sensitive. It was good for me, the right sort of thing to do to get me on my knees, and I was really beginning to accept her dominance over me as she made herself comfortable, propped up on the pillows. She pulled her dress up, showing off expensive panties stretched tight over a plump pussy mound, with a wet patch at the centre betraying her own excitement. I could see that she was eager, her fingers shaking as she pulled the panties aside, and I went straight down, my clamped nipples rubbing on the bed cover as I buried my face in her full, fleshy pussy.

She smelled of perfume, and tasted of it, so strong and sharp it masked the natural tang of her sex. I'd have preferred pussy juice, pee even, but I licked, playing the obedient little slut, with my bottom lifted to show off to her, intent on her pleasure, the pleasure she took in putting me in pain. With my boobs clamped and my face in her pussy it was impossible not to think of my subjugation, my pain, even the way she had insulted me.

My imagination began to run as I tongued her, thinking of how rude I'd look, and how submissive. I was dressed as a schoolgirl, a fat little schoolgirl with her panties pulled down at the back to show her smacked bottom, her boobs squashed naked on the bed cover, her aching nipples chained together, her face buried in an older woman's sex. It was where I belonged, whoever chose to do it to me, used for the amusement of dominant women, however they pleased.

I needed to frig off, but not until she'd come. Her pleasure came first, and when I'd given my all I would frig myself off in front of her, still in my clamps, showing her the state she'd got me into. She gave a low moan and I began to lick harder, no longer teasing her up but right on her clitty, and an instant later she was there, her thighs tightening around my head as she came in my face.

The moment she'd finished I sat back, my breathing deep and even, ready for my own orgasm. I took the nipple chain and tugged it out, watching my flesh stretch and revelling in the pain it brought. She gave a quiet smile as she swung her legs off the bed, but when she spoke it was not what I expected.

'I trust you don't mind entertaining my husband?'

'Your husband? I . . . I'm not sure, I –'

‘He would appreciate it, and I will tell him not to make too much of a pig of himself.’

‘I . . . I don’t know . . . I want to come, Joannie, you’ve turned me on so much. Don’t you want to watch?’

‘Of course, my darling, but I’d much rather watch while you have my husband’s cock in your mouth.’

‘If . . . maybe, if you order me?’ I answered, the words tumbling out, despite my immediate sense of betrayal.

‘I understand,’ she said gently. ‘Perhaps a blindfold, or with your hands tied?’

I nodded gratefully, full of revulsion as I thought of the men downstairs, but knowing just how good the climax would be if I abandoned my self-control and gave in to her, completely, accepting her husband’s horrible cock because she wanted me to, because she had ordered me to . . .

She was going to blindfold me, tie me and make me suck his cock. I needed to do it, badly, but as she went to the table I was playing with my clamped nipples to help myself accept my own needs. They’d gone numb, and I had to pull at them to get the pain back, but the skin of my boobs felt extra sensitive and brought home to me how exposed they were, and how big; fat, like she’d said.

I’d already closed my eyes, and the darkness merely deepened as a length of black cloth from the table was wrapped around my head. It felt right, one more level of responsibility stripped away from me, and then yet another as my hands were taken and eased behind my back to be clipped off in a pair of cuffs. I was helpless, and under orders, Joannie’s little slut, to be used as she wished, by whom she wished.

She laid me down on the bed and I was left, bound and helpless, ready to have a cock stuck in my mouth, or elsewhere, because I couldn't stop it and I wasn't going to try. Even if somebody else came in and just took me it didn't matter. It would just be funny, a joke, for me to get it from some lecherous old bastard, or a string of them, one by one, using me in my mouth, my pussy, my bumhole . . .

It must have been five, maybe ten minutes I lay there, trussed and ready, before I heard the creak of the door, a low, masculine chuckle and the chink of a glass as it was put down. I felt my body stiffen, heard the door catch click, and somebody's weight settled onto the bed. A hand touched me, stroking my hair, and I caught Joannie's voice, low and soothing.

'There, there, darling, you just do as Joannie tells you, and it will be all right.'

She took my shoulders, guiding me around so that I could lay my head in her lap, and once more began to stroke my hair. Again I felt the bed shift, and knew it was him, but my muscles still jumped as his hand touched me, on my thigh, and higher, making my skin crawl as his fingers loitered on my panties. I heard my own whimper as he touched my bum, a knuckle tracing the curve of my cheek, and at last he spoke.

'My, she has been well spanked, hasn't she? Now let's see that little cunt.'

He moved his hand to my knee, and I was being opened, my thighs eased wide to stretch my panties taut between them. His hand closed on them and I thought he would pull them off to let me get my legs open, but he lifted my legs by them instead, rolling me up to show off not just my pussy, but my bumhole too. I was winking at him, my ring twitching, and I couldn't stop it. He chuckled at the sight, and then I felt a fingertip, right in the middle of my anal star, and once again I came within an ace of wetting all over the bed.

I would have done if he hadn't transferred his attention to my pussy, sliding a finger deep into the slippery hole, which tightened on him in reaction, even as his other hand found my boobs. He began to finger fuck me, tugging at the chain on my nipples and squeezing my tits as he did it, with me keeping my own legs up so that he could molest me, and hoping he'd make me come.

A few touches to my clitty and I'd have been there, even a few well-applied smacks. I didn't get it, just his questing touch, exploring my body purely for his own amusement as his wife comforted me. My mouth had come open, expecting to filled with cock, and it was. He lifted from the bed; Joannie took hold of my head to get me in position, and a warm, salty penis was fed to me.

My stomach was twitching as I felt the fleshy tip of his foreskin on my tongue, and then I was rolling it back with my lips, deliberately making the experience worse for myself as the slippery, bulbous mass of his knob emerged into my mouth. I sucked on it, sickened by the thick cock taste but revelling in it at the same time, my legs still up and open, my bound hands eager to get to my pussy.

He began to touch me up again, fondling my boobs as his cock grew slowly erect in my mouth, swelling to a thin, bent erection. I could just imagine how ugly it would be, pink and skinny and twisted, horrible, and in my mouth, to be sucked, to be licked, until he spunked down my throat or in my face.

Only when he pulled it out and didn't start to jerk over me did I realise my fate was to be worse still. I was to be fucked, my pussy used as a slide hole for his horrible old cock, spunked in too. As I felt his weight settle on the bed once more I heard my own groan, of hope and despair both, hope that he would make a thorough job of my fucking and make me come, despair for my own dirty needs.

He took hold of my school pants once more, tugging them down to my knees, to leave me completely vulnerable, my legs held up and open, my pussy splayed to his cock. I tucked them up higher still, making myself ready for fucking as Joannie whispered to tell me what a good girl I was. She had my head tight to her lap, maybe as much to hold me down as to comfort me, robbing me of just that little bit more control.

I groaned again as his cockhead touched my sex, rubbing in the creamy folds and on my clitty, to send shivers up my spine and make my bum cheeks tighten in anticipation of the fucking I was about to get. He slid lower, to my hole, and I felt fluid squash out and trickle down into my anus, and his cock, hot and swollen against that same sensitive little hole, the same slimy, penetrable little hole, my bumhole. Joannie's grip tightened on my head.

As I realised I was going to be buggered I cried out, but there was no fight in me and my ring was already spreading to the pressure of his cock. I made one futile effort to keep myself closed, but it just hurt, and he was already going up. I was gasping and kicking my legs in the taut panties as my ring splayed out on his knob, gaping, wide and wider still, enough to take him. Several inches of hard, hot penis slid abruptly up my bottom and I cried out in pain and shock, but it was right for me, what I needed, to be tied and used, and all the better if it was up my bottom.

They got me, right down, wriggling in my bonds as I was buggered, unable to see, unable to help myself, just jerking feebly on the cock in my rectum as the last couple of inches were packed up. I felt the hairy mass of his ball sac press to my bruised bum cheeks, and knew he was well and truly in, all the way. He switched his grip from my panties to my thighs as he began to move in me, pulling me onto his cock, and off, so I could feel my straining ring move in and out on his shaft.

I felt bloated, my rectum stuffed fit to burst, and for all that I was sobbing bitterly as I was sodomised I wanted to come with it up me, or together, in helpless ecstasy as he spunked in my hole. Joannie was still telling me I was a good girl, and I wanted that too, her comfort as I was buggered, as he came up me, and her touch on my pussy. I tried to speak through the jumble of feelings in my head, to ask to be frigged off, but before I could find my voice he was pulling out, hurting, and my words came as a gasp.

'Frig me . . . frig me, please, Joannie, make me come as he does it,' I managed, and I left my mouth wide.

I was ready for it to be filled, if that was what he wanted, and I braced myself to taste my own bottom, and for the burning shame that would come with it, because I knew I'd suck, willingly, wantonly, like the dirty little slut I am. Only it didn't happen, and as his cock was pushed back up my bumhole with a wet sound he spoke.

'Good idea. Rub her cunt, Joannie, I love to feel it when their arseholes tighten.'

He pushed himself deep up once more, and began to move, his cock squelching in my bumhole as she took hold of my panties, rolling my thighs right up against my clamped boobs. A quick movement and one clamp had been undone, making me cry out at the sudden pain in my nipple, and again as it was refastened, only now with the chain twisted through my lowered panties. I was helpless immediately, forced to keep my legs up or wrench the nipple clamps off, with no choice but to make myself as fully available as possible.

She touched my pussy, spreading my lips to find my clitty, touching, teasing, and rubbing, masturbating me in front of her dirty pig of a husband as he used me up my bum. My body began to tighten almost immediately; my pussy let out a long, wet farting sound; my bumhole began to pulse on his cock, and I was there, screaming and writhing on the bed, juice squirting from my pee hole, my clamps jerking on my nipples, lost in unbearable ecstasy. So was he, grunting loudly with his hands locked hard in the flesh of my thighs and his cock working my gaping, slippery bumhole, and at the very peak of the most glorious orgasm, filling my rectum with spunk.

He stopped, held deep in me as he gave me my filling, my bumhole still in contraction on his cock, fluid still bubbling from my pee hole and into my pussy. I came very, very slowly, down, with feelings of shame and betrayal rising in my head as the orgasm subsided, as I tried to tell myself that I'd only done as I was told by Joannie, that I'd been a good submissive, nothing more and nothing less. She had held me throughout, and at last let go to unfasten my nipple clamps.

'Thank you, Jade, you really are a good girl,' she said. 'Now this may hurt a little.'

It hurt a lot, wrenching a hiss of pain from my lips as the blood flowed back into one squashed nipple, then the other. He began to pull his cock out, which hurt too, and left my bumhole agape and oozing spunk as he stood up from the bed.

'Shit! I wish I'd known she was a squirter!' he complained. 'Better clean up.'

For one awful moment I thought he was going to stick his dirty cock in my mouth after all, but he simply stomped off, leaving Joannie to release me. She was sweet, and even pulled my panties up for me to cover the mess her husband had made. I was shaking badly; my nipples hurt like anything and I was sure my bumhole was bruised, but for all my guilt there was no denying the orgasm had been good, very good. I gave her a kiss and a hug before scampering off to find a bathroom, with the spunk still dribbling out of my bottom hole and into my panties.

It was a while before I felt ready to come downstairs, because the party was in full swing, and Joannie and her husband had brought me far enough down to ensure that it would take much to make me join in. I had betrayed my principles enough for one evening, and went to Harmony's bedroom to borrow a pair of panties and lie down in the dark for a while. It must have been half an hour later when she came in, her face flushed, stark naked but for the torn remains of her school blouse and with her bottom marked with at least two dozen dark-red cane cuts.

'Hi, Jade, there you are,' she said, moving to the dresser. 'I wondered where you'd got to. Are you OK? They weren't too nasty, were they?'

'No . . . not really,' I answered. 'I'm a bit sore, that's all.'

'Me too,' she answered, twisting the lid from a pot of cream, which she began to apply to her bottom as she went on.

'All to the good anyway, and I think we should be able to sort out the mess you made.'

'What mess? I haven't made a mess, not badly –'

'With your cabaret. Morris has just about managed to persuade him that it was his own fault, and Joannie's pleased with you too.'

'Joannie? What's she got to do with it?'

'She's his wife, silly, Mrs Joan Miles, Joannie Lang as was, but she's one of these women who just can't let go of her youth.'

I didn't answer. It could only mean one thing. I had been buggered by Ronnie Miles.

Ten

All the way back to my flat I couldn't even bring myself to speak. Penny had had a fine time, spanked over and over, across lap after lap, with her panties going up and down like a yo-yo, until she was dizzy with submission and need. They'd tied her to Sophie, head to toe and faces to pussies, and watched as the two of them licked each other to orgasm. There had been more too, plenty more, but all of it within her limits, and, if her bottom was a mess and so sore she'd borrowed a cushion to sit on in the car, then she was nothing if not happy about it.

It was only back at the flat I managed to bring myself to tell her what had happened. She did her best, cuddling me and telling me I should concentrate on the pleasure I'd taken in the act rather than fuss over the details. She was right, but that didn't make it any easier.

There was a lot of chagrin too. I'd felt so clever, managing to wriggle out of what had happened at Bolero's, only to end up with Miles's cock up my bum, and it was my own stupid fault. With hindsight I knew I should have figured it out, or just not behaved quite so like a dirty little fuck-pig. Unfortunately it's what I am, and I knew it. I'd betrayed myself. I'd betrayed AJ with a vengeance.

Penny pointed out that I should accept my sexuality as it was, rather than try to be what other people wanted me to be. I'd heard it before, and it didn't work. Part of my submission is the need to be what somebody else wants me to be. I couldn't even blame Morris Rathwell, not really, let alone Melody, or anyone else. It was my fault, pure and simple. Nor was it the first time. Let me near men and I seem to end up on their cocks, and loving it.

In the end Penny got so fed up with me moping that she gave me a rousing spanking, which hurt like anything on my bruises, and only made me feel still more sorry for myself. I didn't let it show, thanking her afterwards, and we went to bed cuddled together, but for all my exhaustion it was gone midnight before I finally fell asleep.

Penny had to be up early to drive home, and left when it was still dark. She kissed me goodbye and was gone with a parting remark, not to worry. I tried, but it was not easy, because there was no getting around the fact that I'd enjoyed being buggered, that I liked being buggered, that if I got high enough again I'd be pulling my own cheeks apart to have the cock put in my bumhole.

It was the same for the rest of the week, trying to decide if I should accept my sexuality as it was, the way Penny did, setting her boundaries only according to what was safe and practical. The choice was to become what I felt I should be, a lifestyle lesbian submissive. I was going to have to make the decision, in the end, but both choices meant losing something.

The Ealing job had become so routine I barely had to pay attention to what I was doing, reading the paperwork and sticking on the labels as an automatic action. It left me plenty of time to think, and by the Wednesday I had made my mind up. Penny was right. I should be me, and let other people react to me as it suited them. Some might disapprove, but that was their problem. AJ for one would never lose interest so long as I still needed to be chased. If I was caught, it might prove a different story. As for Ronnie Miles, he had buggered me and given me a glorious orgasm. What mattered was not Miles, but the orgasm.

Penny was delighted with my decision, and suggested organising a party to celebrate what she saw as my liberation. I agreed, even to inviting Jeff and Monty so that I could be thoroughly dealt with in front of all the girls. It was a scary thought, but undeniably arousing, and as Penny and I lay in each other's arms on the Thursday night, masturbating together, I came as she described to me how it was going to feel with Monty's cock in my mouth as Jeff buggered me.

We initially invited just Melody, Sophie, Poppy and Gabrielle, but word soon spread, and by the Friday evening we had agreed that both the Rathwells could come, along with Harmony and Annabelle, and also June and Teo. That made four men, and four cocks, all of which I was determined to accommodate in my body, not just in my mouth and up my bum either, but in my pussy, which would be my first proper fucking in ages.

There was one other person I wanted to invite, and that was Zoe. I was surprised not to have seen her, as she generally rang quite often, and came round to collect her striptease gear. I called, to find that she'd been away with her parents, but was keen to get back into the swing of things. She happily accepted the invitation, and also suggested I come down to Sugar Babe's. I agreed, eager both to see her and for a good night out.

It was surprisingly warm, and I was keen to avoid the inevitable half hour in the cloakroom queue at the end of the evening. So I put on a pair of pale blue low-rise jeans with bright red panties underneath so that the waistband showed at the back, along with a thick but short top in black. The jeans hugged my bum, making me a little self-conscious on the way in, but I knew I'd be OK in Sugar Babe's, where showing off was appreciated.

I wanted something for my hair, so changed tubes and got off at Tottenham Court Road, walking down Oxford Street, where the shops were still open for the early Christmas crowds. It was busy, and my mind was on what I should buy and how Zoe was going to look.

AJ caught me completely unawares. I never even knew she was there until I heard the low growl of her bike as she drew out of a side street, stopping right in front of me. She was going to do me, I knew she was, from the wicked grin on her face as she lifted her helmet off. I just ran, straight into a group of Japanese tourists coming up behind me, and before I could untangle myself she had me by the arm. I was begging immediately, imploring her not to do it, to take me to Whispers, even to Sugar Babe's.

'. . . not in the street, AJ!' I pleaded. 'Anything, anywhere, but not in the street, not in the street!'

My voice broke off in a bubbling, choking giggle as she stuck her fingers deep into my sides, tickling to send a jolt of pain right through me. I nearly let go, but she stopped and my bladder held, just. Then I had twisted free, and darted away, in the only direction I could, into the brightly lit mouth of a boutique, dodging among displays of red pillar boxes and plastic policemen and model Big Bens, into a space lit brilliant white, crowded with shoppers, and with no way out.

'Good choice, Dumplings,' AJ remarked as she came towards me, 'couldn't have done better myself.'

'You wouldn't, not really?' I managed. 'Not here? Come on, AJ, this isn't fair. I'll be yours, I promise. I'll do anything, I'll –'

'Good. So stand still.'

'No, I mean . . . Ah! No!'

She had me trapped against a display of fat brown and white teddy bears with union-jack hats, her hands digging in under my armpits, deep in. I struggled, squealing stupidly and giggling, praying the shop assistants would stop her, praying that not quite so many of the Japanese tourists were packing into the shop to see what was going on, and praying they hadn't had quite so many cameras.

AJ stopped, leaving me panting, with my thighs crossed and my fists clenched against the expected strain. Her grip changed; she lifted me clear of the floor and I was turned, bum out to the crowd, thrashing in her grip, pleading, begging, my feet kicking in the air . . .

'Tickle, tickle, Dumplings,' she said sweetly and once more her fingers dug in deep.

I clenched my teeth. I clenched my fists. I shut my eyes tight. I squeezed my thighs together and curled my toes up and tightened my bum cheeks and prayed and prayed and prayed, fighting . . .

. . . and losing as I burst into helpless, stupid giggles, my feet stamping on the ground, my toes wiggling in my shoes, my full weight in AJ's arms, desperate to drop into the Vincent's Curtsey that would, that might, save me, and then it was too late. I felt the first squirt erupt into my panty crotch; I heard my own despairing squeal, and I was doing it, pee gushing into my clothes, full force, not just in my panties and jeans, but through them, bubbling out at the crotch in a little yellow fountain, as a chorus of exclamations broke out behind me.

'She's peeing herself!'

'Excuse me, lady, your friend –'

'She's wet her pants!'

'See, down her legs!'

'No! She can't be!'

'She is!'

There was more, in Japanese, fast and full of excitement, shock and sympathy and embarrassment, but delight too, with little squeaks from the girls and crowing from the men. Some were even taking pictures, flashes popping around me as the urine squirted into my panties and through, running down both legs and into my boots, pattering on the shop floor and soaking up over my bum.

I burst into tears, beating my fists on AJ's chest and calling her a bitch over and over, but she'd stopped, and was apologising, making me look like a complete baby, not just wetting myself but going into a tantrum over it too. I couldn't stop the pee either, because my whole body was shaking with great, heavy sobs, my pussy squirting with every one, to leave a trail of yellow urine on the shop floor as AJ quickly led me out.

The angry voice of someone in the shop reached me as we pushed through the tourists, the owner finally realising what had happened. I didn't care, and I wasn't stopping, my vision blurred with tears as AJ hustled me away, pee still dripping from my crotch, down the alley she'd parked in, and into the blessed darkness of another, smaller passageway. She led me deep in to where a huge zinc bin blocked the view from the alley, and pushed me against the wall. I sank down, sobbing bitterly, my back to the rough brick. My pee had stopped, but I could feel it, soggy and warm around my pussy and over my bum.

I knew what she wanted, and there was quite simply nothing I could do to stop it. For the anger and confusion in my head, she had me, and as the zip on her leathers rasped down I was already pressing my tearstained face forwards, broken and willing to bring the pleasure she had taken in my humiliation to a peak. She pushed down her leathers and thrust out her hips, adding the scent of pussy to that of London back alley. She was right in my face, my nose touching the bulge of her tattooed mound, my lips to hers, the metal bead of a piercing touching my skin.

'Lick, fast,' she ordered, and sighed in bliss as my tongue found her clitoris.

She took my hair, twisting hard enough to hurt, but she didn't need to. I was hers, licking pussy in utter submission, my bottom fat and warm in soggy panties, my pussy ready for my fingers, her fist. I took hold of her, clutching at the firm cheeks of her bum, cool in the night air, and she began to speak.

'That's right, hold me like that. You're enjoying it, aren't you, you little slut, you little dirt-bag bitch, yes you are, and you knew you would, Miss Pissy-Knickers . . .'

I licked harder, eager to be told what a slut I was, what an utter filthy, grovelling little slut, to be getting off on wetting myself, on being made to wet myself, in public, photographed, filmed, with pee spurting out between my legs, soaking in over the fat, denim-clad ball of my bum, soiled and disgraced in public and then on ten thousand computer screens from Tokyo to Cape Town.

She started to come with a low groan as her fist twisted harder still in my hair and I was licking for all I was worth, and wishing she'd made it worse, held me still and taken my jeans down to be inspected, made me strip and mop it up with my clothes, made me lick it off the shop floor, lapping up my own piss in front of a crowd of laughing, pointing tourists.

I could feel the muscles of her pussy working against my face as she came, and the instant it stopped my hands were between my legs, rubbing in the pee-soaked crease where my jeans had pulled up tight into my pussy. She realised, and laughed at my helpless, dirty reaction to her cruelty. My face was kept in, pulled hard to her sex; her hand stayed in my hair, hurting me, twisted so tight I could feel the strands pulling out. I would have screamed, but my face was smothered in moist, fleshy pussy, and I could barely breathe.

What had been done to me rose up in my head as I started to come, a clear image of me in the shop, held by AJ, squirming in her grip, doing my ridiculous little tickle dance with my hands waving and my feet kicking up and down, my bottom a fat blue ball, my red panties showing at the top, and piss squirting from between my legs as I wet myself.

I held the thought as I rode my orgasm: me peeing my panties, pissing my knickers, wetting myself, having an accident in my pants. Every detail was clear, as if I'd been watching myself, the little yellow fountain bubbling out through my jeans, the dark trickles running down the insides of my thighs, the stain growing across my bottom and up my pussy.

When AJ finally let go there was hair in her fist. She gave a pleased grunt as she realised and held tight to it as she quickly pulled up her trousers. I was slumped back against the wall, my ecstasy slowly dying to let the awkward reality of being in central London in pissed jeans sink in. AJ was the only person who could possibly help, but she was quite capable of deciding I had not been punished enough.

'AJ . . . Mistress,' I ventured, 'do you think –'

'Hang on,' she interrupted, and I realised what she was doing.

She had stepped back into a pool of dull red light coming from a neon sign far above our heads, and was twisting the hair she'd pulled out into a braid. Pressing her wrist against one leg, she carefully tied the ends off to make a bracelet, spent a moment admiring the effect in the light, and turned to me.

'What's up?'

'I . . . I was hoping you . . . you'd be nice, and maybe help me home? It really shows, and –'

'Sure. Hop on the bike. I've got a spare lid.'

'On the bike? But –'

'Take it or leave it. Take it, and you're mine, completely. Leave it, you can do as you please.'

I took it, in no condition to argue over details. It still meant travelling the eight miles or so from central London to Turnpike Lane clinging onto her with my bottom stuck out behind and my wet patch blatantly visible to every single one of the hundreds upon hundreds of people we passed. The way she drove I would have had every reason to wet myself, out of fear, but that was small consolation.

AJ spent the night, and made me sleep on the floor, my ankles cuffed off on the bed post, with the taste of her sex thick in my mouth after she'd fucked me with my own strap-on and queened me. It gave me a taste of what it would be like living with her, much as it was in my fantasies: cold, uncomfortable and generally unpleasant, with moments of agonising ecstasy. That was fine for sex, in fact necessary at times, but not much fun as I was huddled shivering on the hard floor and she was snoozing comfortably in my bed, under my duvet and on my pillows. The life of a sex slave was not for me.

Fortunately, with Christmas coming up she had to go to work in the morning, otherwise it would have been awkward. As it was she booted me awake before seven in the morning and made me bring her breakfast in bed, then spanked me because her egg was too hard. I wasn't allowed to dress either, although it was freezing, and I was left stark naked and rubbing a rosy bottom as I watched her bike pull away from the window.

The flat was a mess, but as soon as I'd put the heating on and made myself bacon and eggs I went back to bed. As I quickly drifted towards much needed sleep I was thinking of scenes I'd read in books, generally with one hand between my legs, in which hapless heroines are chained in stone-floored dungeons and brought out as needed to be abused. Not me, I'd have dozed off on the branding table.

I was woken by the insistent ringing of the doorbell, and dragged myself to the window to find Penny below and that it was nearly two in the afternoon. The flat looked like a bomb had hit it, and as soon as I'd made her a coffee we began to tidy up. I told her what AJ had done to me, and she responded just as I had thought she would, with disapproval of the way it had been done, but delight at the act. It was just the sort of humiliation that appeals to her, and she was quiet for a long while afterwards, doubtless reflecting on how she'd have felt in my position.

We had the flat immaculate in a couple of hours, then showered and changed. She seldom bothers to dress for sex, unless asked specifically, but she knew the boys' tastes and had gone for a deliberately tarty sailor suit, with a flared skirt to show off her panties, a big collar and even a little hat. With white knee socks and black shoes it looked both foolish and cute, so much so that just putting it on had her blushing.

I'd already decided on my army uniform, with the jacket but no skirt or blouse, so that I had plenty of cleavage bare and my panties were visible under the flared tail. It set off my waist nicely too, and was a match for Penny's sailor suit. Just being dressed was enough to start me feeling horny, but I wasn't sure if I would have the courage to ask for what I really wanted. Besides, it's always best when it just happens, and what I say or do doesn't matter a damn.

So I asked Penny to take over, and to make sure I had no control whatever over what was done to me. She agreed, and if it wasn't mentioned I knew I could rely on her to stick to sensible limits. Having given away my control over my own body I felt ready, but very, very nervous. My attitude to men and their cocks hadn't changed, just my acceptance of them. I was going to be made to fuck and suck, and the knowledge made me feel as uneasy, and as dirty, as it ever had.

I opened a bottle of wine, sure that a few glasses would make what was coming to me a lot easier to take, and we were still sipping our first glasses when the bell went. It was Monty, and he'd brought Gabrielle and Poppy with him. Penny was playing hostess, and soon had them comfortable, while I just watched Monty moving about my flat, wondering if I could ever have made the choice to let him have sex with me without being tied up, given to him, or tricked in some way.

He was oblivious, pinching my bum as he came in and complimenting me on the depth of my cleavage. Poppy wasn't much better, teasing me and calling me a turncoat, and suggesting that I should be made to wear a green L-plate over my pussy. Only Gabrielle seemed to have any real sympathy, asking how I was coping with my giggle micturition and listening intently as I described what AJ had done to me.

We'd finished the wine and opened a second bottle when Zoe turned up, as cute as ever in heels and tight black cords that hugged her bum and left a hint of bright green panties showing behind. She was a little flustered, and followed me into the bedroom when I went to fetch the spanking brush, speaking even as she closed the door.

'Naomi caught me, the bitch.'

'Me too. She dragged me onto Hampstead Heath and queened me, then . . . then she pissed all over me. And she made me wet myself.'

'That all? She got me in the toilets at Whispers last night, and . . . well, it was pretty sick.'

'I can guess,' I answered.

From the look in her eyes it seemed likely she'd been given much the same treatment I had, or something similar. I gave her a feeling grimace, but she said nothing, just shaking her head.

'Seen anyone else?' I asked.

'No,' she admitted. 'You? Did they catch up with you, AJ and that?'

'Yes,' I admitted, 'and then some. Sorry about last night.'

'That's OK . . . only it was because you weren't at Sugar Babe's I went on to Whispers.'

'Oh. Sorry . . . you can take it out on me if it makes you feel better?'

'I'd rather take it out on Naomi, but thanks.'

The bell went again: it was June and Teo, and Jeff had joined them at the door before I'd recovered the keys. That left only the Rathwells' group to come, and my stomach was fluttering dreadfully as I helped to sort out drinks for them. Four more people had to arrive and I would be getting a fucking in front of all of them, even if I lost my nerve and had to be held down, or tied, or spanked until I was ready . . .

We'd cleared the centre of the living room, making space for me to get it, and so everyone could watch. Just walking across it set my pussy and bumhole twitching, and my nipples were so hard they showed through the thick material of my uniform jacket. The boys didn't know, or not the details anyway, although Monty and Jeff always took the attitude that it was worth trying to get into a girl's knickers whatever the circumstances.

I wanted it to start, because I was getting more and more nervous. Penny was starting to look at her watch too, and wouldn't sit down. June was already in Teo's lap, with her plump, coffee-cream boobs pulled out of her top, and Zoe seemed to be negotiating the loan of Poppy with Gabrielle, which was probably going to get her more than she'd bargained for. That was all fine, but it was my night, and I went into the kitchen after Penny to find her opening the last of the bottles of wine.

'Let's go,' I suggested.

She just nodded, leaving the bottle and walking into the main room. I came behind, my stomach absolutely tying itself in knots. Penny clapped her hands together, which had no effect at all, then spoke, which did.

'Put her down, Teo, or at least leave her until later. We have a little show first. Jeff, Monty, Teo, you're to fuck Jade. I want her spanked first, then put in the middle of the carpet and . . . well, you can do as you like. Just take what you want, because she's feeling a little shy, OK?'

All three of them looked surprised, even Teo, who didn't know me that well. He glanced at June too, but she hesitated only a moment before replying. 'Go on, fuck the little tart, see if I care, but just in her mouth, yeah?'

'Her bum is mine then,' Monty put in. 'I love her bum.'

'Yeah, nice,' Teo agreed. 'You're underneath then, Jeff.'

'Suits me, the lazy man's fuck,' Jeff answered, feigning a yawn as he heaved himself to his feet.

I couldn't bring myself to step forwards, but I didn't have to. Penny stepped back, as if she was returning to the kitchen, but the moment she was behind me she gave me a hard push, sending me staggering into the middle of the room. Teo caught me, his massive hands closing on my shoulders; Jeff's hand came up under my jacket tail to close on my bum; Monty's slid down the back of my panties, and I was theirs.

My jacket was opened, Teo popping the button to let my boobs into his hands, his splayed fingers wide enough to hold them properly. I closed my eyes as he began to rub my nipples with his thumbs, then to bounce them in his hands, as if unable to believe their size and weight. He growled something about how big they were, then buried his face between them, squashing them in his hands.

The other two had my panties down, all the way to my feet. Monty ducked low; my cheeks had been opened and he was licking my bumhole, not as an act of submission, not the way Penny or I would do it, but to get me ready for his cock. It felt good though, scary but good, and I couldn't resist sticking it out a little to let him get further in. My ring opened to his tongue as Jeff's hand cupped my sex, and I was being frigged as the three of them began to ease me down on the carpet.

'Nice arsehole, rubbery,' Monty commented as he pulled back. 'Better lube you up properly though.'

He left me to the others, Jeff already down on the floor with his hands on his fly. I sat on his legs, hoping they wouldn't let go of me, and they didn't. Teo had pulled his cock out one handed, and fed it into my mouth, making my eyes pop in surprise at the sheer bulk of it. I'd sucked him before, but he was nearly as big limp as stiff, and he felt so heavy, with the full weight of his prick lying on my tongue.

He took my hair and began to fuck my mouth, his cock growing quickly hard, as Jeff readied his own, eyes fixed to my boobs as he wanked. In no time he was ready, holding his cock up, but for all that I knew I should mount him I couldn't. He solved the problem, taking me by the hips and pulling me forwards to sit me on his cock, his balls against my bum, the crease of my pussy spread open on the thick shaft. I moved a little, balancing myself, and then he had lifted me again, my body gripped in his hands as he eased me up, and down, onto his cock, and for the first time in so, so long I felt my pussy filled with hot, hard cock.

The girls began to clap and cheer as they saw I was well and truly fucked, and I was grinning shyly as Teo pulled his cock out of my mouth to let me ride, with Jeff bucking beneath me to bounce me up and down on his erection. Teo moved back, June taking his wet cock in her hand as he joined her and I was in clear view, riding on Jeff's cock with my boobs bouncing and the tails of my jacket slapping on my bare bum.

Jeff took my waist as I heard Monty's voice behind me, and a sharp stab of fear went through me. My bumhole was next, and Monty was a lot bigger than Ronnie Miles, his cock a thick trunk of flesh that I knew would stretch my poor little hole to the limit. He was holding it, nursing a full erection, with a tub of margarine in the other hand. In went his cock, pushed down to scoop out a thick blob of the yellowish spread, and he was advancing on me, grinning.

I began to panic a bit as Jeff started to pull me down, but he held on tight, his strength far too great to resist. Monty waddled over as I was put in position for sodomy, held to Jeff's great belly and broad chest, his cock still in me, my bum flaunted, my cheeks apart, offering my anus for entry. I shut my eyes and hid my face in Jeff's chest, unable to look as Monty sank down over my bum in an obscene squat, with his cock and balls lying in my crease.

He began to rub, smearing margarine between my cheeks, his balls slapping right over my bumhole. I wondered if he could hold it, if he'd just spunk in my crease, but no, his knuckles pushed into the slippery groove as he took his cock in hand; the head of his cock travelled slowly down, towards the little hole he was about to penetrate, and on it. My ring tightened by instinct, only to spread to a blob of half-molten margarine as it was pressed in, and up, my hole opening to the grease as I forced myself to loosen up.

'That's right, push it out, like you're on the bog,' Monty said, and shoved hard.

I cried out at the sudden, dull pain as my anal ring spread open on his knob, but it was mercifully quick, and he was already inside, his fat helmet swelling out in my rectum. He grunted as he pushed some more in, making me gasp once more, and I was clinging hard to Jeff as it was forced slowly up past my greasy, straining ring, bloating me out, heavy and fat in my gut. Even with it half in I was clutching at Jeff's body and curling my toes, in pain, in ecstasy, and filled with an agonising need to go to the loo. My mind was already burning with shame and my utter helplessness, then Jeff spoke.

'Here, Monty, I can feel your prick going up her shitter, you fat perve!'

Both of them laughed and a great jolt of humiliation hit me. They were fucking me, pussy and bumhole both, my body bloated with their cocks, and they were laughing and joking as they used me, getting their kicks over something that already had me on the edge. Then I had been pushed over it as I was taken firmly by the hair and my head dragged around for Teo to feed his fat black cock into my mouth.

They just had me, my body a conveniently shaped lump of meat for their huge cocks, fucking in my mouth, pumping in my juicy pussy, squelching in my greasy bumhole. I could do absolutely nothing, sandwiched between their massive bodies, the breath squeezed out of me with each pump as they fucked me, a little dirty fuck-doll good only to be used, to be spunked in.

Teo did it first, maybe because he'd been in June's mouth while Monty got his cock up my bumhole. I wasn't sucking, I was having my head fucked. His erection was jammed into my throat so deep I was panting through my nose to breathe, and suddenly he'd come and my gullet was full of thick, salty spunk. It set me gagging, my throat going into frantic, agonising spasms on his cock to milk the spunk down, choking me, and exploding from my nose. He just held it in, indifferent to the mess of snot and spunk bubbles I was blowing all over his cock shaft and balls, and withdrawing only when he had quite finished.

Monty and Jeff never even broke their pace, their cocks still working in my holes even as I coughed and retched over Teo's spunk. I was jammed down hard, most of Monty's weight in my back, making it even harder to breathe, my head swimming, my vision blurred. I still felt Jeff's spunk squirt out from around the mouth of my pussy, and heard his deep groan as he unloaded himself inside me, the first man to come up my pussy in what seemed an age.

I didn't have time to thank him, still breathless, and he slipped out with his final push, his cock jamming hard up between my sex lips to make me cry out in an ecstasy close to orgasm. Not that it was going to take me long, as Monty's pushes were now rubbing my spunk-soiled pussy onto Jeff's cock and balls, my clitty on his still-hard prick. I began to squirm, needing to come with Monty's cock still in my gut, and as he began to babble I realised it might even be together.

'I've got to do it . . . do it . . . right up her . . . up her dirt box . . .'

His words hit me, bringing home just how unspeakably filthy it is for a girl to let a man stick his cock up her bum, in her dirt box, and I was there. I screamed, pissy fluid squirted from my pee hole all over Jeff's cock and balls as Monty went frantic, ramming himself into me in a series of hard, sudden thrusts, only to stop, gasping for breath.

'Don't . . . not yet . . . bugger me, you bastard!' I squealed. 'Bugger me hard!'

Monty just grunted as he spread my cheeks with his thumbs and pulled himself slowly out of my bottom. I was still rubbing on Jeff, but half-heartedly, my orgasm broken right at the peak, sobbing with need. Something had to go up my bum, something big, and as I swung my leg off Monty I was casting around for the strap-on AJ had used to fuck me, hardly aware of Monty's panted words.

'I can't . . . not like that . . . I'm knackered! Be a darling and give me a suck, yeah?'

Time seemed to freeze. Monty was sat there, fat legs spread, vast belly bulging out under his top, his trousers wide, his huge, dirty cock steaming in the cool air, from the heat of my rectum, the skin glistening with my juices. He wanted me to take it in my mouth, suck it, swallow . . .

The next instant I was down on it, my mouth full of the taste of my buggered bottom, my hips up, my twin holes open to everyone, open and juicy, because I'd just been fucked and buggered, by men, by the man in my mouth, the man who had fucked my dirt box and made me suck his soiled cock, suck and swallow, suck and swallow . . .

I was doing it, spurt after spurt of thick, slimy come erupting into my mouth even as I snatched at my pussy, rubbing frantically, my body already tight in orgasm. Something fat and smooth and cool was pushed deep into my pussy hole, something else up my bottom as the girls came to my rescue and I was there, in perfect ecstasy as I mouthed on Monty's cock, revelling in the taste of spunk and margarine and my own bumhole as my body shook to climax after climax, hands on my boobs, my bum slapped, my holes fucked, just the dirtiest, filthiest, most abandoned little slut there ever was.

Monty had pumped every last drop of his spunk down my throat long before I came off him. Some of them had been clapping too, but it had barely sunk in. It was Penny and Sophie who'd helped me, with a cucumber, the handle of my spanking brush and by hand, and they helped me up and into the bathroom too. I was still cleaning up when the doorbell went again, and as I buttoned my uniform jacket once more Melody Rathwell appeared at the door.

'So what's this Penny tells me?' she asked. 'Miss Lesbian Lifestyle just took three cocks?'

'Yes,' I admitted, blushing.

'Sensible girl,' she answered. 'Why restrict yourself, yeah? I need to change, can I borrow your bedroom?'

'Sure, make yourself at home.'

She moved away from the door and I went back to the living room to retrieve my panties. Annabelle was there, and she didn't need to change, stark naked but for a pair of black ankle boots chained together to make a hobble. Her hands were chained behind her back too, leaving the tattoo on her pussy mound that marked her as Mel's property plainly visible.

'Morris and Harmony are parking the car,' Penny explained.

'Can I be next?' Sophie asked. 'That's got me well horny, Jade.'

'Lick each other or something,' Jeff advised. 'We need refuelling, we do. I'm going to get a pizza off Dough Boy. Anyone else?'

'I'm up for that,' Monty responded instantly. 'Let's get some more booze in too. Who wants what?'

'I'll do the drink,' Teo offered. 'You girls get yourselves ready.'

I'd had mine, at least for the time being, so I gave them my spare keys and pinched the comfy chair as Jeff vacated it. Sophie and Penny were already kissing. Poppy was cuddled up to Gabrielle with Zoe beside them. June looked a little sulky, but Annabelle was talking to her and I could tell there was a spark between them. It was going to be a good night, and a feast for the men, and for Melody, with nine submissive girls to play with.

The boys had barely been gone a minute when the doorbell went again, and I assumed it would be Morris and Harmony, only to find AJ's bike parked outside the door and AJ herself scowling up at me.

'Hi,' I ventured, wondering what I could possibly say.

She'd made it fairly clear the night before that I was now hers completely, but she hadn't said anything about coming back, so I hadn't expected her to.

'Get down here,' she ordered. 'We're going to The Pumps.'

'I . . . er . . . I've got company,' I answered.

'What, Muffet? She can drive us then. It's about time she learned how big girls play.'

'Not just Penny, no, Sophie and Zoe, and my friends Poppy and –'

'What is this, the National Union of Submissive Sluts? Let me up.'

'But –'

'The keys, Dumplings, now!'

I threw them down. After all, she was my Mistress, and, if she didn't like me having men round, then she'd just have to punish me again, and again, and again. I went back to my chair, determined to go through with it even though my fingers were shaking hard, and telling myself I'd had no choice. It was true. She wouldn't have gone away, and the boys would be back from the shops within minutes.

'AJ?' Penny asked.

'AJ,' I confirmed as the door pushed open.

Every one of us was looking at her as she came in, and she was looking back, her face set in a calm, cruel smile.

'Eight little baby dykes,' she said as she put her helmet down, 'well, eight little sluts anyway. I wonder which I should have first?'

She was in full leathers, and as she slowly peeled the zip down to the level of her belly it became obvious she had nothing underneath. Sophie gave a little purr at the sight, clearly willing, but AJ ignored her, looking at each of us in turn as if inspecting a tray of steaks or pork chops. Finally her gaze came to rest on Annabelle, and she spoke.

'If it isn't Black Mel's little slave girl, out on her own. Maybe I should send you home with the taste of my cunt in your mouth, just for her? Maybe –'

'Maybe you should learn some fucking manners,' Melody answered as she stepped from my bedroom.

AJ turned sharply, shock showing on her face for just an instant before her expression hardened. Mel stepped forwards. Just a moment before I'd been thinking how tough AJ looked. Mel was in a different league – two inches taller, maybe three stone heavier, and a lot more muscular. She was in her wrestling outfit, a bright blue singlet and silky gold shorts, with her brawny arms folded beneath her heavy breasts, her brown skin glistening in the light, grinning.

'Annabelle is mine,' she stated.

'Yeah, well, plenty to go round,' AJ said hastily.

'Yeah, plenty,' Mel answered, 'and I know who I'm having – you.'

'I don't switch. I –'

'You,' Mel went on, advancing towards AJ, 'put Sophie out of action last week, Jade too.'

'Yeah, well,' AJ answered, 'I can spank Jade when I like, Sophie too, she's not –'

'She'd been asked to stay ready,' Mel answered, 'and, because she wasn't, I had to take her place. I got a spanking, over some dirty old bastard's knee, on the bare, and more . . .'

'He washed her mouth out with soap,' Sophie added helpfully.

AJ laughed. It was only a nervous titter, but it was a big mistake.

'I was going to make you kiss my boots,' Mel went on. 'Now you get a spanking, in the nude. Strip.'

'Go fuck yourself!' AJ spat, but there was fear in her voice, and she was backing for the door.

She never made it. Mel snatched out, catching the collar of AJ's leathers, to pull her off balance, trip her and send her sprawling on the floor. The rest of us moved back out of the way just as fast as we possibly could, and Mel dropped herself on AJ, grabbing for a wrestling hold. She got it, and the contest was over, really, only AJ wouldn't admit it. She fought like a wildcat, kicking and scratching and swearing, as she was calmly and methodically stripped naked, her leathers tugged down, her boots wrenched off, even her socks removed.

With her leathers pulled off her feet she was left in just her panties, a plain white pair more like men's briefs than anything. Mel paused, tightening the arm lock she'd applied, to roll AJ face down, still fighting, her body twisting and her legs kicking on the carpet, her little round bottom quivering in her panties. She was still swearing too.

'. . . don't you fucking dare, you fat black bitch! I'll fucking have you, I'll –'

'Now, now,' Mel interrupted sweetly as she caught her breath, 'that's no way for a little lady who's about to have her botty spanked to talk, is it?'

'Fuck off, bitch!' AJ shouted. 'Just fuck off! Fuck off!'

'Temper, temper,' Mel answered. 'Now, Alice Jemima, I said in the nude, so I suppose you had better be in the nude. Let's have these little panties down, shall we?'

'Fuck you!' AJ screamed, but her voice was starting to crack, filled with fear and misery as well as anger as Mel took hold of the waistband of her panties.

Her struggles redoubled, but Mel held on, one

hand gripping both of AJ's wrists in a steel grip as she began slowly to peel the panties down to a crescendo of screams and swearing.

'. . . get off me, you bitch . . . you . . . no! You can't! I'm a dominant. You –'

The whole of the tattoo in the small of AJ's back was showing.

'– can't do this! No! Fuck off! Fuck off! Fuck off!'

I could see the neat little V at the top of AJ's bum crease.

'Just fuck off, bitch! No! No!'

Both round little bum cheeks were bare, all but the tuck, and then the tight pink anus I had been made to kiss so often was visible.

'N–no . . . please . . . no! Fuck you, you black bitch!'

It was all showing, the panties right down, the rear pouch of AJ's pussy bare along with her bumhole. Her hips were squirming in desperation, her lower legs cocked wide in a last, pathetic effort to stop her panties being pulled off completely, and she finally shut up, her face setting into furious consternation as the panties were whisked off, and she was nude.

'My, what a fuss!' Mel said happily. 'There's nothing to be ashamed of, you have a very pretty bottom, and you do need spanking.'

AJ's answering scream was so full of rage it was incoherent. She was red in the face, and her body was still jerking in Melody's grip, but she couldn't break free. Mel began to spank, not hard at all, just little pats and, as the little round bottom cheeks began to bounce and quiver, she started to sing:

Pat-a-cake, Pat-a-cake, Baker's man,
Bake me a cake as quick as you can,
Pat it and prick it and mark it with P,
And pop in the oven for baby and me.

She laughed as she finished. AJ had gone completely berserk, spitting like a wildcat and thrashing her body about, but succeeding only in making a yet ruder display of her pussy and bumhole. I was trying not to laugh, for all that I could feel something of her outrage, but the others had no such reserve. Every one of them was giggling, with Poppy and Sophie and June laughing openly, and clapping. Mel continued to spank, aiming gentle pats at the frantically wriggling bottom beneath her with her fingertips.

Slowly AJ's bum began to pink up, warming under what was obviously going to be a long, slow spanking. I knew why, and it was so outrageous I almost spoke up, but the thought of how I had felt held in her grip while the piss squirted into my panties in front of a crowd of goggling tourists came back to me. Sure enough, Mel was still spanking happily away when I heard a heavy tread on the stairs. The key grated in the lock, the door pushed open and the boys tumbled in, Fat Jeff, Monty, Teo – and Dough Boy.

'We brought Romeo up –' Jeff began, and stopped.

AJ had been so wrapped up in her spanking she hadn't heard the door, but when she heard Jeff's voice she twisted violently around, and screamed. I thought she'd screamed before, and I'd thought she'd put up a fight, but it was nothing to the state she went into the instant she realised that she had four men watching her bare-bottom spanking.

'Girl fight, cool!' Monty sang out.

For one moment I thought AJ would escape, but Mel reacted fast, throwing one powerful thigh across her back to pin her down, bottom on her neck. One arm was free, briefly, then Mel had it trapped again, kneeling on it to wring a gasp of pain from AJ's lips. A quick, powerful jerk, another anguished squeak and the other arm was trapped the same way, pinned under Melody's weight. Jeff gave a cheer at the manoeuvre and he and Monty began to clap in time as once more Melody's hand began to rise and fall on her victim's bare bottom. For a moment AJ took it, then lurched violently against Mel, bringing her knees up in an attempt to get the strength of her legs into play, a position that left her bottom flaunted to all four men. Still Mel held on, and Dough Boy gave a crow of delight at the sudden and complete exposure of bald pink pussy and wrinkled anal star, calling out as he dropped his pizza boxes hurriedly on the table.

'English spanking! Cunt show too! I love it! Naughty girl! Naughty, naughty girl! Yes, yes, spank her good!'

Mel complied, laying in harder to the wriggling pink bum and AJ's screams grew louder still, her struggles more frantic. In answer Mel hissed a swearword and snatched quickly for the discarded panties, reaching back to stuff them into AJ's mouth, only to have them spat out immediately. Mel just laughed and laid in harder still. Dough Boy began to caper around them, kicking his fat legs up in a bizarre, posturing dance and clapping his hands. With that, AJ began to reach the end of her tether, still struggling, but only in blind reaction to what was being done to her. I could feel for her. She'd been stripped, spanked, and there were men watching, which had to be the final degradation.

Mel had other ideas. Leaning forwards she reached under AJ's tummy, her fingers curling around the wet pink pussy as she continued to spank. AJ's screams rang out anew as she realised she was to be brought off in front of everyone, but there was absolutely nothing she could do, pinned helpless with Mel's experienced fingers working her sex. She was going to come, and that was all there was to it. The muscles of her legs and bottom began to twitch; her bumhole started to wink; her pussy was tightening. Still her face was set in fury, then her mouth was open and she was going through a grunting, hissing orgasm, unable to hold it back as her pussy was frigged and her bottom slapped, with every person in the room cheering and laughing and clapping as she came.

That should have been it, her punishment complete, but as Mel finally stopped the spanking Dough Boy lifted his apron and I realised his cock was out, and erect. I called out in protest, and so did others, but he was jerking furiously at it, the fat red knob pointed up over AJ's bum. Mel realised, spun around and yelled out an angry command, but too late.

'Watch me spunk! Watch me spunk!' he crowed and a fountain of it erupted from the tip of his cock.

I watched in horror as the spunk arched high in the air, spurt after spurt, to patter down on AJ's hot cheeks. She twisted her head back and gave one long wail of utter despair as she realised she'd been spunked on, and she finally broke. All the fight went out of her and she burst into tears, shivers running through her body and her feet kicking feebly on the carpet but otherwise still as the dribbles of spunk ran slowly down over the red ball of her spanked bum like cream on a Christmas pudding.

Mel climbed off, and AJ hauled herself to her feet. She was streaming tears, and for one moment she let Mel cuddle her, only to pull away, rounding on Dough Boy, her fists clenched. Mel grabbed her, holding her back, and Jeff and Teo quickly hustled Dough Boy out, his cock still hanging out over the top of his trousers as he was helped from the door with a well-aimed boot.

'Time out, now!' Mel yelled as the door closed behind Dough Boy, and AJ abruptly stopped struggling. 'That was out of order, right? But you deserved that spanking, girl!'

She let go and AJ broke away, immediately snatching up her panties to wipe her bottom, then her leathers. Her eyes were still full of tears, but for all her misery and humiliation they still blazed with the desire for revenge as she turned to me.

'You, you are dead meat, Jade –' she began as she pushed one leg into her leathers.

Just half an hour before the same words would have had me tongue tied and grovelling, unable to speak. Now it was different. I'd seen her spanked to tears, and I found my voice, interrupting her.

'Hang on, stop! You can do what you like to me, AJ, you know that, but one thing. Not in front of straights, OK?'

'No fucking way! I do as I –'

She hesitated, sudden doubt on her face. I knew what was going through her head – how it felt to have her will broken. Either that or what would happen if her butch friends found out she'd had her panties taken down for her and her bare bottom spanked in front of an audience.

'OK,' she answered.

'And . . . and could we drop the possession bit?' I went on. 'I mean, you can take me up to The Pumps, or clubs, or whatever, and I'll be ever such a good girl, but . . . but I just want you to be playful, maybe give me a cuddle now and then, when we're alone, and Penny too?'

She nodded as she pulled her zip up to leave her no longer a spanked brat but once more a leather-clad biker girl.

'That's a deal. Now get in the bathroom . . . no, the kitchen.'

I hung my head, not in submission, but to hide my smile. Now I had what I wanted, exactly what I wanted. AJ was going to give me hell, again and again, because if she punished me ten thousand times it would never make up for her single bare-bottom spanking, never mind being spunked on. Yet, whatever she did, she knew she had to keep me happy, because otherwise I might just tell. She'd been spanked, the ultimate come down for her, and it had been inevitable, from the moment I'd got Mel involved, if not at my party, then some other night. So I'd got my way after all, devious little brat that I am, and, if I'd betrayed AJ, then I was about to get my just desserts.

AJ took my hand and I was led away, the others following, all keen to watch whatever horrible fate she had in store for me. They were all making suggestions, but I knew what I wanted, and managed to gesture to Penny before AJ put me down on my knees. Penny stepped forwards, so that I could whisper into her ear. AJ smiled and reached down, taking me by the scruff of my neck.

My pussy seemed to swell as I was dragged roughly across the floor to the bin. It was full, piled to the brim with all the rubbish of my daily life, the surface bits of eggshell and bacon rind sticking up from a layer of yoghurt, from AJ's breakfast, and mine. For one awful, glorious moment she held my head over it, and then I was in, my face pushed down into the muck, my hair soiled, my tightly closed eyes, my nose, my cheeks, my lips, all covered in squashy, slimy mess.

'Stay,' AJ ordered, and let go of my hair.

I stayed, already shaking hard, and thinking of the orgasm I would have as she made me eat what my face was in. Her hands came under my chest, to unfasten my uniform jacket and pull it wide, flopping my boobs free. It was tugged down my back, trapping my arms to leave my weight on my knees, and on my face in the rubbish. Already I wanted to frig myself, in front of all of them, with the scent of decay in my nose and the humiliation of being put in a waste bin burning in my head as I came. I held back, waiting like the obedient little slut I am, my control given over completely.

No order came, but I could hear AJ rummaging in the drawers, and I realised I was to be beaten. Sure enough, the noise stopped, a hand closed in the seat of my panties and they were hauled tight up between my cheeks and the lips of my pussy, lifting me and dropping my head still further into the bin. I cried out at the sudden, sharp pain as the first blow hit me, and I was getting it, spanked with a spoon, head down in a rubbish bin – exactly what I deserved.

My mouth had filled with eggshells so I opened it, but the spanking hurt too much to let me do anything but gasp out my pain into the mess, snorting and blowing, with a bit of bacon rind up one nostril. I was going to come too, with my panties tight in my crease and rubbing my clitty with every hard smack to my poor, jiggling bottom, taking me higher, and higher.

She began to bounce me in my panties, making my bottom and boobs wobble and drawing giggles and deep, masculine laughter from the watchers. I just came, the orgasm hitting me in a great rush of ecstatic humiliation. There I was, head down in a rubbish bin, my big bottom spanked, my fat boobs bouncing naked under my chest, my panties tight up my pussy, and they were laughing at me. It was so good, and I held it for ages, all the while with the spoon smacking down hard on my sweet spot and my panties jerking in my crease.

It hurt like anything, and finally broke to raw pain, forcing me to pull my head up from the muck and squeal for mercy. I got it, but I was still thinking of what a ridiculous sight I would look as I came slowly down from my orgasm, ready for more just as soon as I'd recovered. It had been too quick, and AJ thought so too. Even as I gulped down air she put her foot on my neck, pressing me firmly back into the rubbish, her voice full of malign satisfaction as she spoke.

'Get down there, I'm not finished with you yet, Dumplings.'

She trod on my head, to push it deeper still, until I could barely breathe. With the first ecstasy gone my stomach had begun to tighten at the stench of rotting vegetables and sour yoghurt, but she kept me down, her foot on the back of my neck as she began to issue orders.

'Muffet, get me a beer. Pig, pull Dumplings's panties out of her slit and grease her arse.'

'Are you going to bugger her?' Sophie asked in delight.

'What sort?' Penny queried.

'Never mind what sort, you silly tart,' AJ answered. 'It doesn't matter, because I'm not going to bugger her. I'm going to give her an enema.'

A sharp pang of fear and chagrin struck me at her words and I felt my bumhole tighten by instinct, and again as I caught their voices, Monty, Jeff, Gabrielle, and others.

'Nice one!'

'Cool, you're going to make her spurt, yeah?'

'Should we put her in a towel for a nappy?'

'No,' AJ answered them. 'I have a better idea. I'm going to tickle her, and make her do it in her panties.'

I swallowed hard at her words, feeling sicker still, but she had me, and I knew how good it would be.

My whole body was shaking as my panties were tugged out of my bum crease and pulled down to my thighs. Sophie turned my jacket tail up too, exposing the full, fat moon of my bottom, my cheeks open, my bumhole showing at the centre, pink and wrinkly, still slimy from my bum fucking . . .

That didn't stop Sophie greasing me.

'Bum up,' she ordered, and as I lifted my haunches I felt something cool and unctuous touch between my cheeks, some pooling in my anus, some running down into my open pussy, some the other way, onto my back.

'Enough with the olive oil, Sophie!' Mel laughed. 'You're getting her ready for an enema, not an elephant.'

'Shame,' Monty answered. 'I'd love to see that, well, not an elephant maybe, but –'

'Shut up, you pervert,' AJ cut him off as Sophie slid a finger up my bottom hole. 'Muffet, get me a funnel.'

Sophie eased a second finger into my anus, and a third.

'A funnel?' Jeff queried. 'It won't work, not unless she blows off.'

I felt my ring stretch as Sophie spread her fingers and a dribble of olive oil ran down into my open bumhole.

'Loose, isn't she?' Annabelle remarked.

'Monty just buggered her,' Jeff pointed out. 'You'd be loose and all.'

'Why won't a funnel work?' AJ demanded, Sophie still easing my anus wider and looser as my humiliation rose up and up to their words, to the stink of the bin, to my exposure . . .

'Because her tube's closed,' Jeff explained, 'or full of shit, depending. There's no room for the beer, unless you push it up.'

'What if you were to sort of fuck her with it?' Teo asked.

'It would go everywhere, except up her arse,' Jeff told him. 'One of those turkey basters, that's what you want.'

'Have you got a turkey baster, Dumplings?' AJ demanded.

I shook my head as best I could with my face pressed deep in the rubbish and half Sophie's fist up my greasy bottom.

'Or one of those bags you do cake icing with?' Poppy suggested. 'That's what Anna always used on me.'

'The beer would come out through the bag,' Monty objected.

'We could use cake mix,' Poppy went on, 'or custard, or –'

'It wouldn't squirt so well then.'

'Yeah, but that doesn't matter if she's going to be made to do it in her panties . . .'

'Yes it does . . .'

'No it doesn't, not if she's being tickled.'

'Right, you know what she's like . . .'

'Just do me, please!' I wailed, dragging my head up from the bin.

'Shut up!' AJ answered, and trod on my head again, squashing my face back into the mess. At the same instant Sophie finally forced the full bulk of her hand up my bottom.

My mouth came open in shock, to be instantly filled with a mixture of bacon rind and eggshell in yoghurt, which I was struggling to spit out as they carried on arguing, heedless of my distress or the state I was in. For a moment I was too far gone to understand what they were saying, and then AJ was speaking again.

'Get your fingers out, Pig.'

Sophie withdrew her fist with a soggy noise, to leave my bumhole gaping and sore, a wet pink cavity between my cheeks, ready to be filled. I forced myself to relax, keeping it open, but my cheeks still tightened as something touched between them, something hard but slippery, and someone's fingers, easing it in up my bum.

'Good thinking, Pen, and she can wipe up after with the paper,' Jeff said and I realised what was going up my bum – the inside from a toilet roll.

'Shame Jade hasn't got a hamster!' Monty laughed. 'I've never seen a felching.'

'You are one fucking pervert, Hartle!' Jeff laughed. 'Look, you can see right up her box.'

They could, I knew. I could feel myself gaping, my anus stretched wide, ready to be filled. I heard the pop of the beer can, felt the cool liquid on my ring and the weight in my gut as she began to pour. It spilled over, running down my pussy, cold and wet, and in my hole, then more, slowly filling my rectum as I farted, quite unable to control myself. Jeff laughed, one of the girls gave a disgusted giggle and yet more beer was being poured into my body as the loo roll inside was slowly withdrawn.

It came free, I felt my ring close on my load, and they'd done it, putting the best part of a can of beer in me, strong beer too, because I could already feel the hit of alcohol as my gut absorbed it. Even as Sophie tugged my panties back up my head was swimming. The last of my ill feelings went, pushed aside in my drunken ecstasy, and I wanted to do it, to be made to do it. As AJ's finger slipped in under my armpits I was babbling into the muck under my face, to be made to come as I squirted into my panties. Sophie took pity, a knuckle pushing my panty crotch in between my sex lips, Penny too, taking my boobs in her hands. Sophie found my clitty and my mouth was already wide in the mess as AJ spoke.

'Tickle, tickle, Dumplings, darling.'

My whole body jerked as her fingers dug in, painfully deep. I burst into uncontrollable giggles, struggling to hold it as I heard a knock on the door – Morris and Harmony, come to add one last touch to my degradation. They would see me, head down in the rubbish, coming in blind, helpless ecstasy as I was made to wet myself, and to release my enema in my panties, and it was going to happen. Mucus was spraying from my nose as I squirmed my face in the rubbish, my feet were kicking, my bladder was in agony, the beer in my gut felt like a huge, heavy ball, my anus was pulsing . . .

. . . and opening, to squirt my enema out at the same instant my bladder went and I was writhing and bucking in their grip, piss and beer erupting behind me, straight into my panties. I felt the cotton swell, bulging, fat and heavy, then collapse as the sides gave and it spurted out over the floor and down my thighs. More came, and yet more, my bladder emptying, my gut too, until my panties had begun to bulge again, with solid. It was glorious, stuck in the rubbish and tickled until I filled my panties, and even through the blinding ecstasy a little calm voice was telling me I should never, ever try to destroy my gift, the gift of pissing myself when I'm tickled. It gave me what I need – helplessness – and as AJ's fingers did their work and my bladder and rectum emptied into my filthy panties without me needing to push at all I knew I'd reached my ideal. It didn't stop either, Penny still teasing my nipples, Sophie still rubbing through the mush in my panties, to keep me so high, in helpless, filthy ecstasy as I loaded my knickers in full view of my friends.

Not just my friends, as I realised when my orgasm finally broke and I heard a dry, clipped voice from behind me.

'I am from Noise Abatement. Which of you is Jade Shelton?'

NEXUS NEW BOOKS

To be published in September 2004:

ALICE IN CHAINS
Adriana Arden

Fresh from the adventures chronicled in *The Obediant Alice*, young Alice Brown returns home to find that she has sprouted bird feathers where her own hair should be. Only another trip to Underland can solve the problem, and her bedroom mirror is the only means of return. Used once more as a pawn by the Red Queen, this time literally, and enslaved by the greedy Tweedledum and Tweedledee, Alice must use her willingness to submit to any of the bizarre demands made of her if she is to succeed in returning to normal. And that's before she's met the Jabberwock. A delightfully perverse retelling of a classic tale.

£6.99 ISBN 0 352 33908 X

SIN'S APPRENTICE
Aishling Morgan

Poor young Ysette is an orphan. Having been raised in an especially strict and unworldly nunnery, she is sent out to have her obliging nature taken advantage of again and again. First she is to learn the bizarre sexual byways of witchcraft. Then, travelling as a Sin Eater, she is tasked to remove the sin that men contain within their seed. Finally, she is taken by an elderly and perverted priest before finding her redemption. A novel of sex, superstition and religious punishment, inspired by the classics of SM literature.

£6.99 ISBN 0 352 33909 8